The Old Boys Club

Christopher Masterman

To my lovely and patient wife, Elizabeth, who once again has provided invaluable comment and patiently read through the text to negate the effects of my ever-worsening dyslexia.

And to my three oldest school friends who continue to purchase my books and may well find of parts of
'The Old Boys Club'
amusing and, hopefully, interesting:
Michael Curtis
John (Jeep) Jackson
Richard (Rick) Sheldon

Also by Christopher Masterman

Non-Fiction
An Average Pilot
An affectionate history of Cedric Masterman OBE, DFC

Fiction
Secrets From Norway
Travelling to Tincup
Deathly Confessions
The Bridge at Braunau-am-Inn*
(*Reissued as Crossing The Bridge)
The Convent Girl

Book One

Setting the HOOK
to return a body

Chapter 1

In the 1960s the Cold War was at its height and many people were genuinely fearful that an all-out nuclear war was imminent. Stalinism, eagerly praised in the 1930s by those who had not had to suffer under it, had been discredited, and the attraction of Communism to intellectuals and dilettantes was waning. Left and Right Wing politics in Britain and elsewhere became more distinct and entrenched. Tolerance of each adherent to the other's views withered. Spies were being recruited, discovered, turned, imprisoned or executed on both sides of the Iron Curtain

At 6.30 pm on the 22nd of October 1966 a rope ladder was thrown over the high wall of London's Wormwood Scrubs prison from the freedom side. Climbing through a prison window that he had just broken, a man slid down a low roof onto the ground. The area that he had to cross to reach the perimeter wall was clear of warders and other prisoners; they were all watching the weekly film inside the prison buildings. The escapee ran to the wall, climbed over it using the ladder, the treads of which were made of thick knitting needles, jumped to the outside and into the arms of his accomplice, fracturing his wrist as he did so.

George Blake, Soviet Spy and ex-member of MI6 had escaped from his would-be 42-year prison sentence. Within three weeks he was ensconced in the Soviet Union, joining a bevy of other British members of the intelligence establishment who had turned their coats.

I, David Shawyer, had just turned 24-years of age. I was living in London as an insurance broker but soon to depart to Australia to follow a girl who was tormenting me with unrequited love.

George Blake was nothing to me then.

Chapter 2

Six months later, in mid-April 1967, I returned to London. As soon as I walked through the doors of my company's City-of-London headquarters James Harrington called me into his palatial office-cum-conference room.. 30 years older than I, impeccably dressed, film star-looks and deep, plummy Harrovian accent, he was totally admired and held in awe by me, and by most people I would suppose. Sometimes I felt inadequate in his presence and could see that if one had to be like him to become a partner member of Lloyds Insurance then I was probably neither going to make the grade nor own a Bentley as he did. But he was a good boss and usually very affable to both me and the rest of his twenty-five or so office staff.

I had anticipated such an interview with him ever since I had departed Perth airport in Western Australia, and the anticipation had turned to anxiousness during the second leg of my return journey which had commenced from Singapore. I had no idea how much I should tell him about my Australian adventure; I had officially been on holiday so perhaps, I reasoned, it was no business of his to know. But what had happened out there could, I thought, affect the much anticipated contract to insure a large, Singaporean Government, harbour infrastructure for which the company was competing. I and my mentor, Henry Souch, had worked for months preparing the company's proposal – all possibly for naught because of the girl in Broome, Western Australia, and her probably enraged government-lawyer-father in Singapore.

James settled himself back into his imposing looking leather chair behind his even more imposing mahogany desk; his smile was broad and genuine as he indicated for me to sit down opposite him. In the seven years I had worked for him I had been into this office many times to speak with him or to attend meetings around the oval elm-wood table which, with its eight chairs, filled much of the remainder of the room.

'So, how was Australia?' He began. 'Did you have a good visit?'

'It was interesting,' I answered guardedly.

'You didn't stay long. I thought you asked for two weeks holiday there after you had departed Singapore? But here you are back after just a week.

'Yes, things happened rather more quickly in Australia than I had anticipated, so I came home. I had dropped our proposal into the Singapore Government on my way out, so there was nothing else to keep me in Singapore or away from my office here.'

There was silence as James waited for me to say more. I didn't. His face became sympathetic.

'It's about the girl, isn't it? He offered.

I nodded. I could feel my eyes starting to fill.

'It's not still on with her then? Your father told me that he was sure you would be coming back engaged. If not actually married.'

I got myself under control. 'We broke up, that's the simplest way of putting it.'

'Well I'm very sorry. She was bright and lively, and of course, so beautiful. The loveliest Chinese girl I have seen.'

'Yes, so beautiful to look at, and actually more Japanese than Chinese.'

'Really?'

I wanted the conversation to stop; it was hurting me, and there was no way I would, or could, describe what had happened between myself and the girl in that Western Australia outpost of humanity – Broome – or about her Japanese connections. Now she was in Hong Kong and I was back in London, and the studio below my apartment in Earls Court where she used to live was empty. I had not told my parents in Spain the details of what had taken place and doubted I ever would – they knew the girl too, and had loved her. I was certainly not going to let James extract anything more from me. He saw the signals plain across my face and thankfully changed the subject to one much more acceptable and pleasant to me.

'I had a phone call from our man in Singapore, your man really, George, last Friday evening. He was querying why you didn't see him on your way back from Australia; he had exciting news that he wanted to give you. He told me that the Singaporeans have had a first look at our proposal for insuring the dry dock project. They are pleased with what we have offered and indicated that we will get a significant share of the eventual contract which should be issued within six months. So well done you! I know how much time and effort you put into that proposal.'

'Together with Henry Souch,' I added. 'I could not have done it without him.'

'Yes, Henry. Our Eminence Gris. He's been your mentor for most of the time you have been with us, hasn't he? He will be a great loss when he retires later this year; he will be 70 in two years' time you know.'

I didn't know. He looked much younger than 68. Perhaps, I considered, because he had never married. I had been to West End theatres with him several times – he particularly loved musicals. And no matter which theatre we went to, often with a couple of other members of our Company, he knew the girls behind the bars or taking the hats and coats or checking the tickets. Women of well-preserved years who looked on him kindly with the eyes of past lovers. A lovely man and very wise.

'So,' James continued 'You will receive a token of appreciation in your pay at the end of this month, five hundred pounds let's say, and a further one thousand when we receive our first contract from the Singaporeans.'

I stuttered out some thanks. It was a very generous reaction to my work but typical of the man; perhaps, I thought, I would look again at buying my first car.

James rose from his seat which I took, correctly, to indicate that his chat with me was over; I followed suit. With his hand on my shoulder, he guided me back to my desk in the open-plan office that formed the heart of his company - one of the 'Associates' of the Lloyds of London insurance conglomerate; I was greeted with a thin round of applause from my colleagues – common practice whenever a new contract had been won. James then went to speak to Mavis who, as the Company Secretary and a Member of the Governing Board, had her own small office outside of the room where I sat, perhaps to arrange my bonus for she was also the company's book keeper.

Aware that the time in Singapore was seven hours in advance of Britain's, my first task was to telephone George. I made some feeble excuse for why I had not contacted him on my way back from Australia to London. As I was nominally his boss – albeit very hands-off – I didn't care much whether I was convincing or not. He told me much the same news as I had just heard from James. Nothing new had happened vis-à-vis the dock project over the past few days; we were in what he called 'the waiting phase' although first rumblings from the bid assessors seemed positive towards our offering. He knew enough about my private life to realise that I would probably move out to Singapore if our bid proved successful, and enough from my activities during my visits to Singapore to know that there was a local girl I was keen on, a girl that I wanted to marry. But his knowledge was out of date – I had wanted to marry her but, after our time together in Australia, no longer.

The rest of that day I spent catching up with Henry and receiving updates from some of the other staff on their work.

I left the office at about 4 pm, an hour earlier than the notional cease-work time, and made my usual way by tube train to my apartment in Earls Court Gardens, just off the Earls Court Road. I lived by myself except for when my parents returned from their villa in Spain for two weeks or so every few months. Then they occupied the spacious self-contained studio that comprised the basement under my space, the same studio in which that girl had lived for a year. I crashed out in front of the television as I fought my last battle against the lingering effects of the jet lag from my flight home.

---///---

My work during the following three months was taken up with a combination of answering questions from the Singapore Government which were forwarded by George and assisting with the insurance work of some of my office contemporaries. The usual pattern of short working days and after-hours forays to City pubs prevailed, as they always had during my time as a member of James Harrington's staff – the only job I had had since leaving school at 18. It was a good life for a 25-year old like me with no personal ties and a liking for watching sport, attending parties and visiting pubs, of which there was a plethora in and around my area of Earls Court and Kensington. But I sensed there was every chance the latter half of my twenties could see me becoming more and more feckless.

The loss of the oriental girl whom I had taken to be my putative wife, and the manner of the loss, had been a severe shock. That she had abandoned me, just as I thought our joint Australian ordeal had cemented our relationship, had shattered my confidence and made me wary of getting close to another lover. And, of course, we had not been lovers in the absolute sense – that I had proved impotent at the one time she had wanted us to be conjugal was another blow to my young pride. I realised that it was the circumstances of the attempt that had caused my failure – I had never had that problem with prior girlfriends – but nevertheless, I knew I would cloak myself in wariness if a new attraction with a girl was to develop.

The close male friends I had were all hangovers from my London schooldays, and they had been getting fewer as they moved to other places or got married. One of them, sensing that I was becoming personally aimless outside of my work, suggested that I joined the Questors theatre group that operated from a superb new theatre in Ealing, almost within spitting distance of my apartment. I had occasionally joined in with the theatre group at my school and was quite accomplished as a set builder, although I had never ventured on stage myself.

So I joined Questors as a member of their stage crew and spent two or three evenings and some weekends working there. This activity much reduced the time that I spent in local pubs. I even neglected my favourite, 'The Marquis of Zetland Arms' in South Kensington, which had once been owned by Charlie Chaplin, but the Questors had an excellent bar much frequented by the actors and stage hands alike and the theatre became a centre of recreation and activity for me during those first months after my return.

As soon as I had arrived back from Australia, I had phoned my parents and informed them I was not going to be getting married anytime soon, and certainly not to the girl that they favoured. I made it clear that I would not, could not, discuss why things had fallen through, and I took that resolution with me when I spent two weeks in Spain with them in June. They stuck with the boundaries I had set up about my personal life throughout my stay in their Malaga home. I swam in their private pool, played golf with my father and traipsed around with my mother to various of her ex-patriot friends who had daughters of a suitable age for me to marry – judging from the photos I was shown, their ages were the only things going for them.

I got on well with both my parents, I always had. Being their only child, I suppose that they doted on me but, in that curious English manner of their generation, in a sort of 'hands-off' way. My father had started off as a policeman but at some point in his career, probably during the years of the Second World War, his activities became covert in essence and nobody's business but his and his masters - of whom I knew nothing. These activities were never discussed by the family, or anyone else for that matter, but even in his retirement he seemed to keep in touch with powerful and influential people, some of whom may have been counted as friends. Often during the times that we got together, either in Spain or when he came to stay in the Earls Court apartment which he owned together with its basement studio, he would have a serious talk with me about my career or personal plans. The latter was off limits during this visit of mine to Spain but he did offer some career advice. He knew my boss, James Harrington, very well; in fact, it was their friendship that provided the opportunity for me to join the insurance world and earn my articles in the profession.

'David, your golf is improving. Have you joined a golf club and taken lessons from a professional?'

'No, I only play when I'm with you – so about twice a year.'

'Well you should join a club, there are plenty in and around London, and take lessons. There is probably one associated with the London insurance world, perhaps Lloyds itself has a golfing society.'

'So I can get a handicap? I hardly need one to play with you – you always beat me in any case.'

'Not so easily these days. No, it's not all to do with having a handicap.'

This was a classic ploy of his and was probably practiced by him in his police work. Get me interested by asking seemingly innocent questions and then come out with some pearl of wisdom or an agenda of his own which would benefit me.

I took the cue. 'What are you driving at?' I asked.

'You see, there are hundreds of people working in the London insurance market, and many more in associated professions such as foreign exchange broking, the stock market, commodities markets or shipping, to name just a few examples, so –'

I waited for the punch line.

'How are you going to distinguish yourself from all of those people? How is young David Shawyer going to become a James Harrington type?'

'I don't know. I have never thought about it. I'm only 25, I'm good at my job, I think.' (I had told him about my bonuses). 'Looking that far ahead? It's never crossed my mind.'

'But it should have. At your age most mathematical prodigies have produced their best work and are starting to burn out, and 25 would have been quite old for a Battle of Britain pilot.'

'Then what are you driving at? You never have a conversation like this with me unless you have some telling point to make.' I said and smiled.

'Am I that obvious?'

'Not exactly obvious, but you have an established method of making your views known or persuading somebody of something.'

'Look David, it's all down to networking. It's not what you know but who you know … coupled with ability of course, and you have plenty of that.'

'Thank you.'

'You could join a golf club, that might help. Or you could join the Freemasons. You haven't done that already, have you?'

'No. Have you?'

'Never. Freemasonry was, probably still is, endemic in the Police Force. I was not attracted to secret handshakes and mystic rituals; that view may have reduced my promotion prospects and probably helped my decision to leave the more conventional aspects of policing. I know, of course, that Masons do a great deal of good, charities and all that.'

'But more good to themselves.'

'Ah! So you do have an opinion on Freemasons?'

'Yes, but nothing attracts me to them. Admirable in many ways I suppose, but not for me. Not them, not any sort of secret society.'

My father went into one of his speaking pauses, thinking perhaps or, more probably, to make his audience think and then react. But he broke first. 'You could join a good club.' He suggested.

'I belong to a drama club – I've told you about Questors.'

'Admirable organisation, but I don't think building stage sets is going to advance your chosen career.'

'You are right, and the same might be said about my cricket and rugby supporters' clubs.'

'Actually, they might serve you better, dependant of course on who the other members are.'

'Mainly watchers, cheerers and beer-in-the-clubhouse-after-match swillers.'

'Like you.'

'Not quite so much these days.'

My father stoked his chin. I knew from this habit of his that the real words of wisdom were about to emerge.

'Instead of trying to join a suitable, established network group, you could create your own. Attract people of influence to you instead of the other way around.'

'How on earth would I do that?'

'By having some special attribute or talent, something that is needed by, or attractive to, others.'

'Like a pop star?'

'No, no! I'm trying to be serious. Special ability is what I'm talking about. You start off in your career with knowledge, then you gain experience, then the combination of these two equates to wisdom; and wisdom is attractive and valuable.'

'You don't get wisdom, as you call it, at my age. Henry Souch has wisdom, but not me.'

'Yes, Henry certainly has wisdom … and in areas you are not aware of.'

'Really?'

'That's enough about Henry and this career counselling interview.'

The serious part of the conversation was over. But I had got the hint: my father had been talking to James, and James was going to talk to me about my career when I got back to London.

Chapter 3

The talk with James did not take place until the first week in September. At about 11 in the morning he passed by my desk saying, 'Lunch is on me today, something special, just the two of us. Meet downstairs in the lobby at exactly noon.'

I arrived as he was hailing a taxi and I heard him tell the cabbie 'De Hems, China Town – do you know it?'

'Certainly do. About ten minutes, hop in,' came the reply.

Sitting side-by-side in the back of the vehicle, James asked if I had ever been to De Hems.

'No,' I replied. 'But I've heard of it. Something to do with oysters? Sounds Dutch.'

'Which it is, a sort of Dutch Café-cum-Oyster Bar.'

'What's the occasion?'

'The Singapore contract, it's through.'

'What, all of it?'

'No, I never thought we would get the whole thing. The Singaporeans will want to split their risk and bring in at least one local insurance business. I got a fax this morning which I decided to keep to myself until now. Henry is away for a few days as you know, so you are the first to be told, although I expect George will know by now also. The total insurance task is to be split three ways. Our portion is about half of the total business, so a huge boost to the firm. It will bring several millions each year for at least five years and, even allowing for the elements that we have to lay off to others, it will still represent an increase in our company's revenue of at least fifteen percent. So congratulations!'

James shook my hand enthusiastically over the arm rest that separated us.

The taxi drew up outside De Hems. James paid the cabbie then led me inside the building which looked almost medieval. He was greeted at the doorway as if he were a regular patron. We were ushered into a grotto-like room with walls completely covered in oyster shells and thence into a private booth. A bottle of Krug was already open and standing within a silver cooler on our table.

James poured two flutes of champagne. He clinked his glass against mine. 'To success. Do you know the saying that oysters should only be eaten when there is an 'R' in the month?'

I nodded in between sips of the cold drink that had formed beads of moisture on the outside of my glass.

'One of the patrons of this place,' James noted, 'when it was known as The Macclesfield although owned by Mynheer De Hem, composed a little poem:

> *When oysters to September yield,*
> *and grace the grotto'd Macclesfield,*
> *I will be there, my dear De Hem,*
> *to wish you well and sample them.*

The place was much frequented by members of the Dutch Resistance during the war. Another patron then was Kim Philby'

'The Spy?'

'Yes, but well before he was found out. Anyway, as the month is September and equipped with an 'R' all is fine for oysters. But the other choices of food here are all good, steaks or ribs for example. I think I'll go for half a dozen oysters on the shell followed by a rare tournedos with salad.'

I was still bemused by the occasion and the environment, so could only agree 'The same for me, please.'

A waiter mysteriously appeared, took the order, placed huge white bibs around our neck and went to a counter where he shucked a dozen oysters in front of us.

'When would you like your steaks, Sir?' asked the waiter of James.

'In about fifteen minutes would suit, thank you. We have things to discuss and we are in no hurry.'

I had never eaten raw oysters off the half-shell before so I took my cues from James, checking that the meat was properly detached from the shell with a small fork, adding seasoning, a drop of Tabasco, then an admiring look at each item to be eaten, tilting back my head and dropping the mollusc into my mouth. One quick bite, swallow then a smile of enjoyment and a wipe of the chin with the bib. I loved them.

James started to speak. 'Let's eat these slowly, savour them, while we, mainly I, talk.'

I nodded my agreement and dried my fingertips on my bib.

He opened with, 'You don't want to go back to Singapore, do you? I had thought that once the contract was in the bag you would want to marry that girl and live with her there, next to your business so to speak, but it's all over with her, isn't it?.'

'You are correct. No, I have no desire to go out there permanently, or even for a visit until I've got her completely out of my head.'

'I understand, I sympathise. We have all been disappointed in love at some time in life. Do you think that George can handle it all?'

'If he keeps us, that's me or Henry, in the loop at all times then, yes, yes I think he can.'

'Alright, accepted. Now what are we going to do with you instead? No, don't answer because I know what I want you to do'

He swallowed two more oysters; I followed him.

'The world is changing all around us, business, even such traditional enterprises as insurance, must advance with the times. Computers are being moved into the basements of banks and Government offices, in time even into ours I expect, and within a couple of years men may well be on the moon. Buildings, aeroplanes and ships are being designed and built by processes quite different from those of even ten years ago. These are the things that we insure, but I don't believe our industry is aware of what is happening and is going to continue to happen at an ever increasing pace. We of the insurance trade are traditionalists and change is often antipathy to us, for we are steeped in history and rely upon it for our guidance. Let me ask you, How do we evaluate risk so as to establish insurance premiums?'

James finished the last of his oysters as I replied.

'Well, for life insurance, which we don't do but which can serve as a starting point, we use actuarial tables which tell us the likely life span of people of differing ages, engaged in different occupations, living in different areas and engaged in different lifestyles. We also look at their health habits of course. Basically, we use actuarial tables leavened with our own nous.'

I finished my oysters, feeling quite pleased with my off-the-cuff exposition.

'So we don't look at their parents?'

'We do, sometimes, if they are dead, but not when they are still alive. Itis taken to be a good sign if they are.'

The silent and swift waiter whisked away our plates and bibs. James told him that we would take the steaks as soon as they could be made ready and then we topped up our glasses, finishing the champagne.

'We could have a nice Rioja red to go with our meat,' James suggested.

I declined, I wanted to keep a clear mind and it was already a little fuzzy from the half bottle of champagne I had just drunk.

'Then we will have something to go with our cheese later. Now, I concur with what you have said about life insurance. But what about entities in our own field: Ships, cargoes, dock side equipment, buildings, bridges and other infrastructure, what then?

'Basically, we look at records, we scrutinize what has happened to similar items before, how often have they failed and for what reason. And we will look at the owner's insurance history.'

'So statistics again, a bit like actuarial data?'

'Yes, which is why I started off with life insurance as an example.'

'Well, you are right, and that's the problem. We are using Victorian methods in a late 20th century business. We rely on history, and if the type of entity has no history, like these new computers for instance, what then? We have to do better.'

James puts his elbows on the table, entwined his fingers as if in prayer and stared at me either thinking hard or making his mind up about something difficult. I returned his stare and saw that his steel-grey eyes didn't blink. His countenance was exactly as I had seen in the faces of Formula One racing drivers waiting on the grid for a Grand Prix to start. They stare straight ahead and at the starter's flag; their gaze is unwavering, blink free and somewhat disturbing to observe.

'What we have to do David,' he said after a silence that must have lasted just half a minute but seemed to me much longer, 'is to predict what may happen to the things we insure. And to do this we need a technique. A technique that puts our syndicate ahead of our competitors. We must be able to know, with a reasonable degree of certainty, how, when and why something we insure is likely, or not likely, to fail or be lost in some way. This will enable us to tailor our premiums to circumstances far more closely than at present and make us more profitable than our competitors. Do you get the picture?'

'Yes, yes I think I do.'

Our tournedos arrived, the waiter laying fresh napkins on our laps. We slowly started on our meat, mine was perfectly cooked; pink on the inside and crisp on the outside, just as I liked as too, it seemed, did James judging by the little 'Oooh' he let out at his first mouthful.

'Would you like to be the person in our company, possibly one of the very few in the whole world of the London insurance market, who knows about the technique and how to use it?'

'Yes, yes I would.' I was thinking what my father had said in Spain, about me acquiring some sort of discriminator that would set me apart from others and boost my career prospects. I had guessed right; he must have known what was on James mind and he had set me up to accept – just like that damn girl used to do with me.

'Good. However, the bad news is that, of course, the technique, the process, call it what you will – doesn't exist as yet. Well, not as far as I know. But, thinking that you would be agreeable and no doubt with some pushing by your dad, I collared one of my Government chums, a civilian tied up with defence somehow, and he came up with two courses of instruction that should set you on your way. The rest will be up to you.'

We stayed silent while we finished our steaks and the champagne. I couldn't comment until James had explained some more about these courses.

As the waiter came to clear away our plates, James broke the silence with, 'How about some stilton to end up with and a glass of port?'

'Sounds just right,' I replied.

The waiter glided off to get our finales.

'One of the courses follows on from the other and most of the students will attend both. About 12 people in all, mostly Royal Air Force but a few civil service scientists or engineers as well, and you. The first will be at the Aeronautical College at Cranfield in Bedfordshire, do you know of it?'

I shook my head. James pulled out a small, leather bound notebook from his jacket's inside pocket and flipped it open to a page marked with a paper clip.

'It will last one week and there is accommodation in the facility. An old RAF barracks I expect. It starts on the 2nd of October, just under a month from now. The objective is to look at how and why things fail prematurely and what can be done to predict and prevent such failures. Apparently, it all springs from the space business where things that are blasted off from earth not only have to be very light but also mustn't fail.' James squinted at the open page of his notebook. 'It's all to do with 'single failure points' and 'redundancy', and I have no idea what either of those things mean in the real world.'

I had no idea either, but I recognized that the course sounded as if it would be important to insurance assessment.

The waiter arrived with two large glasses of port the colour of dried blood, and two small plates each bearing a healthy wedge of Stilton cheese. He put a basket of wafer biscuits between us and a dish of butter which James waved away. 'If the cheese is as good as it looks, it won't need butter.'

After checking his notebook again, James continued his talk once the waiter was out of earshot. 'The second course starts the following Monday at the Royal Aeronautical Establishment, RAE, at Farnborough. It lasts just three days so you will have to put up in a hotel nearby. Farnborough is easily and quickly reached by train from London. It will comprise an introduction to why aircraft crash; my pal told me it's all to do with accident investigation and, he says, fascinating. And although I know that we have never insured aircraft, apparently the examination of the chains of events that lead to aircraft misfortunes can be extrapolated to buildings and other civil engineering structures as well as machines.'

What James had said about the courses had no relation to anything in my career so far, but I could see that that they might well in the future; he had definitely got my attention and it looked as if I would have a very interesting and stimulating October.

'However,' James interrupted my self-centred thoughts. 'There is one small snag about attending the courses. Not really a snag, more a condition.'

'What's that?' I asked.

'You have to become a Civil Servant.'

I nearly choked on the last crumbs of my cheese.

'Your Pa was a Civil Servant, of sorts; it's really not that bad. But I'm pulling your leg a bit. In order to attend the courses you have to be working for the Government, either Armed Services or Civil Servant, or be a specially invited defence contractor. You are not the first or the last of these so Civil Servant it must be, but only 'For the Duration'.

'What does that mean?'

'You are not familiar with that war-time phrase? Oh! The innocence of youth! You will sign a paper that puts you on secondment to some obscure branch of Government for a short period of time. That's all. You still get paid by me just as you do now, nothing else changes.'

I pondered for no more than a few seconds. 'Sounds fine,' I replied. 'What do I need to do to before the 2nd of October?'

'I'll make the necessary phone calls tomorrow. You will probably have to go to some dust-laden Victorian office to complete the paperwork later this month. I am very glad that you have agreed, although I never had any doubt you would … there is a lot of your father in you. But not a word to anyone else in the office. This is just between you and me for the present.'

I nodded my agreement.

James paid for our meals with his Diners Club card, and I thanked him for having taken me to such a distinctive place to eat. When we returned to the office the staff rose and clapped vigorously to mark the success of the Singapore contract which they had been told about by Henry Souch while James and I had been lunching.

Chapter 4

I had a long chat with my parents by phone that evening. I told my father about the Singapore contract coming through and then about James' plan for me to become an insurance incident cause and effect expert. It was no surprise when he told me that James' initiative would result in me becoming distinct from my insurance broker peers.

'Better than joining a Golf Club,' he remarked.

'Or the Masons,' I re-joined.

My mother, as she often did, drove our conversation towards my love life.

'Absolutely nothing at all,' I told her. 'I've gone all celibate and not looking out for anyone and, you know, I feel better for it. Once bitten, twice shy.' She seemed to accept it as an explanation.

As I watched the news on the television later, finishing the last of a bottle of wine that I had opened the previous evening whilst digesting a ham sandwich for a light dinner, given the earlier ample lunch at De Hems, I suddenly realised that I really had been following a rather monk-like existence. The girls that had entertained me in my bedroom the previous year had no successors and I was going out to pubs in the evening far less frequently; these activities having been replaced by my set building at Questors. Although I still regarded socialising with my male friends at Summer Sunday cricket matches as sacrosanct, as were the Rugby Club roistering during the winter months, I realised that as this group of friends, like those from my London school days, became progressively smaller there would be fewer visits to sports venues with them.

My conclusion that evening was that all in all my physical and mental health had probably benefitted from the collapse of my engagement. I resolved to put my physical and mental energy into fulfilling James' plan for my education and future career. To cement my resolution, I bought myself a nearly new Rover 2000 the next day.

---///---

Two weeks after our lunch together, James invited me into his office again and introduced me to a lady dressed in an elegant but formal two-piece suit tailored from some sober, tweedy material. She was tall, just a couple of inches short of my six feet, despite wearing almost flat, highly polished black shoes. Her hair was dark brown, cut short and bore some natural silver coloured streaks. I guessed at her being in her mid-forties. She was what my mother would have described as 'handsome' to which I would have added 'impressive'. James introduced me to her, calling her Miss Hathaway.

'Jean,' she said as she offered her hand for me to shake.

'Jean Hathaway is going to turn you into a Civil Servant,' James said, indicating for us all to sit at the Board table.

'Temporary Civil Servant,' corrected Jean. 'You will be gazetted as an Executive Officer attached to the Treasury.'

'That sound impressive,' I commented.

'Not really,' Jean replied. 'As an Executive Officer you will be able to regard yourself as equal to the RAF Flight

24

Lieutenants or Squadron Leaders you will mix with on your courses. And as for the Treasury,' she smiled. 'No one really knows all that they do in that organization, or completely understands its functions. Just pretend to the other students that you are a 'Risk Advisor' with a background in insurance.'

'And how long am I to be signed on for?' I asked her.

'Oh! As long as it takes. We can sack you when the courses are over, or you can stay on our rolls if you like. You will be counted as a supernumerary and as unpaid you will not affect our Establishment.'

'Establishment?' I queried.

'That's very much a Government concept. It means the number of staff and the categories that an organization is supposed to have, as opposed to what it actually has. If you are identified as a supernumerary then you are not counted as being part of the Establishment and you don't have to be declared to the pen-pushers. In fact, you might find it to your advantage to stay on our rolls because you could possibly get to go on other courses. Also, we might get to pick your brains about insurance and risk mitigation without having to sign confidentiality agreements. The arrangement could be beneficial to both parties.'

'So you are expecting to get some return from me for sponsoring my attendance at the courses?'

'Certainly. Nothing is for free in this world. Now, two bits of paper to be signed by you.'

The first form that Jean handed me was an acceptance by me of the temporary employment she had described. I signed it.

The second collection of papers was headed 'Official Secrets Act'. The top sheet was to be signed by me and witnessed by Jean and James. My name and theirs had already being typed in. I started to read the other pages.

'You really don't need to read all that stuff,' Jean commented immediately.

'Why? What is it?'

'It simply, well hardly simply I suppose, tells you what you are supposed not to do and the penalties if you do do what you are not supposed to.' She took the pages from my grasp. 'It's all common sense really, nobody actually reads all this bumf, we will be here all day if you do.'

'But I do have to sign if I want to go on the courses?'

'Yes, you do. But it's really only to put you on the same footing as the other attendees, otherwise they will find it hard to chat with you after school.'

I signed the Official Secrets Act, as did my two witnesses. I didn't ask how long I would be bound by the Act. I suppose I assumed it would be for as long as I was a quasi-civil servant; I was wrong.

The next day I received a letter giving me what was described as 'Joining Instructions' for the two courses; Government procedures and nomenclatures continued to surprise me, but I started to see the sense of some of them.

I drove to Cranfield in my new car on the afternoon of Sunday the 1st of October. I found what was clearly an ex-RAF airfield off the M1 motorway about 45 miles north of London and quite near to Bedford. I was given a room in what had been the Officers Mess and joined the other course attendees in the bar before a communal dinner. I learned that there were ten people on the course of which seven were from the RAF (they were not wearing uniform that evening, but did so during the daylight hours of instruction) comprising five Flight Lieutenants and two Squadron leaders, one of the latter was a woman from the Education Branch who lectured at the RAF College at Cranwell, the remainder were Engineering Officers. Of the two civilians other than myself, one was from Farnborough and would be instructing us there the following week; the other was from a company called Hawker Sidley and engaged in the development of guided missiles. While the latter was distinctly guarded about his job, the others course members described their work quite openly after they had ascertained that I was a Civil Servant and had signed the Official Secrets Act. I must have seemed guarded to them about my work- because I had no Government work to talk about.

I found the Cranfield course fascinating. It was entitled 'Guarding against Failure'. The dry instruction was leavened with films, slide shows, case studies and hardware examples. We looked at all the things that could go wrong in the design and manufacture of aerospace hardware, and were taught ways to prevent or mitigate them. Important topics that stand out in my memory included Human Factors or how a person could unintentionally screw-up the best efforts of designers, single point failures, failure detection, self-repair in computer software, and 'design for redundancy', which was explained by a visiting British Aircraft Company designer from Bristol. He brought along a complex piece of mechanism from the Concorde aerodynamic control system and described how it had been designed with triple redundancy, as in there were three separate load paths throughout the structure. Two independent structural failures could be tolerated without hazarding the aircraft. The mechanism, he emphasised, had to meet rigorous weight parameters and at the same time tolerate the aircraft expanding its length in flight by more than a foot due to aerodynamic heating.

Although the course was almost entirely aeronautics centred, I did get to chat with the instructors out-of-school and learnt that the same principles could be applied to any sort of structure and even to non-tangible things. I began to recognize the questions I could pose to someone designing a bridge that my company might insure – 'What happens if those rivets fail, or are not to the specified strength, or the riveter is incompetent?'

The course ended on the Thursday and that evening I returned to my apartment very much looking forward to investigating failures at RAE Farnborough the following week.

---///---

As no accommodation had been arranged for me at Farnborough, I booked three nights in a Trust House hotel situated almost opposite the entrance to the RAE site. I arrived by car on the Sunday evening in time for dinner. I knew from my four days at Cranfield that I would be the only one on the Farnborough course not staying in the RAF Officers Mess.

The next day I drove into the site following the sketch map that had been included in the joining instructions. I passed near to a long, wide runway and could see that the RAE site contained very many buildings of all sorts of shapes and sizes dotted across a wide area. I also saw a jet fighter take off. This, I anticipated, was to be an exciting place for me to visit. After parking the car, I walked into the entrance lobby of a large brick building that looked as if it had been built well before WW2, perhaps even during WW1. The décor, worn creams and browns, substantiated its age. I was asked to sign into a visitors' book which wanted not only my home address but also the hotel at which I was staying. I was then escorted to a small lecture theatre which I was told would be my principal place of instruction for the next three days. Two of the RAF officers from Cranfield were already seated, and rose to greet me; the other six attendees arrived over the next few minutes. At 9 am we were welcomed by a middle-aged civilian man dressed in a brown laboratory coat and an RAF Squadron Leader who wore pilots' wings above his uniform tunic breast pocket; he introduced himself as a member of the RAE staff.

The core of the course was the technical investigation of aircraft accidents and took all of the first day and half of the second. We were told the principal reasons that aircraft crashed – generally pilot error, engineering failure or weather – and taken to see the wreckage of a civilian passenger aircraft which had been reassembled from its broken bits. We were told how analysis of these bits often provided the clues and evidence of the cause of an accident. Back in the lecture theatre we were shown mangled parts with evidence of fatigue failure, hydraulic actuators that indicated the position of flying controls at the time of the crash and instruments which, from the marks left on the inside of their glass fronts by bent, painted needles, showed what the dial had been displaying at the moment of impact. All of this was of interest to me, but I could not equate it to the business of calculating insurance premiums.

After lunch on the Tuesday which, as on all three days, was taken in the RAE staff management dining room, the Squadron Leader described how the RAF investigated aircraft accidents and other flying malfunctions, some but not all of which resulted in damage to the aircraft or the aircrew. He started off by saying that he was a pilot, General Duties I think he called his branch of the RAF, and was not going to cover anything to do with aircraft engineering which, he suggested, we had probably had had enough of during the previous day and a half. I heard the gently mocking boos from the RAF engineers in his audience.

'Now,' began the pilot. 'If anyone amongst you lot in uniform has formed part of an accident Board of Enquiry I want you to keep quiet for the next few minutes.'

'Suppose,' he went on, 'You are investigating the cause of a non-fatal crash. A helicopter, say, hitting trees in clear weather with its rotor blades. It sustained severe damage as it fell to the ground but the pilot and crew were protected from serious injury by their seat restraints and the strength of the cockpit enclosure. 'What would be the first question to ask the pilot?'

''What went wrong?' Asked a wit.

'Did the controls malfunction?' Asked another RAF officer.

'Did something cause you to lose sight of the trees?' Was my contribution.

'OK, enough already. You've said enough to kick off my spiel exactly as I want. You are focusing on the events at or just before the accident. What I'm going to show you is that that is not nearly enough. Particularly where pilot error is suspected, the whole chain of events leading up to the error has to be defined and analysed, in a time line starting well before the pilot took off on his fateful mission. Questions to ask of him, or of others, might include: had he been to a dinner at the Officers Mess the night before and was thus suffering a hangover? Did he have breakfast that morning, or was he suffering from a sugar low? Has he had a row with his wife? Was he in debt? Had he taken leave recently? And a myriad of other questions. The answers to these sorts of questions will sometimes tell you why a pilot acted in an atypical way and thereby hazarded himself to the point of precipitating an accident. I am going to tell you what to ask and why, and give you true-life examples. But don't think we are just going to concentrate on poor airmanship, perhaps the pilot makes a poor choice, notice I have said a poor choice, not a bad choice, words are important, because of the confusing layout of his cockpit or perhaps the type of emergency he faced had not been covered during his training. For a final thought before I begin, we are talking about male pilots because that's all we have in the Service at present. But when women start flying military aircraft, as they surely will and perhaps not too far in the future even though they delivered such aircraft all during WW2, the nature of some of the questions will probably change. And for my final, final thought, much of what I describe could be applied to technicians whose actions, or lack thereof, lead to an aircraft incident.'

His presentation held me in rapt attention for the whole of that Tuesday afternoon and most of the following day. Although they were exclusively based on RAF experience and military aircraft, I could see right away how the principles he expounded of following a chain backwards could uncover the root cause of an accident. But what was of even greater interest was his discourse on the compounding of seemingly innocuous aberrations into a series of events that would inevitably end in disaster: '*He was feeling this, so that happened, but then this other thing happened which he ignored, at the same time the ?? occurred which caused ?? – and so a disaster became inevitable.*' The relevance to the preventing, or finding the cause of, insurance losses became self-evident to me; that riveter that I had imagined after the course at Cranfield causing a bridge failure should be asked if his home life was happy.

The last session of the three-day Farnborough course was again presented by the RAF pilot. A screen was set up in the lecture room and, on the wall to the rear of where I was seated, I could see a small window with a projector behind.

'Now for something different,' began the pilot. 'Which of you know about the Vulcan 'V' bomber that broke up in mid-air, in 1958, over RAF Syerston?'

Most of the RAF Officers in the room put up their hands.

'Right, now which of you that just put up your hands witnessed the crash, or attended the Board of Enquiry, or have seen a film of what happened?'

No one spoke or put up their hands.

'Excellent,' said the pilot. 'Now, what we are going to do is to watch what happened.'

The lights went out and immediately a grainy, black and white film lasting just half a minute appeared on the screen. A large military aircraft, immediately recognisable from its delta wing as a Vulcan, flew from right to left; it manoeuvred, broke up in mid-air, and the film clip was over. The lights went up again.

The audience buzzed into low conversation as the pilot passed out small slips of paper to each of them.

'Without conferring or cribbing from each other, or identifying the paper with your name, I want you to write down the answers to two questions. Question number one, how many people bailed out? And number two, did anything fall off the aircraft before its final breakup? You've got thirty seconds, then fold your slips tightly and I'll collect them.'

The pilot collected up the folded papers, took them back to his lectern and read them while making a couple of notes on his notepad. He looked up to address his eager audience. 'First of all, why did the aircraft break up? Does anyone know?'

The civilian from Hawker Sidley answered immediately. 'The pilot attempted two manoeuvres at the same time. A partial roll combined with a hard pull up.'

'But surely,' the pilot lecturer responded, 'A military aircraft, even a bomber should be capable of conducting a half roll and a pull-up.'

'Yes,' came the civilian's reply. 'The one after the other, but not combined into one manoeuvre, that's a recipe for over-stress and structural failure'

'You are quite right, that's what happened. And how do you know that?'

'Because I am a structures analysist. We don't even let our guided missiles do that.'

'Yes, it was pilot error. Showing-off before an audience on the ground, a prime candidate for all those chain of event questions I told you about. Now to your observations. All of your answers are distributed between zero and three for the number of bailouts. I suppose most of you know that of the five crew members in a Vulcan only the two pilots have ejector seats, the poor Joes in the back have to scramble out as best they can. I am not going to tell you what the correct answer is, but less than half of you got it right.

As for the second question, six of you got the correct answer. Again, I'm not going to tell you what it is or let you watch the film again. But what I am going to do is to scold the lot of you. You are all on an accident investigation course, all but two of you are engineers in the aeronautics business, you all knew that you were going to watch a film of an aircraft crashing. And yet half of you could not accurately describe what actually took place.'

The resulting silence filled the room.

'But the significant thing is that your performance today is essentially the same as those of the previous six courses I have taught. The lesson, which we still have time today to discuss further, is to be very wary of what eyewitnesses may tell you. Another lesson, which again we should discuss further, is how you should pose questions to potential witnesses.'

He referred to his notes for a moment. 'The second question I put to you was, did anything fall off the aircraft before its final breakup? And I got your answers. But if I had asked, What was the first thing that fell off the aircraft? Then, on my past experience, I would have got different answers, and again many would have been wrong.'

Straight away I could see that the Vulcan crash observation experiment could be useful in sifting through reports on insurance related failures. *Did that construction crane really blow over in the wind as reported, or was it nudged by the passing cement truck?*

At 4 pm on the Wednesday afternoon I said my goodbyes to my fellow students and headed home, mentally thanking James for the stimulus he had provided me.

Chapter 5

I hadn't been in the office more than an hour the following day before James called me into his office.

'How did it go?' he asked. 'Were the two courses worth it? Have you learned anything of use to us?'

'You mean you want me to give you a debrief,' I countered.

'Debrief? What kind of word is that?'

'It's used by the RAF officers I met and the Civil Servants too, of which I am now one, remember? But yes, most useful. Even though centred on aircraft, the courses reviewed many methods, techniques and cases that could be extrapolated to our insurance work. Almost everything was to do with the detection, management and avoidance of risk. Just the sort of things you were telling me were needed at that De Hem's lunch. Yes, all very relevant but needing to be put into the context of our work, rather than that of the RAF.'

'Excellent, just what I hoped you would say. So, no more 'debriefing' now; instead, what I want you to do is prepare some sort of primer based on what you have learned for our staff to use. A list of things to be checked before we take on the insuring of significant, even unfamiliar, infra-structure. You may have to do some additional reading or research.'

'Yes, I may.'

'So, go away for the next two weeks. I'll tell the others that you've had to head off to Singapore in a hurry, then come back with a presentation to give to everyone in our company. You can use this office to deliver it. Prepare some handouts and use the vu-foil projector. But no more than an hour before taking questions.'

---///---

I gave my presentation on Monday morning, the 30th of October, to about eighteen people who were rather crammed into James' office-cum-boardroom. I used his desk as my lectern and placed the projector so that it shone on to the white wall behind me; the large reproduction of Turner's painting of the Pool of London that usually hung there having been temporarily removed.

My audience was comprised mostly of my fellow workers along with James and the Company Secretary, Mavis. Enough chairs had been found for all of them to sit in a straggly arrangement in front of me and the screen. Two others however, a man and a woman, came in just as I was about to start speaking and stood in the corner of the room furthest away from me. The woman I recognized as Jean Hathaway, the person who had signed me up as a temporary civil servant (which made me wonder if, with the two courses well past, I still was); the man I had never seen before.

At the end of my allotted hour my targeted audience seemed enthused with the techniques I had described and eager to try out the checklist of questions I had developed. James was effusive with praise of me. He asked me to remain in the office and speak with Jean and her companion while the others departed back into the main office, taking their chairs with them.

'Jean Hathaway you know, of course,' James began. 'But not, I think, Mr Rupert Noakes.'

The man reached out his hand to me. He was tall, spare, in his fifties, a little older than James perhaps, very smartly dressed in a dark pin-striped suit, white shirt with a separate collar, a dark tie, the pattern of which was not obviously connected to any organisation that I knew of, and, providing a full stop to his corporate 'uniform', a pair of highly polished black shoes. Described in those terms he should have appeared identical to James, but he didn't have the slight flashiness of James' appearance nor the pleasant smile that normally adorned the latter's face. There was a grimness about Mr Noakes and, for a moment, I was reminded of my father. But he smiled at me as I shook his hand. 'Just call me Noakes,' he said. 'I always think first names are a bit superfluous and often seem over-familiar.'

Jean, who I now immediately wanted to call 'Hathaway', said, 'While I arranged all the paperwork for you to attend those courses, which, by the way you have done a fine job in absorbing, distilling and re-aligning to your own needs.'

'Fine job,' echoed Noakes.

'It was Noakes who actually pulled open the doors to let you attend those courses.' Jean added.

I thanked Mr Noakes, exchanged a few more pleasantries and returned to my desk.

At a little past 5 pm that evening, I pushed through the revolving door of the lobby of the office block that housed my company's second floor offices and walked onto the street pavement. The area was already thronged with people either starting their homeward journeys or making for one of the City pubs that would do a thriving post-work trade until 8 pm at which time they would close. There was no staff beer call initiated by James that evening, so I set off for the five-minute walk to the Cannons Street underground station, there to catch a District Line train direct to Earls Court followed by a short stroll to my apartment.

The day had been fine but was now starting to become cold; I paused to button up my newly bought, double - breasted navy Burberry coat. A black taxicab stopped beside me; I saw that the 'For Hire' sign on its roof was unlit and thus was not surprised when its passenger door opened and a man stepped out onto the payment.

'David' the man called out; I looked up from struggling with a tight buttonhole and recognized Mr Noakes. He reached out his arm, just as he had earlier that afternoon, and with the same rather fixed smile. I freed my fingers from the recalcitrant button and took his offered hand. His fingers tightened around mine. Involuntarily, I made to free my hand from his grip and take a step backwards but as I did so a large man who had been acting as the taxi driver appeared by my side and put his arm around my shoulders. Noakes tightened his grip on me. It all looked, I'm sure, as though I was being greeted by old friends but effectively I couldn't move.

'I don't mean to startle you David, but you and I need to have a chat. We can speak in the cab; Charles,' he inclined his head towards the man with his arm around my shoulder, 'will drive us to somewhere quiet. Where do you suggest, Charles?'

'There's that side street leading into Sloan Square,' Charles replied with a distinct Essex accent. 'Not far from your place, Mr Noakes.'

'That will do fine, let's go then,' Noakes replied. With a swift pull from him and a coordinated push from Charles, I found myself in the back of the taxi. Noakes eased himself onto the fold-down seat opposite me while Charles re-occupied the driver's position. I heard the locks of the cab doors either side of me click shut. I looked nervously around. The windows in the doors were heavily tinted as was the glass separating the front of the cab from the rear; the rear window though clear was very small. I could see little of the outside world, and that world was practically blind to me sitting inside the cab.

Noakes continued to smile at me as Charles took the cab back into the City traffic. 'We will be there in ten minutes,' he told me. 'Then a little talk. A short discussion and you will be on your way back with Charles to your very nice apartment in Earls Court Gardens, with its bright red front door and the blue one below it leading into the basement studio.'

This guy is a policeman, I thought to myself, *that's why he's told me right away that he knows where I live. He has probably walked past and peered in. He is trying to intimidate me.*

Contact with the police was always going to make me uneasy in case that business in Broome six months earlier had come to light. But dealing with the girl there had taught me to keep my mouth closed to prevent it becoming choked by my own foot. I gazed at his still smiling face and confined my reply to, 'I look forward to that. Getting home I mean.'

Although we were travelling in the rush hour and the narrow City streets were starting to clog with traffic and pedestrians, it was clear from the motion of the cab that Charles was an expert driver used to weaving in and out of stalled vehicles. *Perhaps he really is a licensed London cabbie,* I reasoned.

After the predicted ten minutes' drive the cab drew to a halt and Charles called over his shoulder 'Here we are, Mr Noakes. Just around the corner from Sloan Square and no-one too near.'

Had I known then what I know now about interrogation tactics, I would have guessed correctly that Noakes was going to start his conversation with something designed to put me entirely off balance.

'Now David, just a few questions I need to put to you. All to do with the Official Secrets Act and associated nonsense I'm afraid.'

For Gods' sake, I thought, *I don't know any bloody Official Secrets. Or is it my talk today about risk management? Did I give away something that I'd learned at Farnborough?* I thought I had disguised my sources, so-as-to speak, pretty well, and I never mentioned the V-Bomber crash. He had got me off balance sure enough and with his opening question, was about to make me topple over, but not straight away.

'Do you know a young woman called Penelope?

The name didn't ring any bells. I mentally went through what was a fairly short list of past girlfriends and was certain that none bore that name. 'No,' I replied. 'I can't recall anyone of that name.'

'How about Penny then?'

I thought once more and came up with the same answer. 'No again. No Pennies in the purse,' I said, trying to defuse the situation with a little humour. Noakes completely ignored it.

'Otherwise known as, Poppy?'

Bullseye! And I was toppled.

'Poppy Khosla?' I stumbled over the name though not due to unfamiliarity.

'The very person. You knew her very well?'

'Yes, very well,' I agreed, remembering that last night together in Broome, in each other's arms, and then the despair of the next day. 'But I haven't seen her in six months.'

'Not since flying out of Perth last March?'

'No, not since then.' I answered freely, but then my spine stiffened. *What was my relationship with Poppy to do with this uber-cool policeman in front of me, and why the hell was I suddenly sitting inside a cab with him when I should have been almost home by now?*

'Are you a Policeman?' I asked, deciding on a more aggressive posture. 'You have no right to keep me inside this locked taxi.'

The smile returned to Noakes' face as he leaned forward towards me. 'You are not locked in.' The door nearest to me opened a few inches as he turned its handle. 'See, no locks when the engine is turned off. Of course, you can get out and make your way home right now if you wish. Although I shall seek you out again. Or you can answer a few more questions and have a little discussion with me about your future.'

The prospect of the open door allowed me to relax a little back into me seat. 'What's my future as an insurance broker got to do with you, or with Poppy Khosla?'

'Certainly, your insurance career is your own business, but you are also a pro-temp civil servant. We need to talk about how we can combine the two trajectories. But first to Poppy, she is the key to all of this.'

She always was the key to my life, I thought. *And this civil servant thing is just so much crap. I can't be held to that piece of paper given me by Ms Hathaway.* That thought gave me an opening.

'Where is Jean Hathaway?' I asked. 'I presume she is in this along with you, whatever 'this' may be.'

'In a way, yes. But back to Poppy, please. She is in trouble and needs your help. How does her being in trouble sit with you?'

I thought of the last time she had pleaded for my help; complying with that request resulted in me losing a fiancée and my honour, such as it ever was. 'I don't want to help her;

I helped her before and it all ended very badly.' I stated as firmly as I could.

'Badly for you, because you thought you and she were going to get married, but much more badly for Mr Okada.'

Oh Jeez, I thought as I felt a shiver of fear like a gush of cold water coursing down my spine. *He knows, he bloody well knows; I'm about to be blackmailed.* I could think of no other action than to hold my peace.

The forced smile had gone from Noakes face. I was going to get a lecture from him. For a moment I was reminded of my headmaster chastising me when he had seen me coming out of a pub in uniform during my last term at school; I was about to be lectured.

He started. 'Your girlfriend Penelope, 'Poppy' as you call her, whom you had known since attending the same primary school in Singapore, lured you to the pearling town of Broome, Western Australia in March this year. There she had arranged for the Japanese policeman who had raped her Chinese mother during the occupation of Singapore to be confronted by his son, her own half-brother, who worked locally as a diver. While you watched, Poppy and another girl, Liu Chi, forced Okada to admit to the rape of her mother, who had died during the resulting birth, and to other crimes while a member of the notorious Japanese military police, the Kempeitai. How am I doing so far?'

He had got it exactly right. I involuntarily nodded my agreement.

'Your supposed reward was to get to marry Penelope, which had been your ambition for a long time. You were supposed to make your getaway together from Australia, leaving father and brother relatively unharmed, physically at least, and fly off to meet up with her adoptive parents in Singapore.'

'The Khoslas,' I offered, and suddenly realised that I was starting to cooperate with Noakes..

'Yes, well known to you of course, for they are friends of your parents. But she slipped away from you in Perth airport after which you flew straight back to London. Am I still on the right track?'

There was little point denying any of it. Not with the level of detail he already knew. 'Yes, yes that's all about right.' And then my inevitable question. 'But how do you know all this? I haven't had any contact with her since she dumped me. For all I know she is still in Hong Kong where she fled to from Perth. You must have spoken to her, or perhaps to Lucy, Liu Chi, she is quite a devious one too.'

'To her only, not the other girl.' Noakes looked at his watch. 'This has all taken rather longer than I thought, sorry about that, and sorry that we still have a way yet to go.'

Now that the story was out, a story than I had never shared with anyone, I strangely felt quite relaxed. All in all, my couple of years of relationship with Poppy as an adult were neither happy nor honourable on either side; a shameful episode for me really. I was glad it was all over and that I had, hopefully, learned from it and grown up. I didn't want to hear any more from Mr Noakes, but knew I was about to. Otherwise, what was I doing sitting in the damn taxicab?

Noakes settled back into his seat indicating, I thought, that the more intense part of our conversation, as he had called it, was over. 'I started off by saying that Penelope needs your help, so now I am going to tell you why. You probably thought that leaving Mr Okada in Broome was, for you and the two girls, the end of the story, but it wasn't. He got back to Japan after the son had effectively disowned him. The son stayed in Broome and avoided jail time for a pearl theft, the ins and outs of which I don't fully understand, neither did the judge I expect.'

Noakes paused and fixed me with an interrogator's look. 'And then, just a few weeks later, Okada killed himself. Suicide.'

I had a picture of him slicing his stomach open, Hara-kiri style; Noakes must have guessed what I was thinking as he shook his head.

'He shot himself. Apparently, his son's rejection was too much to bear. The shame too much for him to continue living among his fishing community where he had been a successful businessman.'

But how would Noakes have known that? I immediately wondered. Surely Poppy would not have told him, even if she had known, because she was the clear cause of his death. She had made it clear to me that her objective had been the bringing of shame to Okada for the rape of her mother. Well, she had certainly succeeded in that!

Noakes was way ahead of me. 'So Penelope, your 'Poppy', was the cause of him taking his own life.'

I nodded.

'And you, with Liu Chi, were accomplices. You, because you did nothing to prevent the shaming.'

'Why should I have? What should I have done?'

'Oh! I don't think you need any help from me in deciding that. Let's end this session here and continue tomorrow – in your apartment might be suitable, I know you live there on your own. I'll call by at nine o'clock tomorrow. Don't worry about the office, James knows that you won't be in. I want you to give me your answer tomorrow about helping Penelope out of her jam.'

'What jam?' I retorted. 'He's dead and I don't suppose that son of his is heartbroken.'

'Yes he is dead, but she is now in the sights of an organisation that wants to avenge him.' Noakes opened the door and exited the cab saying, 'You can help her get out of her predicament. Think on it overnight, I need your decision in the morning. Charles will drive you home now.'

---///---

The drive from Sloan Square to my apartment took just a few minutes through the easing rush-hour traffic. The cab drew up behind my shiny new car. My thoughts during that short time were totally confused and added nothing to my comprehension of what was happening to me. Charles said nothing as I got out of the cab and opened my wrought iron front gate. Once inside my home I poured a whisky and slumped into my favourite armchair opposite the television in the lounge. I twisted to look out of the bay window facing the street, the black cab had gone.

My reaction now to Noakes' revelations was one of anger. What the hell was it to do with me? Yes, I will admit, I was there when Poppy had forced her birth father, using some degree of physical pressure, but more psychological I had comforted myself at the time, to tell his son how he had come to father her. But that he chose death because of dishonour was surely nothing to do with me? But I realized it was – because I had stood by and done nothing. And then, just the very next day, she dumped me – used, spent, to be forgotten by her. Now she needed me again – for what? She could go to hell!

I climbed down the stairs that led to the basement studio where she had lived the whole of the previous year. Ostensibly, she was working in the jewellery department of Harrods to enhance her knowledge of pearls and studying Japanese at night school, but it seems that all that while she had been planning the final confrontation with her birth father. She was good company, and so beautiful that I had a bounce in my stride whenever she was by my side and I revelled in the envious looks of other men. She said she loved me, but platonically. I craved her body but touching it was forbidden and kisses were restricted to pecks on the cheek.

I paused before I opened the door at the bottom of the stairs; there was the keyhole through which I spied on her naked body as she showered in the little bathroom opposite. She had opened the door and caught me but showed no anger, even offered to take baths in my bathroom so I could wash her back and view her nakedness in comfort - an offer that I never took up. In my shame, anger and need to kick back at the celibacy of our relationship, I took several girls in quick succession. Nice girls who didn't seem to resent the transient nature of their time with me and who still remained casual friends.

I walked around the studio. My parents had twice used it since Poppy's departure during their bi-annual visits from their permanent home in Spain; no traces of the girl remained. She was gone from my property, near gone from my mind, and I was living a totally celibate life; this probably as the unconscious result of my last night with her when she finally invited me to make love to her and I had found myself totally incapable.

I returned upstairs and sat down glumly in the armchair with another glass of whisky. A dim light suddenly illuminated in the back of my brain. Just as Poppy had lured me to Broome with a series of seemingly straight forward, unremarkable, actions, events and choices, another similar scenario had been unfolding about me. I had been given a choice by Noakes, more of an ultimatum really, to help Poppy; just as Poppy had presented the choice to me to join her in Australia which had proved irresistible. Perhaps I could discover the path leading to the Noakes' offer by working backwards as I had been taught at Farnborough. Had the pilot had breakfast or a row with his wife before taking off for his fateful flight?

Noakes had been at my presentation earlier in the day, ergo James must have invited him or he knew James enough to ask to attend. James also seemed to know Jean Hathaway when she signed me up to the courses and the Official Secrets Act, and she also was at my presentation. So, some sort of liaison, collusion, between Hathaway and Noakes – a professional relationship perhaps – to which my boss is, perhaps, also a party. Which then begs the question about the Cranfield and Farnborough courses themselves. James had made a persuasive pitch to me about their potential use for introducing the concept of modern risk assessment to the insurance business, and thus presenting a unique opportunity for my future career. Having completed the courses, I had no doubt he was right; but what if there were also another, ulterior, motive? Was I being set up for something, something completely unlikely and involving Poppy? And thinking of her – that was the sort of dance she had led me on which had ended in me watching her break the spirit of her Japanese father in that barn in Broome.

Those thoughts drove me out to the nearby Chinese restaurant owned by the parents of Lucy, Liu Chi, Poppy's co-conspirator who had shared my bed at her own insistence for those last few months of 1966. It had been at the same time as George Blake had made his escape from prison, causing us to make wry comments at how poor Britain was at not only detecting spies but keeping them when caught. I wasn't expecting to see Lucy working in the restaurant – she had gone to Hong Kong the last I had heard – but I looked for Lucy's parents despite remembering that they never came out of the kitchen. However, the waitress I questioned, had never heard of them, or of Lucy. The restaurant had changed hands before she was hired, and everyone working there was new, she added.

I ordered a take-away and returned to my apartment. Later, my initial, automatic reaction to avoid helping the woman that had caused me so much grief in Australia softened over the course of the night. I remembered our charmed childhoods together in Singapore where we had first met at eight years of age and how soon after we had realised our love for each other. An uncomplicated but nonetheless true love. I knew that if she was in trouble that I had no option other than to help her as best I could.

I was watching out of the lounge window the next morning when the black cab pulled up at exactly two minutes before nine. Noakes got out and stepped through the apartment's gate, but I had opened the front door to him before he had finishing climbing the three steps leading up to my porch. I greeted him with a firm, 'Good Morning'.

'Good Morning,' he replied and on my waved invitation settled himself in one of the chairs in the dining room that led off the lounge. I sat opposite him.

'Well?' He began. 'Have you made a decision about helping Penelope?'

'Yes,' I replied. 'And yes, in principle I *will* help her. But first you have to tell me what her situation is and what sort of help she needs.'

'Fair enough. But talking of firsts, I have to remind you that you are still bound by the Official Secrets Act. What I am about to tell you comes under that Act and you are hearing it on a strictly *need to know* basis. Do you understand what that term means?'

'Yes, I mustn't repeat what you tell me to anybody.'

'That's about right, but you also must not tell anybody that we have even had these meetings, although Jean Hathaway of course knows.'

Bingo! I thought. *They are a pair.*

'And your boss, James Harrington.'

Again, Bingo!

'But you still must not discuss our meetings with him. He is also need to know, but his need to know is not quite so much.'

Noakes crossed his legs and fastened his hands around one knee. He looked as if he were about to tell a story – and that's precisely what he did.

'So, Miss Penelope Khosla … she is a naughty girl and she is in a scrape. What do you know about the Kempeitai?'

'They were the Japanese military police and held the population in terror during the occupation of Singapore.'

'Correct,' Noakes said. 'And in many other places that they invaded during World War Two. At the end of the war some were executed for their crimes, some were jailed and others, like Okada were tried but acquitted although not necessarily innocent. Now it is well known that some surviving members of the German SS meet to celebrate the *Old Days*, drink beer, sing the *Horst Wessel* song, whilst blaming the Americans and the British for not joining with Germany in attacking Russia and so avoid the current Cold War. They are tolerated so long as they don't cause trouble or attempt to recruit youngsters to their beliefs. Well, surprise surprise! Ex-members of the Kempeitai, just a very few, act similarly but very much under the radar. They are associated with powerful criminal gangs and are not afraid to perform acts of revenge, including murder.'

Noakes adjusted his position again leaning forward with his elbows on the table but with both hands still intertwined.

The preamble was over, I realized … now for the problem with Poppy.

'And murder is just what they have done.'

'Oh my God! Panic struck me. My face drained of its colour. Poppy was dead. What was my role to be in all this?

Noakes saw my reaction and knew exactly what I was thinking. 'No, it is not Penelope. It was Liu Chi, her friend.'

'Lucy?' I managed. An unworthy sense of relief swept over me.

'They thought she was Penelope and shot her.' He added, almost as an afterthought, 'In Hong Kong.'

I remembered how alike they had looked and not in some stereotypical oriental way. They had been the same height, their figures almost identical, as was the shape and structure of their faces. Almost exact replicas of matching beauty. That was why Poppy wanted me to sleep with Lucy rather than her. 'We look the same naked, and you white guys can't distinguish between Oriental girls anyway,' was her supercilious rationale.

'Who did it?' I asked, still seeing Lucy's face merging with Poppy's in my mind's eye.

'It was probably the Triads working under contract for the Japanese that wanted revenge for Okada's suicide. Apparently, the son spilled the beans on what had happened in Broome which set them onto Poppy's trail. Both girls were staying with Liu Chi's grandparents in a rather seedy area of Hong Kong but the wrong, pardon the expression, girl was targeted. Liu Chi was shot in the midst of a crowd within the city centre. I gather the two girls looked alike?'

'Yes, very alike,' I said, my brain still reeling with the news. 'Where is Poppy now?'

'She is staying in a police compound for her safety although the bush telegraph, the local police are expert at that, are broadcasting that it was Poppy that was killed, not Liu Chi.'

'So now what?'

'Interviews by the Hong Kong police and by a person who, let us just say, is on my payroll, show Miss Penelope Khosla to be a very interesting and adaptive young lady. She is also well connected through her father to important people in Singapore. I could use her talents to do a little task for me, but for that I need to get her to London, to quietly, unobtrusively move her from Hong Kong to here. And, that's where you come in.'

I thought he meant I was to be the bait to lure her to London. But I was not quite right.

Noakes examined his immaculate fingernails and said 'We –'

I stopped him. 'Who are we?'

'Oh, we are a very little team. Just me, Hathaway, the man now in Hong Kong who travels a bit, an office minder, and of course my boss.'

'Who is?'

'Need to know, David, need to know and for that, you don't. Yes, a small team but with extensive other resources available to it, to us. Sometimes people like Penelope or you will do us a one-time favour. Your favour will be to fly to Hong Kong, collect the girl and escort her here safely.'

'But why me, why doesn't that man of yours already there do the job?'

'Because Poppy wants it to be you, specifically and no argument would be entertained. You, otherwise she won't come. And then, knowing now a little about her, she will go after those that killed Liu Chi and in the process will get herself killed. No, she has to be got away from Hong Kong and probably Singapore too. The Triads have a far reach throughout Asia.'

51

This was typical Poppy, I thought, and waited for the next shoe to drop.

'You told me first thing today that you were ready to help her. The plan is for you to go out there and bring her back to England … as your wife.' Noakes paused for my reaction.

'Marry her!' I exploded, thinking, *That's all I ever wanted to do. It's the same bait that she used to lure me to Broome. NO. NO. NO!*

'Well, sort of marry her. We thought that you would attract less attention from the airport watchers on you route if you travelled as man and wife. Her name would have had to be changed anyway to make the journey, she couldn't have travelled as Penelope Khosla, considering that person is meant to have been killed already by the Triads. Much simpler to bury her within your identity. The idea is that your passport, oh do you have it here?'

'Yes,' I nodded testily.

'Good. Your passport will be altered, amended, to include your wife, Penelope Shawyer, British Citizen. You will be provided with a marriage certificate stating that you were married last year in the Wandsworth Registry Office. So, all make believe!' A slightly knowing smile passed over Noakes face. 'Of course, when it's all over you could remain married if you wished. I mean, the paper trail would be robust enough for that, or everything could be made to disappear, leaving you unencumbered with each other once again.' Noakes paused, again waiting for my reaction, then when it wasn't forthcoming said, 'What do you think?'

'I agreed to help her, although I think it's more about helping you, but I'll do what you want. What about my work?'

'Excellent, excellent. Don't you worry about James. Although he doesn't know the details of the plan he does understand that you won't be available for your normal duties for a while. I think he is going to tell everyone that you have gone on one of your courses again. And it's not the first time his company have helped me out, so as to speak. Henry Souch has been of great use on several occasions, all before the Second World War so a long time ago. Perhaps when he finally retires he will tell you about it.'

Why, I thought, *do I detect a maelstrom forming around me?*

'If you give me your passport now it will be returned by the end of tomorrow along with the marriage certificate and on the very next day you will be on your way to Hong Kong. Take the rest of today and tomorrow off. Go to the Zoo or something. A trip to Hampton Court Palace or Greenwich would be nice even at this time of year, but be back here by 6 pm tomorrow. Hathaway will come with all the paperwork, airplane tickets and a little *just in case* spending money. She will give you a thorough briefing on the details of your journey, your hotel in Hong Kong, who will meet you and where. You will have nothing to worry about, you will find her very thorough. You might want to get your car off the street and into a lock-up garage or something while you are away. You don't want it stolen.'

Chapter 6

The weather had turned lousy and the only time I went out was to put my car inside a nearby mews garage that I had rented over the phone. On Thursday the 2nd of November I boarded the first of a series of flights that would end in Hong Kong, a place I had never been to before. Overnight clothes had been packed in a soft-sided bag that travelled with me in the cabin along with a small briefcase containing my and Poppy's return tickets for the day after I my arrival, a voucher for a hotel near to the airport, my passport which was now David and Penelope Shawyer's passport and about 200 pounds worth of banknotes in a variety of foreign currencies … and my marriage certificate.

Jean Hathaway's briefing the previous evening had been very thorough as predicted by Noakes and, somewhat disturbingly, given with a hint of sympathy. She emphasized that I should avoid using the name Poppy while travelling with her until we were safely back in England. 'Behave as if you are married,' she concluded. 'But don't ask me what that entails because I've no experience of that supposedly blissful state.'

First Class tickets had been provided and my route out was fairly straight forward: Eastwards always with stops of an hour or so in the Middle East, India and Thailand. But coming back was to be a different story. Out of Hong Kong to the west coast of America, changing planes and airlines to get across to the east side of the USA, then out of New York back to London direct. . I had queried the return routing with Jean and she explained that the objective was to get Poppy and me out of the Orient as quickly and directly as possible, but I suspected that the real reason was to create as confusing a trail as possible while still travelling approximately in the direction of England.

Almost 24 hours after leaving London I was awed by my aircraft's final approach to land at Kai Tak airport as it seemingly skimmed through the surrounding buildings of Hong Kong. I was met by a young Englishman, about 30 years old I guessed, smartly dressed in an open neck short sleeve white shirt and matching white shorts. He looked and carried himself like a policeman but offered no personal information except his first name, Paul.

He drove me in a small car to the nearby Western style hotel where I was to stay for just one night, then be picked up by him the next morning at 9 am to meet 'The Lady', as he called Poppy, back at the airport. He told me not to leave the hotel at all and by way of less formal conversation said that the Chinese mainland-inspired anti-British riots that had plagued Hong Kong over the past year now seemed to be well and truly over. He then added that the riots had provided good cover for the assassins' attempt on The Lady's life, but they had also provided the confusion in which the report of the actual murder was muzzled and buried.

I obeyed Paul's instructions and spent the time mainly sleeping in my room and eating meals at odd times using room service.

I was sitting in the hotel lobby, packed, my room paid with a voucher given me by Jean Hathaway, and ready to go when Paul arrived to collect me. There was a peak-hatted, Chinese looking driver in the front of a different, larger car than that of the previous evening. Paul sat next to him while I graced the back seat all by myself. My feelings were a mixture of anticipation and dread as we retraced the route to the airport. What would be my first words to Poppy? And what would be hers to me? I wanted to see her although not under these circumstances. But in just a few minutes after parking the car in a space reserved for the Police, Paul guided me through the airport's arrivals hall and into a small, window-less room which was, I think, part of the Customs facilities. There, standing with her hands clasped demurely below the belt cinching a plain cream dress, with a small suitcase by her side, was Poppy.

She didn't move. I also stood still for a moment then moved up to her and said the first silly thing that came into my head. 'Hello Mrs Shawyer.'

She burst into tears. I had only seen her cry once before, not ever when we were young children in Singapore but only as an adult when she told me for the first time about the death of her mother. I faced her not knowing where to put my hands, she flung her arms around my neck sobbing. 'I'm so sorry David, so sorry about everything.'

I could feel her chest heaving against my body. The sobs diminished and she looked up into my face with the trace of the smile that I had so loved. 'You always said you wanted to marry me, well, here we are joined at last.'

She straightened her hair which was still styled like a cloche hat, took out a silver powder compact and checked her appearance in its mirror. A few dabs of powder around her eyes and once again she was the Poppy – No, Penelope! – I knew, ready to face anything. But I had learned from my past times with her that she was never quite all that she seemed and always had secret agendas. I looked at her with different eyes, no longer lovesick, from those of just six months ago. But her beauty was as apparent as ever although, even now, I couldn't be certain if she were aware of its effect on other people; was her face - her secret, but completely overt, weapon? I glanced at Paul, his gaze at her was unabashedly fixed on her face then, as if shaking his head to restore it to action, he told us to move to the First Class lounge after checking-in and await our boarding instructions. He walked us up to the check-in desk and left wishing us, 'Good luck.'

---///---

The journey back to London was tedious and lengthy despite the luxury of our aircraft cabin surroundings. Using some of the money Jean Hathaway had given me, I bought magazines and refreshments for us both during our ground stops. I slept a lot, slumped in my reclining seat, and at other times we chatted trying to act like a married couple – the cabin staff scrupulously addressed her as Mrs Shawyer. We both instinctively knew that certain topics, including many of our shared experiences, were off limits: Lucy, Broome, Mr Okada, his son and the whole of her time living in the studio under my apartment. What was left was our two idyllic childhoods in Singapore. I asked about her adoptive parents who had so wanted us to marry; she said that they were well but had only seen them once this year when she returned from Hong Kong for a short stay. She then closed that topic down. I imagined that her adoptive father, an influential lawyer, would not be well pleased with her and might even had known some of what she had been up to over the past year.

For most of the remainder of the journey we flipped through our magazines and languished with our own thoughts. I had an overwhelming feeling that my involvement with Poppy and Mr Noakes was not going to end in the Arrivals Hall at London Airport. When I glanced at Poppy, as I frequently did when I thought she was not looking at me, I occasionally saw her beautiful face collapsed in grief and I guessed she was thinking of Lucy. I had always thought that there had been a romantic attachment between the two. Was she mourning a lost lover? An hour out of London I wrapped an arm around her shoulders and drew her head into my neck.

'Tell me Poppy, tell me what happened. To Lucy and to you. Don't hold back. We have shared so many secrets in the past. Please let it out, it would make you feel better I think and it's driving me crazy not to know.'

The sobs started again, loudly, bringing a member of the cabin staff to ask if she could do anything to help. I told her that we had had an old friend die in Hong Kong and had been to her funeral. At my request she brought us a large whisky each.

'It was all my fault,' Poppy whispered to me. 'My fault, I don't mean about Okada killing himself, I mean about getting Lucy involved.'

Involved, I thought. *Just like in all your little schemes.'*

She went on. 'You remember Lee in my father's office in Singapore. The man who helped me find my birth father?'

'Yes, I remember you telling me about him. He was tracing members of the Kempeitai who had escaped justice for their actions in Singapore.'

'That's right. Well it was Lee who told me in Hong Kong by phone that Okada had killed himself and that people were after me for retribution. It was he who suggested that Hong Kong Triads would be looking for me there; that was in May.'

'So what did you do?'

'I was terrified of course, you don't mess with the Triads, particularly in their home territory like Hong Kong. I didn't want to flee to Singapore and bring my family under threat, so I went to the British Governor's office and pleaded for help. It wasn't until I mentioned the Triads that I received proper attention. A senior British police officer interviewed me accompanied by a rather spooky man in plain clothes, British again.'

Noakes, I thought to myself. *Or more likely, one of his cohorts.*

'Instead of being offered protection of some sort I was told to carry on as normal, going on with my life such as it was, but under permanent surveillance so that the police could identify who the Triads might be.'

'You were going to be used as bait?'

'Something like that. Anyway, I agreed because I wasn't going to let the ex-Kempeitai thugs get the better of me. It was a very foolish display of bravado on my part. But I did what I had been asked, carried on life as normal with Lucy. She was living with her grandparents, I had a sort of bed-sitter nearby.'

'And what was carrying on as normal?'

'Oh, a bit of this and that, part-time work in jewellery shops, that sort of thing.'

'You've still to tell me about Lucy's death.'

'Yes, I'm sorry. I have been skirting around her a bit. You have heard about the Hong Kong riots this year and, indeed, last year.'

'Yes, it was well reported in the British newspapers. People died, didn't they?'

'Yes, guns, explosives, beatings. The police had a very hard job to keep the peace and root out the perpetrators. It was all orchestrated from mainland China in order to drive the British colonial masters out.'

It seemed to me that Poppy was still trying to delay telling me what had happened with Lucy, perhaps she was hoping the aircraft would land before she got to that part. She must have seen a frown of impatience cross my face.

Poppy started to speak more rapidly. 'We, Lucy and I, got stuck in a mob of people who were trying to get away from a close-by confrontation between rioters and police. We had been separated from each other by the jostling crowd, all I knew was that she was somewhere behind me. Shots rang out from the direction of the confrontation and the crowd started to panic. Another two shots came from behind me. I was overtaken by a feeling of dread. I turned back to try and find Lucy. Pushing against the rushing people I could hardly move more than one small step at a time. The shouting and other loud noises coming from all around me produced total confusion in my mind and I started to panic. And then suddenly a gap formed in the surging crowd and I could see Lucy lying on the ground with a man bent over her, trying to protect her from the feet of the melee.

'When I reached her I could see blood on the ground flowing from a hole in her skull; I was in no doubt that she had been shot dead. The man looked up. It was Paul, the man who saw us off at Hong Kong airport. He was holding a radio-telephone in one hand. He looked up at me and ordered, '*Stay right here, get down on your knees and don't move,*' pulling me down with his free arm. After what seemed an eternity but was probably only about five minutes, a police ambulance nosed its way through the now dissolving crowd and took Lucy, Lucy's body, me and Paul to a police compound where I have been living ever since.

'Paul was one of the officers who had been assigned to provide surveillance of me. He was distraught at what had happened. He explained that he had been trying to keep me in view in the crowd and didn't know where Lucy was until he heard the two shots and saw her on the ground just a few yards away. He never saw her attackers, he said.'

'So it was a targeted killing,' I said, as the full horror of what I had just heard was sinking in. 'In broad daylight, but of the wrong person.'

'The first reaction, obviously, was that it was me the killers were after, but the Police Inspector assigned to the case suggested that perhaps the killing of Lucy was deliberate and intended as a warning to me. I don't suppose we will ever know. The outcome is that here am I in hiding and married to you.'

'You haven't said anything about Lucy's grandparents with whom she was living. What was their reaction to all of this?'

'Police deception, I'm afraid. They were told she was one of the innocent casualties of the riots, there were many others you know, and the local press swallowed, or were persuaded to swallow, the story. Her parents gave up the café in London and returned to Hong Kong as soon as they knew.'

'And she didn't have any other family, I remember her once telling me.'

'No, except me who she looked on as her sister.'

Rather more than that, was my inner reaction.

Poppy pulled away from me, went to the toilet where she freshened up her makeup and returned to her seat for the landing at Heathrow Airport. I now had the full story of Lucy's death as told by Poppy, but to my mind the setting behind it did not quite add up. That was typical of Poppy; she never told you everything at once, truth came from her in dribs and drabs. She didn't tell lies, well, not obvious ones, but she controlled the telling of her plans, dreams and experiences to a pace that suited her rather than her audience. Her story about working casually in jewellery shops in Hong Kong didn't sound like her scene at all. I wondered how the police in Hong Kong had handled the questioning of her? She might even have got the better of them just as she so often had with me.

Jean Hathaway was waiting to meet us on Monday the 6th of November as we cleared immigration at Heathrow Airport without any problems, although the greeting of the officer checking the First Class passengers passports of, 'Welcome back to the United Kingdom, Mr and Mrs Shawyer' did make me think that he had been briefed on our arrival.

There was a car and driver waiting outside the terminal; Jean shepherded us straight to it saying that she was taking Poppy to the place where she would be staying while I was to make my own way home. Her last words were, 'Use some of the money I gave you to take a taxi. I'll probably be seeing you tomorrow, have all your receipts ready to give me and any cash left over. Someone will pick you up early in the morning.'

Book 2

The LINE which leads back to the beginning

Chapter 7

I tumbled into bed at about 6 pm that evening, anticipating that I would be meeting Mr Noakes and his crew sometime on the morrow. I was so tired that I went quickly to sleep after a short but sad thought about how poor, beautiful, Lucy had once graced this very bed.

At 9 am the next morning, Tuesday, I was once again looking out of my lounge window, waiting for a black taxicab to pull up in the light rain typical of London in November. Right at the anticipated time the vehicle arrived, Charles stepped out and knocked on my door. With a little maliciousness I made him wait for three minutes or so while I slowly put on my raincoat.

'I'm taking you to see Mr Noakes,' Charles began as he ushered me into the cab then continued speaking over his shoulder as he lowered himself into the driver's seat. 'We are going to the Air Ministry building in Whitehall, or what was the Air Ministry, I think it's called the Ministry of Defence now, but it's the same old building with the same half-naked, stone women guarding the doors. It's not far from the Cenotaph.'

Charles then said something I didn't catch into a radio microphone hanging from the roof.

Ten minutes later we were pulling up at the white edifice of the Ministry of Defence, the stone guardians seemed to glower down as Charles escorted me through the main door and brought me up to the waiting Jean Hathaway who was standing by a turnstile.

'Is this where you work?' I asked.

'Not really,' she replied with a smile. 'But we are all hoping that you will.'

She handed me a credit-card sized pass that bore my photograph; she told me to keep it ready at all times when in the building. *Photo taken from my passport,* I presumed.

'We will be on the ground floor,' she addressed a waiting uniformed Corps of Commissionaires gentleman as she pushed through the turnstile. 'I know where we are going, there will be no need for you to accompany us.'

Jean led me swiftly through what seemed a maze of corridors. 'If you follow the painted lines on the walls you can't get lost,' she offered. 'Or so they say.'

We arrived at a non-descript brown wooden door at the end of one of the corridors. I noted that the wall line leading there was green. The top half of the door was glass with an embedded screen mesh and painted over in whitewash – nothing could be seen through it. Jean knocked gently on the door and, without waiting for a response from inside, opened it.

The two of us walked into a large room of bare walls and no windows bar the opaque one in the single door. Lighting was by overhead fluorescents. An oblong wooden table with six chairs, probably of wartime 'utility' issue, took up nearly half of the floor space, two small desks each with its own chair together with several empty book shelves, closed filing cabinets and a large safe took up most of the remainder.

Poppy was seated at the table with Noakes alongside her. He got up to greet Jean and me; Poppy didn't rise but smiled at me from a very tired looking face.

Noakes shook my hand, 'Good job, good job, well done, to both of you. Now please, everybody sit down.' Jean and I sat next to each other on one side of the table, facing Noakes and Poppy on the other.

'Now, everyone,' Noakes continued. 'A little reminder, Official Secrets Act and all that stuff. And need to know in particular. What goes on in this room only we four need to know, plus one other and my boss of course.'

I wondered who this other one was. I also wondered who Noakes's boss was and finally, I wondered what on earth Noakes was talking about – I had done my task, got Poppy safely into England, it was time for me to return to the world of insurance. But then another thought struck me, *Wouldn't insurance seem rather dull after my little escapade to Hong Kong and back, and the story of Lucy's death?*

As I should have expected, Noakes was way ahead of me.

'Of course, David, you are wondering what you are doing here when your world is that of selling insurance cover. You are here because we want you to do a job for us, we need you and Penelope to do that job.'

That was too much for me. 'Who the hell are *we*? I've no idea what you are talking about,' I almost spat the words out.

Noakes' response to me was all calmness. 'Just be a little patient David, I'm coming to all of that in a moment. But first we have to follow a path so that things come out in the right order. You know about the importance of tracing the order of things from the little courses we arranged for you at Cranfield and Farnborough. First of all, let's establish who we are not. We are not MI5, MI6 or the police, but we are Government.'

'The Ministry of Defence then, this place, the old Air Ministry?'

'Oh goodness No!'

I actually thought he was about to laugh at my suggestion.

'No, we have simply been lent this spare room by the defence brass for our project.' Noakes raised his arms as if encircling all of us. 'Our project, because we want our work to be, let us say, completely independent from the intelligence boys. But let us start with Penelope, or Poppy as she has told me that she would rather be called, and Lucy . Please correct me, Poppy if I get anything wrong.'

This is going to be interesting, I thought. *Here comes the stuff that she didn't tell me on the plane.*

'I'm sure, David, that Poppy has told you how Lucy died. How she was under surveillance by the Hong Kong police and that, in the melee of a deadly riot, a young policeman lost contact with his charge during which time an assassin took his chance, but found the wrong target. I gather that she also told you that the surveillance had started when she had informed the police she was on a Triad kill list. But that wasn't entirely true was it Poppy? Or at least, not the whole story. Now she can tell you what actually happened, or I can tell you which, now that I know her penchant for reticence, might result in a more complete rendition.'

Poppy said nothing. She didn't squirm in her seat, but merely sat still, hands folded on her lap, showing no emotion, as if she were at a mass in her convent school.

Noakes adopted the same schoolmasterly tone he had used with me in the taxicab.

'Poppy and Lucy came to the attention of the local police not long after their hasty withdrawal from Australia to Hong Kong. It seems that in return for Lucy's help with the episode with her birth father, Poppy agreed to help her find out the fate of relatives of hers that had disappeared during the Japanese occupation of Hong Kong. A sort of tit-for-tat deal. The two of them started to poke around unsavoury characters in unsavoury neighbourhoods and, unwittingly I'll admit, nearly derailed an ongoing police investigation. The pair were dragged in for a stern lecture from a police inspector. This officer, however, was so impressed by the knowledge already possessed by Poppy about the Kempeitai and, for want of a better expression, her natural deviousness, that he decided to use her as an on-the-ground asset, even to pay her a stipend. She, with Lucy in tow, provided good intelligence on the who, what and where of people of interest to the police. They posed as ladies of the night, and I think quite enjoyed themselves up until the time of the death threats. By that time the episode in Broome and the death of Okada was also known to the police who, in their wisdom, decided that Poppy should become a problem for the Intelligence Community rather than for the Hong Kong Police. I was contacted in a round-about way. Coincidently, I had a job to be done by someone with her talents who was completely unknown in Britain. So I decided to extract her. But she would only come if you, David, would fetch her. Payback or love? That's for you to decide'.

I looked at Poppy. She showed no embarrassment for having concealed from me what had just been revealed, but then her face broke into one of those beatific smiles that used to melt my heart – this time it had no effect. But I suddenly realized, even though my knowledge of such matters was zero, that she might be just the sort of person to be of use to a police or intelligence agency, one or other of which was surely Noakes's province.

'Now,' Noakes continued. 'We have dealt with Poppy so we come to you David. I don't know whether or not you have already twigged it, but there is a role for you in Poppy's task. A task for which you have already undergone training.'

He was being too bloody smug and starting to get on my nerves. Well if I only had suspicions before then I have no doubt now. It's all been a charade:. James Harrington setting me up probably with some collusion by my Dad, the risk reduction courses that were in fact to introduce me to detection and deduction of cause and effect and you and Miss Hathaway sitting in on my presentation to see how much I had mastered. Or was it to see how useful I might be to you? So you have some nasty little job that you want me, with Poppy, to do for you.' I'm sure there was more than a touch of scorn in my voice.

'For your country, David, not for me. What I do, what MI5 and MI6 do, often relies on information passed to us by willing assets. That's a horrible word I know. People that are not solely motivated by monetary, or sexual, reward, although there are those of course that want and take such rewards, but rather of feelings of duty and patriotism. We live in dangerous times, such people are vital.

'The country was also in peril in the late 1930s. As an example from those times and your own backyard, your mentor Henry Souch travelled in Europe and elsewhere doing his job of negotiating insurance business. His travels took him to ports where he noted the building of facilities to support naval activities and his reports proved invaluable in predicting the movements of Italian warships and even the harbouring of the Vichy French Navy in North Africa. All the time he was a part-time asset, although the term was not used then, strictly amateur, patriotic and never on the Government's payroll. He is retiring of course and it would be nice to have someone of similar inclinations in James Harrington's organisation to replace him. He has told us that he thinks, as does James, that you would be a good choice to help us, particularly because your character has significantly hardened over the past six months.'

I saw Poppy throw me at glance over those last words of his.

He had succeeded in getting my interest and he had flattered me. I just hoped a journey like the one I had taken to Broome was not involved again.

At that moment a knock came on the door. Jean got up and opened it to reveal a lady pushing a trolley on top of which was a tray laden with the accoutrements for a tea party. Jean turned to us, put a vertical finger to her pursed lips and then invited her in. The lady silently laid out the tea things on the table and then departed. With tea poured and biscuits shared, Noakes started talking again.

'The preciseness of that welcome lady's arrival was accomplished by my pushing a small button by my knee under the table. So this is the position to be,' he said with a smile, his first for a while, 'if you want to control a meeting.'

His smile disappeared as quickly as it had arisen. 'Now we come to the really, really need to know bit. I can't emphasise that enough. What I am about to say can never be repeated or even referred to outside of this room and outside of this company.'

Poppy and I shuffled in our seats as some form of acknowledgement. Jean Hathaway sat stock still, she knew what was coming.

Noakes held up his left hand as a closed fist. As he extended his index finger vertically, he said 'Donald Maclean, ex MI6, defected to Moscow in May 1951, aged 38.'

He extended his middle finger. 'Guy Burgess, ex MI6, defected to Moscow with Maclean when aged 40.'

He extended his third finger. Kim Philby, ex MI6 defected to Moscow in 1963, aged 51.'

He extended his little finger alongside the previous three. 'George Blake, ex MI6, sentenced to 42 years in Wormwood Scrubs Prison in 1961 for spying for the Russians. Escaped to Moscow in 1966, aged 44.'

I had heard of all those Soviet agents of course, the scandal still rolled on and produced occasional speculative and unsubstantiated articles in the Press. I thought Noakes had finished his piece of theatre, but he hadn't.

With all the fingers of his left hand still held vertically, he raised his right fist and extended its index figure. 'A fifth spy still at large, identity unknown to us but probably known to others in MI6.'

He raised the next finger and said: 'A sixth spy, similar remarks as for the fifth one.'

He closed his left hand, extended all the fingers of the right one and waggled them in unison, and with volume, passion and heat said, 'And all the rest of the traitors, probably still lurking in MI5 or MI6.'

My shock showed on my face I'm sure, as it did so plainly on Poppy's. I was about to speak but she beat me to it, the first words she had uttered in that room, they were deliberate and chilling.

'You want David and me to find spies for you? You are fucking crazy.'

I could see Noakes startled reaction to her outburst and distaste of her use of that word. I could also see a slight grin about Jean Hathaway's mouth. I had also been surprised when first I had heard convent-educated Poppy use such expletives during our time together the previous year.

'No, no, well, yes and no,' Noakes fumbled for a moment but then regained his composure. 'You won't be finding spies exactly but, hopefully, you will be finding things out about them, discovering how and why they become double agents. And we are definitely not talking about the yet-to-be identified numbers five and six, half the intelligence communities are already doing that here and in America, and they should probably now be looking within their own nests. What my boss, my country, needs to find out is when and how the known spies were turned. That, I believe, is the preferred expression. And then extrapolate that knowledge to prevent future defections. So it's a bit like those accident or risk prevention techniques you have studied, David.'

'But that's surely a job for the MIs,' Poppy commented. 'I never know which is which, all stupid acronyms.'

Jean stepped in. 'MI, Military Intelligence. MI5 is Military Intelligence Section 5, concerned with domestic security within the British Isles. MI6 is Military Intelligence Section 6, concerned with international security that could pose threats to the British Isles.'

I knew now what she reminded of … a Head Mistress.

'But as I've already told you,' Noakes added. 'All those people I've just numerated were members of, or had been at one time, members of MI6. And now its MI6's own job to find any and all of the others. It's like setting a fox to investigate the killing of chickens, and its exactly the equivalent of the Police investigating police brutality or the Church investigating reports of abused choir boys, it doesn't meet any test of logic or common sense. So we, that is you two with Ms Hathaway and my boss, have been instructed to conduct an independent, sub-judice investigation. We report directly to the Home Secretary. It's because you, Poppy, are effectively unknown in this country and you, David, are in a profession not usually thought of as being associated with intelligence gathering, that the two of you are just what is needed to help this investigation. You are not on either MI5 or MI6's radar.'

I broke in. 'You mean your little cell reports directly to the Cabinet?'

'No. Not even the Cabinet members can all be trusted with knowing what we will be doing. It's exactly what I said: my boss reports directly to the Home Secretary and no-one else. You belong to an exclusive team. But just to make it perfectly clear, you are in, aren't you David?'

He had seduced me with his words, he had instigated a sense of excitement within my psyche, just had Poppy had done when she lured me to Australia. 'Yes, of course,' I replied. 'How could I not be?'

'Exactly,' replied Noakes with a hint of satisfaction in his voice and forced *got you* smile. 'And of course, Poppy, you are in because you now work for Her Majesty's Government who pays you, provides you with a safe place to live and, as promised by the Hong Kong police, will continue to seek the killers of Lucy. As for you David, James has told all of your work associates that as a result of your rendition of Risk Management given in front of two senior Civil Servants you have been asked to assist the Ministry of Defence in assessing risk to some of its more sensitive infrastructures and will not, therefore, be in the office for a while.'

So Noakes had anticipated that he would capture me and had already arranged my absence from James' office. I warned myself that he was not a person that I could ever outwit.

Poppy had calmed herself. 'Ok, I think I get it, so let's get moving along. What do you really want of us and how do we start?'

'We want you to discover if there is some catalyst that precipitated Burgess, Maclean and Philby into the Soviet world. A person, an event, a political occurrence, a sense of destiny, perhaps a change in the world order, like nuclear weapons. Then to extrapolate whatever you come up with to other persons that might have been similarly influenced. Ms

Hathaway can explain more about your task as you called it. Ms Hathaway, please.'

Jean Hathaway stood up and placed a large, very solid looking brief case on the table, like the sort that solicitors place their court briefs into. She extracted four bundles of documents from the case and put them on the table between Poppy and me, each bundle comprised several files bound together by red tape.

She placed her right hand on each in turn saying, 'Burgess, Maclean, Philby, Blake. Now I'll give you a clue to start you off. All except Blake were at Cambridge at the same time in the 1930s as undergraduates. Blake went there after the Second World War for one year to study languages. So Cambridge is a good place to start, but many other people have made that connection between these spies, so although it is a good place to start I don't think that is where you will end up. These files are merely the abstracts about these people, but they are very pertinent and have already been culled of a lot of extraneous bumf. If you need more information on any of them then ask me and I'll try to source it. I've included some paper pads on which you can make notes, with pens, pencils, pins and so on, almost everything you might need for your work I think. I'll be in here at nine every morning at which time you can ask me to get any more information that you might need. When you leave this office you must put everything away in the safe. Remember the combination. 6 6 9 5 9 4. Do not write it down. What is it David?'

'669594,' I replied

'And Poppy?'

'669594,' she echoed.

With Poppy and me kneeling down either side of her, Jean demonstrated how to unlock the safe by moving the rotary dial back and forth between the digits of the number sequence. She then reclosed the safe's door and spun the dial randomly to secure it. 'What now?' she asked.

'Well that's it I suppose until the next time,' I suggested.

'Yes,' agreed Jean. 'Except for one little thing further. Always memorise the number now beneath the pointer. If it is not in the same position when you next look, it gives a hint that somebody other than you has taken an interest in the safe.'

We all stood up again. Jean took out a Yale key on a chain from her handbag. 'This is the key to the door of this room. One of you must be in charge of it. I have its duplicate and there are no others. I was with the locksmith when he fitted a new, very secure lock last week. Always lock this room every time you vacate it. Right, it's now eleven o'clock and I'm off. I will come in a little after nine every morning to arrange all the other documents that you will surely need once you have got through this lot on the table. My telephone number is on the tag attached to this key chain, perhaps as it is Poppy that is living in the safe house , she should have it.'

Jean laid the key on top of the Burgess pile of files. 'If you need to contact me in a hurry, or you don't need me to come in the following day, then just give me a call from the concierge's desk, where we met this morning, David. Good Luck. It's really important what you will be trying to do. And one last thing, continue with your normal lives outside this office. David, you with your amateur theatre productions, you Poppy, well I might suggest you explore the social life of the Police College, remember that you are there as a plain clothes Hong Kong detective helping the Foreign Office here unravel a knotty case of cash laundering.'

She and Noakes left us, closing the door behind them. I and Poppy were alone in our sterile room, a feeling of near incarceration swept over me.

Chapter 8

'What the hell?' said Poppy.

'What the hell?' I replied. 'How the hell did we get into this? More importantly, how did I get into this?'

'Because you wanted to help me.' She put on her most faux-innocent voice.'

'As always. But to be serious, do you really think it's because we are innocents abroad, unknown to the MIs? Or something else?'

'They don't need us for this paper sorting job but for what may come afterwards, when they release us from this room and send us out to do some snooping in public.'

'When we will be untraceable back to whatever department they really represent,' I suggested.

'Yup, that's it. But let's get on with it.'

'Then where do we start?' I asked, looking at all the files with some dismay.

'We each take two of the file stacks and begin with a quick read through, tell each other what we have found out about the characters, and then decide our next move.'

'OK, that seems as good a way as anything,' I agreed. 'You take Burgess and Maclean because we know they were in collusion and defected together. I'll take the other two. One o'clock we stop for lunch.'

I took the Philby papers and started to read them. It was not an easy task to construct a logical flow of information from the mish-mash of documents that Jean had left to synthesise. I flicked through Cabinet briefing papers that were succinct but seemingly quite superficial, then there were detailed reports covering distinct aspects of Philby's career, his postings, his friends, his education, his personal life, his character flaws and a myriad of other things. Finally, there were extracts from other documents, most of which were heavily redacted to disguise their source. I spent about an hour on Philby, concentrating on thoroughly understanding his background and history while making notes of what I considered the most salient points from his papers. I then performed the same process with the Blake files.

'I need lunch,' Poppy said after the near complete silence between us during the preceding two hours. Let's put all this stuff into the safe, lock up the room and ask the man at the front desk where we can find something to eat and drink.'

'I'm all for that,' I replied. 'I've got reader's cramp.'

The Corps of Commissionaires gentleman that had seen me come into the building that morning with Jean, call me Arthur, he said, suggested that we try the Silver Cross Tavern, just a short walk up Whitehall from where we stood. There were what he described as dining facilities in the Ministry of Defence building, but he shook his head and wrinkled his nose as he told us. We took his hint and found ourselves drinking a beer each and eating a sandwich in a 400-year-old pub.

'We need a paper shredder,' said Poppy.

'We can ask Jean the next time she comes in. But from now on whenever we are in public no talking or even thinking about what we are doing in our cell.'

'Vault would be a better word,' Poppy suggested.

'Changing the subject. Now, the topics for this lunch can be, where are you living and how are your parents?'

She told me that she was living in the police training centre at Hendon so would have quite a long Tube journey in and out to work each day. She also confirmed that her parents were well but little more, except she had phoned them from Hendon so they knew how to get hold of her.

'I'll tell you more about them and Hendon if you take me out to dinner this weekend.' She suggested. I ignored the bait. She wrote down her telephone number on a cardboard beer mat which I placed in my jacket pocket but I put the idea of a weekend meeting with her in the '*too hard* drawer.

I was struck that she was already referring to what she was doing in the ' Vault as work, but I rationalised that it was because she was now, unlike me, a bona fide civil servant, a quasi-police officer even. I cautioned myself that perhaps it was more than quasi; I had grown to be wary of Poppy's cloaks over the years. But for me, what she regarded as work was an imposition that I had somehow accepted although, if Poppy's forecast was right, it did promise to get interesting after we had got through our mammoth reading tasks.

During our short walk back to the Vault, she said that she bring her own lunch and snacks into work each day, and offered to do the same for me if I would look after the drinks. Soft ones only, she emphasized. I agreed.

Back at our table inside our locked room, I asked if she were ready to speak about her first impressions of Messrs Burgess and Maclean. She was, she said, but asked me to kick off with my two men first.

'George Blake', I began. 'Does not seem to have any obvious links to the other three spies. Born in 1922 in the Netherlands. Got involved in some way with the Dutch Resistance after the German invasion then escaped to

England and re-joined his mother who had fled Holland earlier. He joined the Royal Navy, but as a linguist with an interesting history he was recruited into MI6 where he married a secretary. He had postings to Hamburg and Seoul, and also spent time at Cambridge where he studied Russian and other languages. He was in South Korea when the war with the North broke out and was captured there by the North Koreans. During his three years of captivity he had some form of epiphany, volunteered to work as a spy for the Communists and became an agent of the Russian KGB.

'On release he was welcomed back to Britain as some kind of hero. He was posted to Berlin where he passed a massive amount of information to the Russians about MI6 agents who were operating through Eastern Europe. He, in turn, was given away by a Polish defector, convicted and sentenced to 42-years in prison. There are notes among these files that some people thought this to be grossly excessive and others believed thoroughly deserved because many of the MI6 agents he betrayed had either disappeared or were confirmed as executed. In prison he met three other men who grew to like him and thought that his overly-long sentence, which was actually composed of individual sentences combined to be consecutively served, was unfair. They plotted to help him escape from Wormwood Scrubs once the three had finished their stretches. And that is what they did by throwing a rope ladder over the prison wall and he promptly clambered to freedom. They hid him for a while in London then moved him by campervan to East Germany and hence to Russia. It's quite a story, isn't it?'

'It certainly is,' Poppy agreed. 'But who were the accomplices?'

'I've only noted so far that two were members of the Campaign for Nuclear Disarmament, CND, and the third was an Irishman named Sean Bourke. Perhaps he was in the

Irish Republican Army? But I don't know why they were in prison or anything else about them. I suspect information about them is all deeply buried within this pile of papers or bumf as Jean Hathaway called them,' I ended, slapping the George Blake pile with the palm of my hand.

'Do you think that the stuff you have on Blake is enough to get us started?'

'It's a start. A sort of throat clearing exercise, but no more than that. Where we go next is the important question to which, at present, I haven't a clue.'

'Me neither.'

'Will you go with one of yours now?' I asked.

'The histories of my two, Burgess and Maclean are very much intertwined so I think I should talk about them together. And from what I have read so far, your Kim Philby is also very much part of their story, a sort of Machiavellian figure in their histories, so perhaps you should cover him before I start.'

'OK,' I agreed. 'Kim Philby, another character with a very interesting story. Born in India in 1912 so 55 years old now. Educated in England and won a scholarship to Cambridge, when there between 1930 to 1933 he became friends with Guy Burgess and Donald Maclean, your two guys.'

Poppy nodded. 'That checks with my stuff.'

'He joined some sort of anti-German fascism organisation soon after graduating. This might have been the start of his pro-communist stance which has lasted throughout his adult life. He took up journalism as a career. While in Vienna he fell for a young Austrian Communist girl whom he married in 1934 and moved with her back to London where he was recruited, possibly with the participation of his wife, by a soviet agent to work for Russian intelligence. He suggested to this agent that both

Burgess and Maclean might also make suitable recruits for the same business.

'He joined a British-German friendship group which involved him making frequent trips to Berlin and, as a journalist, he went to Spain to cover the Civil War and was actually decorated by Franco after surviving the impact of a Republican shell on the car full of journalists in which he was travelling. MI6 thought his background well suited to that organisation's work and recruited him in 1940, seemingly on the recommendation of Guy Burgess.'

'Have you got that about Burgess in your notes, too, Poppy?'

'Yes,' she replied. 'It all fits with what I've got.'

'After which, his life gets very much more complicated and I haven't yet waded through a quarter of what is in front of me. Anyway, he became more and more senior in MI6, served in the Middle East and New York and was often having to get both Burgess and Maclean out of their drunken and homosexual escapades. He was also passing important intelligence, both American and British, to his Russian spymaster, and, because of a warning from Russia that Burgess and Maclean were about to be unmasked, helped in their escape to Moscow.

Eventually he fell under suspicion himself for being a double agent and had to leave MI6 in 1951. He returned to journalism and although under continued suspicion managed to survive enquiries into his past. But in the early 1960s a Soviet agent defected to the West and provided the necessary information about Philby's work for the KGB. He was warned of this by Moscow and managed to escape from Beirut on a ship to Russia in early 1963. He was welcomed there as a hero and given a Colonel's rank within the KGB, for which organization he still works in Moscow.

'Another even more incredible story,' was my final comment.

'I'll just cull my notes a bit before I start on my two so as not to repeat too much of what you have already covered,' Poppy said. 'Why don't you go and find a toilet, I'm getting desperate for a wee.'

I found two sets of toilets not far away from our room of study. The men's set-up was clean, spacious, gloomy, smelled of disinfectant and contained cracked, stained porcelain that looked Victorian; I could not imagine what the Ladies might have been like.

As soon as Poppy returned from her comfort break, she began to talk about her first subject, Burgess.

'Burgess was born in 1911, so a similar age to Philby, and was a sort of semi-toff. His name, Guy Francis de Moncy Burgess gives a clue to his actual and expected life of privilege. His education echoes this privilege. Eton College, followed by the Royal Naval College and finally Trinity College, Cambridge University. There he joined the Communist Party and was recruited to Soviet Intelligence by Philby. He became a close, roistering friend of Maclean and joined the same clubs and organisations. On graduation, he joined the BBC then MI6 before moving to the British Foreign Office in 1944. There he had access to highly sensitive information concerning this country's foreign policy which he passed in huge quantities to Moscow. He was sent to the British Embassy in Washington in 1950 where he became notorious for drunkenness and was sent back to Britain. In 1951 he learned from Philby that Maclean was under suspicion for being a Soviet spy. Thinking that Maclean would, under British interrogation, reveal his own name as a spy he elected to join Maclean on the escape via France to Russia. There he continued to decline into alcoholism and died in 1963 aged just 52 years old.

'So,' Poppy concluded. 'Not nearly such an interesting story as those of Blake and Philby. A tragic life in many ways. The man was obviously clever and would have done very well if not so devoted to Russia and the bottle. He was a bit like one of those Hooray Henrys, as you used to call them when I was living in London last year. The young men living in Mayfair with money, fast cars and a penchant for shouting in the street late at night and slamming car doors.'

'Yes,' I agreed. 'Rather like them. I wonder if there is a clue there.'

'Could be, but let's get on to Donald Maclean.

'Now here is a man who, it seems, wanted nothing more than to betray his country's secrets to the Soviets, and did so for all of his adult life. Born into privilege, like Burgess, his father was a Knight, a Member of Parliament and a Cabinet Minister. Maclean's schools included St Ronan's and Gresham's. Have you heard of either of them?'

'No,' I replied.

'He was accepted into Trinity Hall, Cambridge University on a scholarship in 1931 to study modern languages. He straight away became associated with radical communist elements and was openly very left wing. By the time of his graduation with a first class honours degree, he had been recruited into the Russian People's Commissariat for Internal Affairs, or NKVD, the precursor to the KGB. He met and socialized with both Philby and Burgess while at Cambridge. Russia told Maclean to join the British Diplomatic Service. He passed the Civil Service examinations and at the subsequent interview board he denied ever having been a committed communist. He started off in the Foreign Office in London and immediately started to send documents to Moscow. In 1938 he was posted to Paris where again he had access to sensitive information which he passed to Russia. He met and married an American woman there, Melinda Marling. The two escaped back to England as the Germans entered Paris and he continued to work on very sensitive, war related information which again he passed on to his Russian masters. He also began to descend into what is termed in the texts I've read, a debauched lifestyle. I've not found the details of that yet, and they are probably not important, but I think the word is code for homosexual activities. Nevertheless he was known as a very hard and effective worker, an opinion that continued when he was posted to Washington in 1944. Again he had access to most secret information, including the nuclear bomb program, details of which he forwarded to Moscow. Many Americans with which he was associated knew he was by having random, casual homosexual encounters and was drinking heavily.

In 1948 he was posted to Cairo as Head of Chancery, a very important position that made him the youngest person in the Foreign Service to have attained that rank. But his personal life was falling apart. Other than his bi-sexual activities his drinking got ever heavier and he even got into fights. He was still in contact with Moscow, however. Melinda, who had been with her husband in Paris, Washington and Cairo, told his superiors that he was ill and needed to return to London.

Back in London he was, incredibly, promoted again to be Head of the American Department of the Foreign Office, and was still passing on stuff to Russia. But by 1951 the net was closing in on him and, warned by Philby, he made his escape with Maclean.

'And all the time Melinda was with him, in Paris, London, Cairo, Washington and of course back in London. She knew of his activities on behalf of the Russians and of his and Burgess' escape plans. She and their three children joined him in Moscow about a year later.'

'Another incredible story,' was my initial comment.

'Yes, and I've only scratched the surface. These files,' she said, thumping the top of the hands-breadth high papers in front of her, 'go on and on. The detail is incredible and they in turn are only an extract of what's available, according to Jean Hathaway.'

'So what now?' I asked.

'I suppose we know about as much as an interested newspaper reader would have gleaned while the Philby, Burgess, Maclean scandal was going on. In other words, nothing new, everything already in the public domain.'

'But we do now have a knowledge of their history and backgrounds that we did not have before.'

'Of which, the Cambridge link and the attraction of Communism were part of Noakes' opening talk to us.' Poppy said a little disconsolately.

'Then we have to dig back deeper, go back further, retrace the track from where the lure of Communism and the urge to support its spread overrode any feelings of loyalty to Britain that they may originally have had. In other words, what happened at Cambridge and who caused it to happen.'

'My two sets of files identify numerous people as having been associated with Burgess and Maclean, but their names mean nothing to me.'

'Much the same with my two. I think we should start by listing all of them and then seeing whose names are common to two or more of our four men, and then finding out who they were and why they are associated with them.'

'Well, that will be a proper start on something original for us to bring to the table, so as to speak,' agreed Poppy. 'But who knows if MI5 or 6 have not already done that?'

'I expect that they may have already done so. But what we are attempting to do is not to emulate the Intelligence community's investigations who, judging from what Noakes said, may not wish to share their findings if they are engaged in some sort of cover-up, smoke and mirrors operation. We are working, covertly and independently, directly for the Home Secretary.'

'We will need big sheets of paper to make up our lists that we can stick on the walls, I'll ask Jean.'

'They will have to be taken down and stored in that safe at days end.'

'Yes, of course. Now,' Poppy went on. 'I have had it for today. It's nearly five. Let's go out for a drink and have supper together.'

'We'll pack up now, but no dinner tonight or the rest of this week. Firstly there are my Questor's commitments in Ealing most evenings and secondly to avoid the temptation of discussing our work out of this office. But as for the weekend, let's make up our minds later.'

She pulled a face at me. All documents and notes were put in the safe with the position of the dial noted after locking it, we then vacated the room with Poppy locking the door and pocketing the key. As we left the building, she to walk to the nearest tube station, me to find a bus stop, she reminded me to bring drinks for us for the next day while she would look after food.

Chapter 9

I returned to the Ministry of Defence building the next day with a bag laden with soft drinks, instant coffee, a small electric kettle and plastic cups, all bought in the Earls Court Road on my way home the previous evening. Poppy was in the lobby speaking to the Commissionaire, Arthur, who was peering into the shopping bag she was holding. 'Our food, David,' she called to me.

'All OK, miss,' said Arthur. 'And I suppose you have food in your bag too, Mr Shawyer.'

I showed him the bag's contents.

'Don't leave food around in your office,' he warned. 'We have a plague of mice at the moment.'

So the Vault was now to be called our office, the change suited me. Reading all those files the previous day and discovering how our four traitors had deceived and damaged their country and professions, I had realised just how serious, important even, this task of mine and Poppy's actually was.

Arthur pointed at some objects behind him. 'This easel thing, the electric shredder, the rolls of paper and box of crayons all arrived for you a short time ago. Would you like me to help carry them to your office?'

'Yes,' said Poppy and, as we traipsed along to our room following the green line on the wall, she told me that she had phoned Jean Hathaway when she got back to Hendon the evening before and discussed the sort of 'visual aids, as Jean had called them, that we would need for our work. 'She arranged for all this stuff overnight and also told me that a telephone would be installed during the day. She asked if we would want her here this morning but I told her probably not, we would phone if we needed anything.'

With Arthur gone, we unlocked the safe, the rotary dial being set just as we had left it, and placed all of the contents back onto the central table.

'Why don't we use the individual desks as our work stations, to sit there making up our notes and a place to think in silent contemplation, and keep the table as our sort of library,' suggested Poppy.

I supported that idea of hers, but then posed the question 'So what now?'

'What you suggested last thing yesterday seems the only way forward. Or in your parlance, working backward. List out all the associates and look for the common ones.'

'But remembering that our four men all started on their paths of betrayal before they started their MI6 careers, I think we should concentrate on their early adult lives. Cambridge is the obvious common denominator for three of them but we should also examine non-Cambridge friends and associates from around the same time.'

'Right, let's go for that route,' agreed Poppy. 'It will greatly reduce the number of names.'

It took the whole morning for us to examine all the files again, digging out more detail than the previous day and making up our individual lists. We took a mid-morning break when a man brought a telephone to our office, connected it and checked it was working. 'Your number is on the dial,' he offered as he departed. 'Just dial an 'O' first for an outside line.'

The electric kettle worked so we could make instant black coffee. 'Get milk in future,' suggested Poppy as she broke open a packet of Bourbon biscuits.

Midday approached and passed and still we kept at it, searching for names, jotting notes down at our desks, hardly passing a word with each other until Poppy called time.

We ate the sandwiches and chocolate bars that Poppy had bought on her way in that morning and broached my collection of canned drinks. But we could not rest, and after no more than a quarter of an hour of sitting around the big table, Poppy asked, 'Are you ready with your list of our spies' associates?'

'Yes,' I replied. 'Blake is a bit of an odd ball compared with the other three so I could start with him. It's a short list in any case. You put that pad of paper onto the easel, I call out the names in alphabetical surname order and you write them down under his name. Leave space for the other three by his side.

'My Blake names don't really meet the criteria of concentrating on his earlier life, but they are all I have. That is except for the first, Henri Curiel, who Blake met while in school in Cairo, the city in which Blake was born. Curiel was communist and a leader of a local socialist movement. He could definitely have influenced the young Blake and probably did. However, it appears that Blakes's true turning point was while a prisoner of war in North Korea when he saw American bombers pounding indefensible villages. Perhaps you should record his communist sympathies by his name.

'The next on the list is Michael MccGwire.' I took the time to explain the unusual spelling for Poppy.

I heard Poppy suck her teeth. 'Tsch Tsch'. I ignored her sibilant rebuke, and continued.

'He is a naval officer and appears to specialize in intelligence and foreign policy. There is a note to say that he appears about to leave the Royal Navy and follow a more academic career, but its undated. He had a very active wartime service after which, in 1947, he was sent to Downing College, Cambridge to learn Russian. That's where he met Blake.

'The final three names are those of Blake's prison mates who facilitated his escape. Sean Bourke, an Irishman, was a petty criminal who decided to send a bomb to a policeman he disliked. The bomb exploded without causing any injury and he was sentenced to seven years in prison in 1961, the same year that Blake was convicted. Michael Randle and Patrick Pottle were, probably still are, highly involved with CND, the Campaign for Nuclear Disarmament. They were sentenced to 18 months in prison for being instrumental in illegal marches and demonstrations outside nuclear military facilities. The three of them were outraged at the seemingly sadistic 42-year sentence that Blake was serving and facilitated his escape. Do you know anything about CND?'

'Nothing really,' Poppy replied. 'It didn't make many headlines in Singapore or Hong Kong, and I didn't spend much time reading newspapers when I lived in London last year. I know its peace symbol, it's rather effective.'

'I suppose some might regard it is as a subversive movement, perhaps with Communist links. I think we should get Jean or somebody to brief us on its importance within the world of intelligence. Meantime, put CND by their names.'

BLAKE	PHILBY	MACLEAN	BURGESS
Curiel, Henri (Com.)			
MccGwire, Michael			
Bourke, Sean			
Randle, Michael (CND)			
Pottle, Patrick (CND)			

'So that's Blake done. There is no direct correlation with my Philby,' I continued

'Or my two,' replied Poppy.

'Nevertheless, we won't ignore him. It was Noakes that brought his name up. So now on to Philby. His pile of files here contains a huge number of names, but let's start with the two obvious ones, put Burgess and Maclean on the list under his name, communists of course. Now, most of the many others that I have had to wade through pop up well after Philby had become an established agent, so none of them were the reason why he turned traitor. We have to concentrate on his Cambridge set and a couple of years or so after he left. I have four names that fall into that category. The first is Maurice Dobb, he was a Fellow of Kings College, Cambridge at the time of Philby's studies there, and of course of Burgess and Maclean, so put his name up under all three. He was a declared and vigorous Marxist Communist and a leading light in an anti-fascist organization in the 1930s aimed at helping Nazi victims in Germany. It was known as the World Federation for the Relief of the Victims of German Fascism in Paris, now there's a mouthful. So the add the communist suffix. The notes in these files say he was a great influence on the young Philby.

'The next person is Willi Munzenburg.' I spelled his name out to Poppy and she added it to the list without rebuke. 'He was a German member of parliament who fled to France in 1933 because of his vehement anti-Nazi and committed communist views. He was the head of Dobb's World Federation for the Relief etcetera. Initially a Soviet agent, he later turned against Stalin and was murdered in France during the war by either Russian or Gestapo agents. I am just guessing that there may have been some connection between him and Philby through Dobb, but I haven't found it yet.

'But there is no doubt about the significance of the next man, Arnold Deutsch. He is almost certainly the person that recruited Philby at Cambridge.'

'And probably Burgess and Maclean also,' interjected Poppy. 'He comes up in my files also.'

'Really? But then hardly surprising. All these people seem to be interweaved'. I commented to her. 'I don't know if this is also among your files, but he was of Central European origin. No one seems to be able to authenticate his place of birth but he is believed born in 1903. While studying at Vienna University he became a committed communist and an agent of the Soviet Union. In the 1930's he was in England ostensibly studying psychology in London but actually engaged in recruiting agents for the Soviets. He died during the war, possible murdered by either Nazis or Russians right at the end of the conflict. So, while we know his role in all this we are, of course, still trying to discover what influenced our four guys to be recruited. It all seems to point to the Cambridge environment.

'And another person for the Philby list is his wife Litzi Freidman.'

'I've seen her name, so I can spell it,' said Poppy a little tartly.

I ignored the jibe. 'She was a card carrying communist in Vienna well before Philby arrived there. They married in 1934 and it appears that she had a significant influence on Philby's political leanings. They split up within a couple of years however, perhaps so that Philby could more easily enter the world of British Intelligence than if being encumbered with a known communist wife, but the two remained in irregular contact with each other until divorcing in 1947. So let's have her on the list too.

'My final offering is Edith Tudor-Hart, that's hyphenated.'

Poppy raised her eyebrows at me and pursed her lips. I smiled a little and went on.

'She was a Viennese Jew, although not practicing because she was another committed communist, and born in 1908 as Edith Suschitzky. She was a friend of the aforesaid Litzi Freidman in Vienna and thus of Philby. She married a British doctor named Tudor-Hart and moved to Britain in 1934. She was a person of interest to British Intelligence because of Litzi's communist activities. The files are not too explicit about her activities for the Soviet Union, but it appears she was pally with Arnold Deutsch and may have actually participated in the recruitment of Philby, Burgess and Maclean. So put her on the list for all three. Well, that's about it for me. Now it's your turn.'

BLAKE	PHILBY	MACLEAN	BURGESS
Curiel, Henri (Com.)	Maclean	Philby	Philby
MacGuire, Michael	Burgess	Burgess	Maclean
Bourke, Sean	Dobb, Maurice (Com.)	Dobb, Maurice (Com.)	Dobb Maurice (Com.)
Randle, Michael (CND)	Munzenberg, Willi (Com.)	Munzenberg, Willi (Com.)	Munzenberg, Willi Com.)
Pottle, Patrick (CND)	Deutsch, Arnold (Com.)	Deutsch, Arnold (Com.)	Deutsch, Arnold (Com.)
	Friedman, Litzi (Com.)		
	Tudor-Hart, Edith (Com.)	Tudor-Hart, Edith (Com.)	Tudor-Hart, Edith (Com.)

'Just give me a few minutes to sort myself out,' she asked.

I browsed the copy of *The Telegraph* that I had got at the newsagent near my bus stop in Earls Court while she went through her notes on Burgess and Maclean, making alterations, I guessed, based on what I had just said about Philby and his influencers.

'Now onto my lot,' Poppy began to speak after about ten minutes of silence. 'I'm going to treat Burgess and Maclean as a single subject. They were at Cambridge together, were recruited at much the same time, and escaped together. Friends and acquaintances would have been largely mutual and almost certainly known to each other. Let's start with two brothers, Roger and Brian Simon.

'Roger, born in 1913, was the elder son of Baron Simon of Wythenshawe. He was entitled to use that title when his father died in 1960, but he didn't. Because he became a committed communist and left-wing activist while at Cambridge, he would have regarded a hereditary title as inappropriate, as would his associates I imagine. A solicitor by trade, he was also a left-wing journalist and one of the founders of CND. We are beginning to see this organization popping up quite often.

'His brother Brian followed a similar trajectory but trained as a teacher after graduating from Cambridge. In addition to knowing Maclean, he also went with Burgess to Moscow in 1939 on some sort of education conference. So these two offspring of the British privileged classes joined others who were trying to slough their guilt for their upbringings by supporting, indeed extolling, communism.'

I was quite surprised at this unexpected social commentary by Poppy but held my tongue as she continued. 'So I think these two Simons are worthy of much deeper scrutiny. Now onto James Klugman. Born in 1912 into an upper middle-class family living in Hampstead, he had a brilliant intellect and achieved a double first at Cambridge.'

I thought immediately of the humorous right-wing social commentary column by Peter Simple in *The Daily Telegraph*. James Klugman would have been one of what Simple called a *Hampstead Thinker*.

'He joined the Communist Party of Great Britain in 1933, presumable while at Cambridge along with all those contemporaries that we have been tracking. He became Secretary to the World Student Organization in 1935 and moved to Paris. Sometime later he met our friend Arnold Deutsch. He had an adventurous time during the war as a Special Operations Executive and spent time in the Balkans, but he was under suspicion of being a Soviet agent and is now regarded as being pivotal in the recruitment of Maclean et al. He, like Roger Simon, now works as a left-wing journalist and flouts his communist adherence.

'As in your piles of documents there are a host of other names mentioned, but they all seem to arise after the Cambridge period, so I have discounted them. And then there is one, Robert Medley, that has cropped up a couple of times, nothing about Cambridge or having direct contact with Burgess or Maclean so I don't know why he is in there. Let's put his name on the list and maybe try to find out some more about him, perhaps from Jean.'

BLAKE	PHILBY	MACLEAN	BURGESS
Curiel, Henri (Com.)	Maclean	Philby	Philby
McGwire, Michael	Burgess	Burgess	Maclean
Bourke, Sean	Dobb, Maurice (Com.)	Dobb, Maurice (Com.)	Dobb Maurice (Com.)
Randle, Michael (CND)	Munzenberg, Willi (Com.)	Munzenberg, Willi (Com.)	Munzenberg, Willi Com.)
Pottle, Patrick (CND)	Deutsch, Arnold (Com)	Deutsch, Arnold (Com)	Deutsch, Arnold (Com)
	Friedman, Litzi (Com)		
	Tudor-Hart, Edith (Com)	Tudor-Hart, Edith (Com)	Tudor-Hart, Edith (Com)
		Simon, Roger (Com.CND)	Simon, Roger (Com.CND)
		Simon, Brian (Com.)	Simon, Brian (CND)
		Klugman, James (Com.)	Klugman, James (Com.)
		Medley, Robert (??)	Medley, Robert (??)

'We don't have many names, do we?' I posed.

'That's true, but what I think is significant amongst these numerous bits of information we have trolled through, is the number of people who are fingered as being influencers on Philby, Burgess and Maclean embracing communism and Soviet service in their early lives.'

'They couldn't all have been responsible, could they? Surely just one or two of them would have been the real activators,' I replied. 'In which case –'

'In which case,' Poppy said slowly and deliberately, 'some body or some agency has deliberately tried to muddy the waters, to create uncertainty and confusion.'

'Which supports Noakes contention that the MIs, or whoever, may still have a dubious character or two lurking within.'

'Your euphemisms are as weak as usual. But away from such speculation, I think we have quite enough names, to begin with anyway, because we don't know, or at least I don't know, where we take this exercise next,' replied Poppy.

'Neither do I,' I agreed. 'We are trying to see who or what persuaded our four to take the courses they did with their lives. It could be one or more of these skeletons in their cupboards, the ones now on this table of ours, or it could be someone that we haven't identified who knew these people, if you get my meaning.'

'Yes, I think I do. But then there are the influences around them and the societies they joined. If your set of notes are anything like mine there are all sorts of other factors to consider other than simply communism. Some, and I'm talking of our four spies and of their associates, were pacifists, or witnessed, participated in even, the Spanish Civil War, or served Britain well during the Second World War, or belong to CND, or were perhaps homosexual. There are so many factors and variables, I really don't how we are going to progress. So, what I'm going to do now, it being three o'clock, is to do what any sensible girl does in a time of crisis; I'm going to go shopping.'

'Shopping?' I echoed.

'You saw how small my bag that I travelled with on the plane was. Well, that bag contained all my clothes and toiletries. I am now going to go to Oxford and Carnaby Streets and have a good splurge. I think I'll keep the key if you don't mind because I seem to get here earlier than you in the morning.'

She walked over to the door. 'Look at the lock mechanism here. If you press this lever down before you leave then the door will lock itself as you shut it behind you. Remember this and don't go for a wee because you will have to leave the door open which is a no-no. Do you need to go now? I'll hang on until you've got back.'

I didn't.

'And don't forget to stash away all our stuff in the safe before you leave.' And with that, she was gone.

---///---

I made myself another cup of coffee and pondered how we might unravel our Gordian Knot, or at least loosen it. The risk management course at Cranfield had included topics related to finding a solution to a problem by analysing a conglomeration of seemingly unrelated variables. I decided to see if these techniques could in any way help Poppy and me. I would use a form of logic array first, I decided, and confine my analysis to just a few of the names on our list to see if the techniques could be made to work. First, I depicted who knew whom in my array.

	Donald McClean	Roger Simon	Brian Simon	James Klugman
Donald McClean	■	X	X	X
Roger Simon	X	■	X	
Brian Simon	X	X	■	
James Klugman	X			■

This immediately begged the question, did James Klugman know the Simon brothers? The answer, I realized, to this obvious question was yes, but the matrix might have other less easy questions to answer once I added all the other names. But before that, I wanted to see if I added the factors that Poppy had mentioned would that also add to the potential usefulness of the array.

	University Contemporary	Communist	Spanish Civil War	Pacifist or Con.Objector	CND
Donald McClean	CAMBS	X		X	
Roger Simon	CAMBS	X	X		X
Brian Simon	CAMBS	X	X		
James Klugman	CAMBS	X	X		

This second of my trial arrays certainly presented information in an easily accessible way, although what to do with such information was still moot. I decided to make up a third array on one of the large sheets from the paper pads that we had been given. I used the cardboard backing of the pad as ruler to line up all the little boxes I was about to create. The array proved too big to fit on just one sheet.

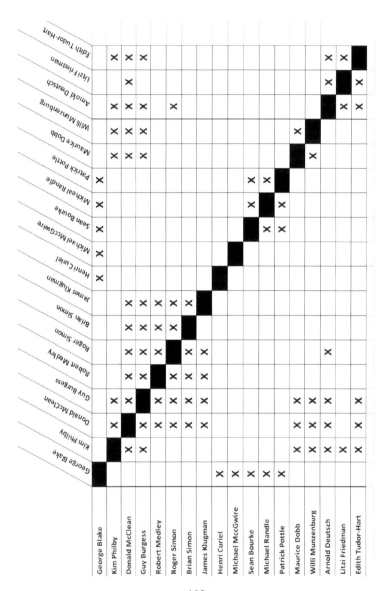

Name	University Contemporary	Communist	Spanish Civil War	Pacifist or Con. Objector	WW2 Participant	Homosexual	CND
George Blake		X			X		
Kim Philby	CAMBS	X	X				
Donald McClean	CAMBS	X				X	
Guy Burgess	CAMBS	X		X			
Robert Medley		X				X	
Roger Simon	CAMBS	X			X		X
Brian Simon	CAMBS	X			X		
James Klugman	CAMBS	X			X		
Henri Curiel		X					
Michael MccGwire							
Sean Bourke							
Michael Randle							X
Patrick Pottle							X
Maurice Dobb		X					
Willi Munzenburg		X					
Arnold Deutsch		X					
Litzi Friedman		X					
Edith Tudor-Hart		X					

I stared at what I had created. More and more information and I had no idea how to use it. The combination of the associations between the people named and their attributes, or failings, seemed to be a step too far for me to be able to manipulate. My diagram enabled me to see easily the principal characteristics of all the players and the people that they knew and probably influenced, but what I seemed to need was a predominate combination of peoples' associates and characteristics. A way, perhaps, of defining or recognizing a would-be traitor.

A knock came on the door. I glanced at my watch and to my surprise it said seven o'clock. I flipped over all the sheets that Poppy and I had been working on and opened the door. One of the Commissionaires, not Arthur, stood in front of me with a clip board in his hand.

'Good evening Mr Shawyer,' he began. 'Are you the only person here at the moment?'

'Yes,' I replied.

'It's seven o'clock and time for the night watch to take over. If you want to continue working here this evening you will have to sign this register.'

He flourished the clip board at me.

'And be disturbed every hour of the evening by a security officer until you decide to leave.'

'I am packing up right now. I'll be down at your desk in no more than five minutes and on my way home.'

'Very good, Sir,' he said turning on his heel.

I packed up, secured all the papers and made sure the door closed securely behind me. I was out of the building in exactly the five minutes I had promised.

---///---

Getting off my bus at the usual stop in the Earls Court Road, I went into my favourite Italian restaurant. I ordered the three-course, pasta-based set meal of the evening and an expensive bottle of Italian wine. I deserved a treat I had decided. Service was protracted, which suited me – I had a whole evening to fritter away – and I settled into drinking all of my wine. But my mind would not stop thinking about my endeavours, seemingly fruitless, of that day. A sudden inspiration came around my third glass of the character filled, coarse would be a better description, Chianti and the arrival of the rigatoni: Venn diagrams! The things that Cranfield had introduced me to as a method of sorting and characterising things. My napkin was paper and I began to draw on it, firstly a simple representation of three characteristics, Communist, CND, Cambridge, belonging totally or in part to five people that I simply identified as A,B,C, D and E.

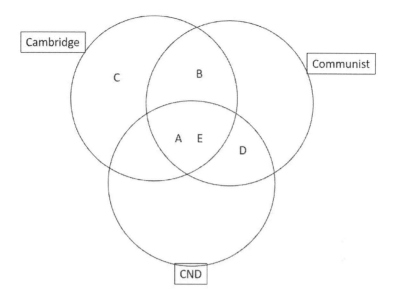

After a couple of false starts, my helpful waiter brought me more napkins, my Venn diagram showed quite clearly that 'C' had been at Cambridge but was neither a Communist nor a member of the CND. 'B' had also been at Cambridge, was a Communist but not in CND. 'D' was also a Communist and a member of CND but had not been at Cambridge. Both 'A' and 'E', on the other hand, possessed all three characteristics. I was satisfied that in principle this was a clearer depiction than that of my complicated array now locked away in the office safe, but I had included just three characteristics whereas my array already had seven with perhaps more to come. I doubted that a Venn diagram with seven, or more, interlocking circles would either be easy to construct or to interpret.

I finished my meal and left for the ten minute walk through freezing weather back to my apartment, the napkin drawings safely folded into my coat pocket. It was approaching 10 pm by the time I sat down with a large glass of whisky in my hand, once more staring at my Venn circles and wondering how on earth Poppy and I were going to come up with any form of result acceptable to Noakes. I was aware that I had over-indulged in wine and whisky as I climbed into bed, the ceiling above my eyes circled a couple of times before sleep found me.

I woke suddenly at 3 am, my mind as clear as a bell and loaded with just one thought; the words of the crash investigator at Farnborough. 'Go back in time before the aircraft accident, ask the pilot what he had for breakfast'. And I knew exactly what Poppy and I should do next.

Chapter 10

I woke early and hurried to work, but still arrived at the office about half an hour after Poppy had opened up. When I entered, she was gazing at the two pages of the large array that I had produced the previous afternoon.

'My, you have been a busy boy!' she exclaimed. 'But what does it all mean?

I quietened my impatience of wanting to tell her about my early morning revelation; instead, I described what I had been trying to achieve with the array and the frustrations that had arisen.

'But the information is all there,' said Poppy, trying to console me

'Maybe, but unusable I had thought,' I replied. 'Until, that is I had a brain wave at 3 am this morning.'

I pulled out my napkin from the Italian restaurant adorned with my trial Venn diagram, stood beside her as I lay it in front of us on the big table, and explained what its purpose had been.

'So basically you have rearranged, at least twice, the deck chairs on the Titanic, but we are still floundering while our ship is foundering.' Poppy commented rather gloomily.

'Until now, until now,' I replied excitedly. 'Look at what I'm drawing now.' I took another large sheet of paper and a black crayon. 'This is a timeline going from left to right. This block in the centre represents the Second World War; the block to the left of it represents Cambridge University in the early 1930s and on the right is Blake and his escape. An arrow representing Communists runs from Cambridge forwards and the second arrow is the CND starting after the war.' You agree that it is a representation of what we have been studying?'

There was a hint of doubt in Poppy's slow reply, 'Yes, yes I do.'

'Now,' I continued let's put a circle around the whole drawing.'

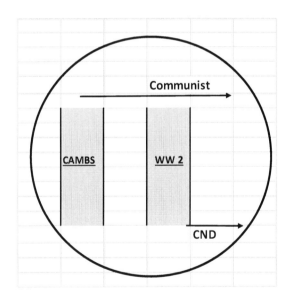

'We have been concentrating on what is inside that circle. But suppose what we are looking for happened outside the circle, to its left, earlier than Cambridge?'

'You mean at school,' said Poppy, cottoning on immediately.

'Yes,' I replied. 'Someone, or some people, were suborned at school by somebody'.

She consulted her handwritten notes. 'Burgess went to Eton College and Maclean to Gresham's, so no convergence there. I presume we are talking about high or senior school or whatever that's called in this country.'

'Yes, whatever might have happened would have been during the subject's later teen years. And Blake went to School in Egypt when he was probably influenced by Henri Curiel whose name does not appear in any of the other three's files, and Philby to Westminster School in London. So again, they all went to different schools. But, and this is my point, it's not so much those four that we have to consider, what we need to do is find out who of all the other people we have listed went to one or more of those four schools.'

Poppy nodded. 'Then we need help, we need to speak to Jean. I could call her from here now we have the phone without, of course, giving too much away. Now! What do you think of my new outfit?'

I hadn't noticed her new clothes because I hadn't looked, being so excited by my 'Schools' theory. She was dressed in a two-piece, light grey suit of sturdy looking material with a yellow blouse, dark stockings and sensible looking black Cuban heeled shoes. 'You look very nice, and expensively clad.'

'Thank you, but you hadn't noticed my clothes at all before I asked. Typical man!. I bought three suits last evening, three pairs of shoes, a new winter coat, sweaters, blouses and other bits and bobs. I spent over 500 pounds plus the taxi to get me and my booty back to Hendon.'

'That's a hell of a lot of money to splash out in one go, did your father subsidise you?'

'No, I sold a pearl in Hong Kong.'

One of the two she had stolen in Broome, I presumed, but made no comment. She had the phone's receiver to her ear in any case and was dialling Jean Hathaway's number. She was very guarded in what she told Jean. We needed help in finding more information on some of the people named in the files. That was all. At one point, Poppy put her hand over the mouthpiece of the phone and softly told me that she was on hold while Jean was sorting something out. She then nodded her head, thanked Jean, and placed the phone back on its cradle.

'There is a young woman called Susan Anderson who will meet us at the British Museum at 11 o'clock today, just over an hour's time. She works with Jean and Noakes and is one of the only four people that know what we are doing. She is a professional librarian, apparently, but works as an archivist and, as Jean put it, *an information gatherer*. She will be in the entrance hall of the Museum and take us into the Reading Room, which is essentially the British Library. She also, apparently knows what we look like.'

'That was quick work,' I remarked.

'I think that Jean was expecting us to call. Anyway, we will have to leave shortly, we can take our lunch with us, but we can't take all this bumf that is scattered around the place. So I suggest we make up lists, on small sheets of paper, of all the people whose schools we want to identify. We should also take note pads with us so we can write things down,'

'Good idea,' I replied. 'Then we should clear everything away as usual as I don't suppose we will be coming back here again today.'

---///---

Our taxi deposited us in front of the British Museum at a few minutes before 11 o'clock. Inspired by the grandeur and importance of the building before us, we somewhat nervously went through the near-overwhelming entrance where a young woman immediately approached and introduced herself as Susan Anderson. She looked to be a similar age to Poppy, about 25, and was dressed in a near-black trouser suit. Her fair hair was short and tightly curled, she wore thickly framed glasses and a pale lipstick seemed to be her only makeup. Her suit was tightly tailored revealing a strong figure that could have been that of an athlete or swimmer. To my eyes she was very attractive although I sensed that she was not a person to be trifled with. Poppy must have seen me sizing Susan up, and gave me a little, knowing smile.

The moment our introductions were over Susan entered a very business-like mode. She had a soft but clear and distinctive voice which I placed as that of a very educated person from Edinburgh. 'My task is to find you information on people whose names you will give me, and I will do this by fetching you written material about these people's lives from the Reading Room into which I shall now take you. I have no wish or need to know what exactly is the information you seek, although I do have a general idea of your mission. Because of my background and current employment, I have unlimited access to the millions of documents available here and I know where to unearth things. I will find a discrete place for you both to work. I will also show you where you can eat your lunch,' she said inclining her head towards the wrapped sandwiches in Poppy's hand. 'I'll also show you where the toilets are. Now, is there anything you wish to ask me before we go in? We should limit our talking to the bare essentials once inside and keep our voices low.'

Poppy and I could think of nothing to ask of her at that time, so we followed her into the Reading Room. I had never seen anything like it, ever. I was completely overawed. Poppy stood and gaped with a half open mouth. The floor space was circular and huge. There was a round open space at the centre of the room from which a multitude of precisely arranged, continuous tables radiated outwards like spokes, almost to the walls. The walls themselves were three stories high, accessed by circular walkways and completely lined with bookshelves. Above these walls a huge dome soared skywards, heavily decorated and pierced with large, ornate windows culminating in another circular window exactly above the centre of the room. It looked Victorian, which it was, with a dash of Byzantine. The long radial tables were provided with chairs so as they could act as individual desks and there were still more desks along the curved sides of the lowest stretch of bookshelves.

'It's quite something, isn't it?' whispered Susan as she settled Poppy and me into a discrete area with adjacent desks for each of us. 'If you give me just two of your names I will get relevant material to you as quickly as possible, and then I'll head off again with another four names, and so on until you call a halt. It may take me about half an hour to come back with the first lot of information, so I suggest you look at the pile of today's newspapers in the centre over there.'

This is one organized person, I thought, with no little admiration.

In less than the predicted thirty minutes she was back with the first of her offerings which allowed Poppy and me to start work. And work we did for most of the rest of the day. We studied almost completely independently of one another, researching not only the names that we had started with but also those of other persons that came up during our near frenzied reading. We took a short lunch break during which we hardly exchanged words. Poppy seemed to be as affected as me, completely engrossed in what we were doing. Susan strode back and forth between us, the bookshelves and a counter where other documents were continually being found for her by library staff. Some three hours into my work I perceived a pattern in what I was reading and was able to tailor my requests to Susan more precisely.

Nearing four o'clock in the afternoon I went for a toilet break. Poppy followed me out of the Reading Room.

'Well?' she asked me.

'Gresham's,' I replied.

'Yes, Gresham's,' she agreed. 'I'll need another half hour, how about you?'

'That will do me fine. Let's tell Susan that we have nearly done.'

---///---

As we waited to hail our respective taxis, Susan asked us if we had been successful.

'Yes, yes,' I answered. 'We have certainly made some progress thanks to your absolutely essential help.'

'Mr Noakes, probably Jean Hathaway also, are coming to see you mid-morning tomorrow, they told me that just before I set out for here. They will be interested in hearing what you have done. I think it might be a good idea if you had my personal telephone number as I do most of the organisational jobs in our little group.' Susan handed both Poppy and I one of her business cards.

I gave her one of mine in return, pointing out that it had both my work and home phone numbers. 'Have this in case you need to contact us.'

'I don't have a card yet,' said Poppy.

Susan took the first taxi that responded to our hailing.

'What shall be do now?' asked Poppy. 'I've a free evening.'

'Sorry,' I replied, although our seeming success together had warmed me towards her, I knew I must never re-enter the entrapment that she had spun around me the previous year. I prevaricated in my reply. 'Tonight, I've got a commitment to that theatre I support, but how about the weekend? Saturday would be best for me as I've got a rugby match to watch with mates on Sunday.'

'Rugby. Ugh!' Poppy exclaimed. 'Let's talk tomorrow about Saturday. More immediately, we must make up some sort of visual presentation to show Noakes. We can do that first thing tomorrow morning, so don't be late.'

A taxi took her to Hendon, another took me to my home.

Chapter 11

The next morning I arrived at our room before Poppy and had to wait for her in the corridor because she had the only entrance key.

She immediately started bustling around getting our paperwork out of the safe and arranging things on the table. 'Let's make a chart that we pin on the wall, a bit like that big array you made of associates and characteristics but showing the names of all those that went to Gresham's School and the years that they were there. I've got people that are not mentioned in any of the files that Jean gave us who, I think, ought to appear.'

'I've got one or two of those as well. If this is to be a presentation to Noakes then I think you should do all the writing of the names, with the school dates alongside, as you are much neater than I.'

We had both come up with the first five names on our list: Maclean, the two Simons, Klugman and Medley.

Then Poppy added Benjamin Britten.

'The composer?' I asked.

'When I started to read about the school itself, I found that he is named as one of the most famous old boys, and he was there with most of the others already listed.'

'And then,' Poppy continued, 'while on the subject of famous old boys there are two others: the writers W.H.Auden and Stephen Spender, and they were there with Robert Medley, so worth including. That's my lot.'

'I had picked up on those two also, but their involvement seems so unlikely that I discounted them.'

'We shouldn't discount anyone at this stage,' Poppy countered. 'Any one of those in our list could possibly be vital, not because of what they did as adults but because of identifying who could have influenced them while at school. That is what we are after, isn't it?'

'Yes,' I conceded. 'But I do have one person to add, Gerald Holtom, the man who designed the brilliant CND symbol carried by anti-nuclear demonstrators all over the world. Blake's CND helpers would have certainly known him and he was at Gresham's with almost all of the others.'

Poppy worked on the large sheet to make it, as she said, into a more visual presentation and, using some drawing pins she had found in one of the desk drawers, pinned it up on the wall in a position where it could not be seen from the corridor when the door was opened.

Greshams Years: 19	21	22	23	24	25	26	27	28	29	30	31
D.Maclean						X	X	X	X	X	
R.Simon						X	X	X	X	X	
B.Simon								X	X	X	X
J.Klugman					X	X	X	X	X		
R.Medley	X	X	X								
B.Britten								X	X		
W.H Auden	X	X	X								
S.Spender			X	X	X						
G.Holtom						X	X	X	X		

'Excellent,' I commented. 'That shows exactly what we discovered yesterday and points us towards who we have to look for. You can trace a line all the way from Medley through to Maclean; I don't really suppose that line goes through the two writers to Klugman and beyond but maybe there was someone else at the school all that time.'

'Like a schoolmaster.'

'Yes, a schoolmaster.'

Poppy pinned another blank sheet of paper onto the wall next to the first.

'I think we should include more information such as membership of CND, like we did before. It might give us a clue to the schoolmaster. She drew columns headed with Communist, Homosexual, CND and Pacifist and together we entered 'Xs' in the appropriate boxes. With Poppy's two tables placed side by side the total effect looked like a cut-down version of the large array that I had drawn up myself two days earlier.

Years: 19	21	22	23	24	25	26	27	28	29	30	31		Comm	Homosexual	CND	Pac
D.Maclean						X	X	X	X	X			X	Bi		
R.Simon						X	X	X	X	X			X			
B.Simon								X	X	X	X		X			
J.Klugman					X	X	X	X	X				x			
R.Medley	X	X	X											X		
B.Britten								X	X					X		X
W.H Auden	X	X	X											X		
S.Spender			X	X	X									Bi		
G.Holtom						X	X	X	X						X	X

The time was approaching 10.30 when we heard a knock on the door. I went to open it while Poppy folded the bottoms of the hanging sheets over their tops and pinned them so the text could not be seen.

Four people walked into the room: Jean Hathaway was followed by Noakes then Susan Anderson who was pushing a trolley laden with teapots, cups, saucers and cakes, and the final person was a tall man of formidable girth, long hair partly flopping over his brow, dressed like an undertaker but with a fresh red rose in his button hole and aged in his late-forties I guessed. Noakes stood to one side as this new person walked straight up to Poppy and offered his hand.

'I am Eugene Russel,' he introduced himself in a very fruity voice full of precise, rounded vowels as he shook her hand. 'And you must be Poppy, Poppy Shawyer or Khosla as you may wish. He turned to me and took my half extended right hand. 'And you are David Shawyer. I met your father once or twice. How is he, and your mother of course?'

'They are both fine,' I rather stuttered at the extravagant manner of this rather imposing man. 'They live in Spain now,' I added lamely.

Eugene Russel took a chair and indicated for Jean and Noakes to sit either side of him; Susan took a seat rather removed from the others and appeared to take charge of the tea trolley.

'Now,' Russel addressed Poppy and me. 'What we have here is the complete team, us four and you two. And it's my privilege to be in charge, so-as-to speak; my master is the Home Secretary. Just us six people involved outside of the British Intelligence Services, trying to complete the job that they couldn't, or didn't want to, do themselves. And I understand you have made some progress over the four days that you have been with us, so please proceed, tell us what you have done and what you have found. Try to do it in fifteen minutes or less and then we will have morning tea.' He settled back into his chair and folded his surprisingly small, beautiful manicured hands across his ample stomach.'

Poppy seemed a bit overawed by Mr Russel, so I jumped in. 'Poppy, if you could find our final big array and pin it on the wall next to those folded sheets of yours, then you and I can go through the work we did to compile it, and say how we got stuck.'

Unrehearsed as we were, Poppy and I managed a fifteen minute double act explaining how we had obtained the listed names, worked out their linkage to one another and categorised their characteristics shared or otherwise. Then we confessed that having produced the array we had run into the issue of how to address all the data it presented.

'At this point then we should get cups of tea and cakes,' said Eugene. 'But settle down again quickly because I'm sure we are going to see something interesting behind those two concealed sheets on the wall.'

As we got our refreshments, Noakes commented that we had done extremely well in compiling our array. Jean chimed in saying, 'I agree, but what it shows, of course, is that it was all down to those years at Cambridge and everyone knows that.'

Poppy seemed a little miffed at that comment. 'So you mean that what we had done to produce that array was worthless?'

Noakes stepped in. 'No, not at all. If nothing else it has provided you with a great insight into how our four friends came to betray their country, who and what their associates and influencers were, and what their characteristics and foibles are. And from that, I believe, you are about to show us something that may not have been realised before.'

Eugene chimed in to pour on a little more soothing oil. 'Definitely not worthless, the array by itself presents information to me in a novel way and I shall certainly ponder upon it. Now let us proceed.'

I suggested to Poppy that she now talk about the covered sheets of paper. She unfurled the left hand one. 'There,' she said striking the data with the flat of one hand. 'It all starts at Gresham's School, a boarding and day school in Norfolk. All the people we have listed went to that school at the dates indicated, to the nearest year.

'I know that Donald Maclean is the only one of the four names you asked us to investigate, but look at the fellow travellers both on this diagram and the array we were discussing before tea. Klugman and Brian Simon for instance both known to Burgess, and so it goes on. If there is to be a place, ' she concluded, stabbing a finger against the chart, 'then the eggs were probably incubated during these years at this school.'

I looked at Jean. 'My God!' she said

'What's that?' asked Eugene.

'My nephew, my sister's son, goes there now. He is sixteen, he loves it.'

Eugene rose heavily towards the chart and asked, 'A very eclectic mixture of people, a sort of broth with a layer of distasteful detritus set among a dazzling array of talents. Which of you came up with this?'

'Both of us,' I replied. 'And we wouldn't have managed it without the help of Susan.'

'Actually,' Poppy added. 'It's was David's idea to look earlier than the period at Cambridge that everyone was focused on. I believe he had a revelation at three o'clock in the morning after a night out on the beer.'

A little chuckle went around our guests. I glanced at Susan, she was smiling at me but then straightened her face as soon as she realized that I was looking in her direction. 'I was just following the timeline backwards, just as taught in those courses you sent me on, Mr Noakes.'

Eugene looked at the chart again for a moment then faced Poppy and me. 'So you think that Benjamin Britten, Stephen Spender and W.H.Auden are all involved? I can see that there is a connecting timeline, but really!'

He turned towards the wall again and pulled out the pins of the right-hand chart so it opened and aligned exactly with the first. 'My God,' he said and turned back to face us. 'You have captured the 'Queens of Gresham's School.'

Eugene captured the frown that came over Poppy's face. I wasn't surprised; I knew that she was attracted as much towards women as men – more so probably had always been my impression.

'My Dear Poppy,' patronised Eugene. 'I am sorry if my use of 'Queen' offends you but my excuse is that it takes one to appreciate another.' He deliberately made a very campy stroke of the loose hair hanging slightly over his face. 'We all make our own way in this world using the raw material with which God has provided for us. Now, I don't readily accept that Britten, Auden or Spender are part of all this, you will have to do much more work to persuade me otherwise; by the way I have had the privilege of meeting all three, on several occasions. And as for Gerald Holtom? He is a fine man, a commercial artist and I would almost regard him as a friend, but I concede that he might have been influenced while at Gresham's to develop his pacifist tendencies and later his participation in the CND. But I can't accept that he might have directly influenced the men that sprung George Blake. What's your opinion Noaksy?'

'Much the same as yours, Eugene. I actually have a lot of time for the CND. They can be a nuisance demonstrating outside nuclear bases and blocking roads, but they have a right to march and demonstrate against something that many people in this country have misgivings about. There are many good, distinguished people in the movement, and it's much easier to keep tabs on the ring leaders when they are out in the open, as they are, rather that acting as 5th Columnists. I think their presence in our society is healthy, even though I don't in any way support their views. And as for homosexuality, so what? Better out in the open than hidden which can offer opportunity for blackmail. The current repressive laws will change in time, I'm sure.'

'There is,' I said. 'One more thing in the same vein. You have both talked about homosexuality and CND but why so many Communists? And why were they permitted to work as members of MI6?'

Eugene replied. 'Times have changed. Nowadays we see Russia, the Soviet Union that is, together with all the communist Iron Curtain countries as our potential enemy. That is why we need nuclear weapons as a deterrent against them, despite the entreaties of the CND. But in the 1930s the world was a very different place. Many people then, particularly intellectuals and over-privileged children of the rich and famous, both sets of whom had no knowledge of real life, believed that Russia was a socialist utopia with a creed to be spread around the world with their help. This belief was genuine and, furthermore, was seen as the antidote to Fascism. The Spanish Civil War was epitomized by many as a struggle between Communism and Fascism, and they were correct. So, being a declared communist was no handicap to personal progression in the 30s, and during the war, of course, we were on the side of Russia, or is it Russia was on the side of us? That's a good topic for debate. And one final point: although, as I have just described, intellectuals and dilettantes took up the communist cause so their mirror images also supported Hitler and Mussolini. Thus MI6 employed known communists, and probably known fascists; that organization has a history of using flawed personalities and putting them into sensitive positions from which great harm could come to this country.'

'So, what are you two suggesting that be done now to crack the riddle of pre-War Gresham's School?' asked Noakes of Poppy and me.

'Somebody has to go up to the school and poke around,' I replied. 'It's in Norfolk, not too far from Norwich I believe.'

'Exactly,' replied Eugene. 'And that somebody has to be you and Poppy. Why? Because you will know what has to be discovered and, more importantly perhaps, you are unknown to any police or spooks that might also have an interest in that place. That, of course, is why we originally recruited you both.'

Poppy entered the discussion with pointed cynicism. 'We should go up to Norfolk and look over the school, speak to the staff, old boys perhaps, find out who was moulding the views of teenagers to their own cause thirty or more years ago?'

'Oh goodness NO!' Eugene said forcibly, rolling his eyes at the same time. 'That would never do. You will have to be far more subtle. Stay away from the teachers and other employees, spin some story about writing a history of pre-war Norfolk schools perhaps and that you are looking for characters of some sort or another that can provide anecdotes. Be casual about the whole thing. Another tack could be that you are considering sending your fictitious son to the school and want opinions from outside people that do not work there. I am sure that you can come up with a plausible story, you in particular, Poppy, you are good at stringing people along, aren't you?'

She certainly is, I thought, remembering my history with her.

Eugene stood up. 'It's lunch time. Noaksy and I have another appointment. Jean and Susan will stay here to sort out your plans for travelling to Norfolk. Please break out five hundred pounds in cash for them Jean, from that special fund. Goodbye to you all, and well done Poppy and David, your work may not lead to anything but then again it may. Perhaps to something quite unexpected.'

'So off you go Norfolk,' said Jean after Eugene and Noakes had departed. 'Can you go next week?'

'Yes, I can,' I said. 'Alright with you Poppy?'

'Yes, fine by me.'

'We will go up in my car on Monday. Perhaps you can find us a hotel to stay in Susan, but perhaps it's better we book it ourselves like any young couple on a sightseeing trip might. You have my number, you can phone me at home this evening to let me know.'

Susan spoke for almost the first time that morning. 'I'll prepare a little brief for you this evening and have it delivered to your door, David, together with the money Eugene mentioned.' She left Poppy and me to our thoughts.

'I guess,' began Poppy. 'That we won't be coming back here for a few days, so we should tidy up before we leave. There is nothing really useful that we can do here until after we have been to Norfolk.'

I agreed with her. We ate the sandwiches Poppy had brought in that morning and finished off the soft drinks that were my contribution to our lunches. We shredded those notes that we no longer regarded as useful and put the long, sinewy scraps in a paper bag that had been delivered with the shredder. We took down the charts from the walls and secured them in the safe along with all the original files of our four subjects and all of our notes.

As we left the room, me carrying the bag of paper scraps to give to the Commissionaire in the lobby, Poppy put her hand on my arm.

'Please let's meet up this weekend, David. We have things to discuss and I miss traipsing around London with you.'

I had expected this request from her and had already decided upon my answer. 'Yes, let's do that. Tomorrow would be best for me.' And quite spontaneously I added. 'You could come around to my place if you like, see your old haunts again.' I immediately regretted making that offer. 'Or we could meet in the West End, do the art galleries or something?'

'I would like to see Earls Court again. I'll meet you for a drink in the Bunch of Grapes, right by where I used to work at Harrods in Kensington, we used to go there after I finished work sometimes, remember? I don't know if they do lunch but if not there are lots of other places to eat all around that area. Then we can go to my old digs.'

'What are you doing for the rest of today and this evening?' I asked meaning it as a genuine enquiry and not as a prelude to a date, but the answer knocked me back.

'There is a sergeant policeman who teaches unarmed combat and physical training at Hendon college. I've a lesson with him later this afternoon and a date with him this evening. I rather fancy him. 'Bye, see you 12 tomorrow at The Bunch.'

And with that she was gone. She hadn't lost that on-again, off-again habit that used to cause me so much grief.

---///---

I went straight home, picked up my bathing trunks and a bath towel and made my way to my local swimming pool. When working at my insurance office employment, I used to go to a nearby swimming club two or three time each week for a strenuous workout during my lunch break. It was as much to maintain my fitness as to avoid the lunch time drinking sessions that were a feature of many young men working in the City of London. The swimming pool near to my Earls Court apartment I used only occasionally, most often to help combat a Sunday morning hangover. But this afternoon I was going swimming so that the adrenaline rush would blank out my thoughts of Poppy making out with some beefy gym instructor. By the time I pulled myself out of the water I had persuaded myself that Poppy having a date was exactly what I had wanted. I had vowed not to chase her anymore and to shut out all carnal thoughts of her body.

After my swim I went into a small supermarket and loaded up with food supplies; all things that I needed for my limited culinary skills. Back home again, I changed into casual but warm clothing and made my way to the big and noisy, Earls Court Tavern. At 6 pm people filled the large bar rooms as they celebrated the end of the week. I knew several of the regulars casually and was soon drawn into a *gemutlich* group of beer swilling, cigarette smoking males. I stayed for about an hour and two pints of London Bitter beer before setting off in a light drizzle to a local Indian restaurant. I drank a lager there as a take-away Chicken Biryani with nan bread was prepared for me. Back in my apartment once more, with my large gas fire turned up, I settled down to eat my meal and start on an entirely inappropriate bottle of Spanish red wine. I had just cleared up when the front doorbell rang.

Standing in my doorway shaking the water off her umbrella was Susan Anderson.

'Hello,' I greeted her. 'Come straight in out of this rain.'

'Thank you,' she answered as she wiped her shoes inside my hall.

I took the umbrella off her. 'Take off your mac as well and hang it on the hat stand there.' I helped it off her shoulders and led the way into my lounge.

'I am sorry about the smell,' I said. 'I've just eaten an Indian take-away and the smell always lingers. Can I offer you a drink? There is red wine open and I can also offer whisky or brandy.'

'I only came to give you your stuff for Norfolk.'

'Well, you can't just drop it and go right away.'

'Alright, thank you. I'll have a glass of wine if I may.' She sat down on the edge of an armchair, one of two in the room along with a matching three-seat sofa.

'How did you get here?'

'By taxi, I can easily find another one in the Earls Court Road to get me home.'

'Which is where?'

'In Putney. I have a flat there just the other side of the river.'

'Where abouts? I know Putney quite well.'

'Millbrook Court, just near East Putney station.'

'I know it, an imposing looking block of flats.'

'Yes, but rather feeling its age these days, although comfortable enough.'

'By yourself?'

'Yes, and you?

'Yes, by myself. Except for when my parents visit from Spain. But they use the studio downstairs, the old basement.'

'Nice.'

'Yes nice.' I handed Susan a large glass of wine and sat down opposite her on the sofa.

'Thank you,' she said with a very attractive smile. I was tempted to say, *You should smile more often,* but restrained myself.

She took a healthy sup of her wine and pulled a manila envelope from her capacious handbag. 'This is the material I have prepared for your and Poppy's trip next week. Can I sit beside you while we go through it?'

I patted the seat of the sofa. 'Come right here, bring your wine over and put it on this other table next to mine.'

Sitting next to me, on the very edge of the sofa as she had been in her chair, she first pulled out a road map. 'Gresham's School is in the market town of Holt. I've ringed it in red pen. You can see it is fairly near the coast and its nearest and much bigger town is Sheringham, right on the sea which, in turn, is dwarfed by the seaside resort of Cromer just a few miles away. Norwich, is about 25 miles by road. The A11, which I have marked in blue, is really the only main road into Norfolk from the south; that's the one you should join on the north side of London. I suggest you drive straight up to Norwich and then take the Holt road, again all marked in blue.'

She passed the map to me and I placed it on my lap. Once again I was impressed the way she prepared and conducted her little briefings. It spoke of a very clear mind and an eye for detail, attributes that I supposed were vital for a person employed directly in a Minister of State's office.

'Here,' she continued, 'is an enlarged ordinance survey map of the town of Holt and its immediate surroundings. The school buildings can be clearly seen and I have annotated them with their names. Big School, Chapel, Library and so on. You can also see that the playing fields, also identified as such by me, are extensive.'

I put the map of Holt on top of the road map.

The next thing Susan produced was a type written address. 'This is the hotel you will be staying at, The Feathers. It is right at the centre of the town, at the market place, and would have been the main coaching inn at one time. It is very old I think but then so is the school, it's over 400 years since the London City merchant Sir Thomas Gresham founded it, as he did the London Royal Exchange. I have booked you and Poppy in for Monday, Tuesday and Wednesday nights, but you can extend or curtail as you wish.'

I saw a faint blush come over her pale face.

'I thought it fitting to book just one double room because you are married, in law if not in actuality, but the room has two separate beds, I was assured.'

'That's just fine,' I answered with a smile. 'Poppy and I have history going back over fifteen years and will have no problems in sharing a room, with separate beds of course.'

The final thing that Susan took from her bag was an envelope containing, she said, five hundred pounds. As she counted out the one hundred five-pound notes she said, 'This is to cover all of your and Poppy's expenses, petrol, the hotel, all meals and drinks and …,' she fixed me with a deliberate stare. 'Any palms you may have to grease.'

She produced a small printed form from the same envelope. 'I need you to sign this receipt for the full amount now, but after that you won't have to produce any receipts to prove your expenses. Just hold onto what you have left over from the Norfolk trip in case you have to go elsewhere or otherwise incur expenses. Dealing with returned money is not something that we can handle easily in our little office.'

I took the money from her, signed her receipt and put everything she had given me on the table next to our drinks. Susan picked up her glass as I did mine.

'Here's to success,' she toasted. I clinked her glass with mine. We sat quietly for a few minutes as we finished our wine. I gazed at her face. *This is one very attractive lady both in beauty and brains,* I thought, then my next words tumbled out by accident. 'You said you live by yourself. Do you have a boyfriend or whatever?'

She smiled at my boldness. 'No, not even a whatever. What about you?'

'Nothing whatsoever, since Poppy and I parted ways. Months ago now.'

'I did know about that.' She drained her glass and got to her feet. 'But I'm glad you told me off your own bat. Sort of clears the air doesn't it? Now I must be off.'

I walked her to the Earls Court Road. The rain had stopped so her umbrella remained closed. She hailed a passing taxi straight away and as she climbed in she mouthed, good luck, to me.

I had a little lift in my step as I walked back home.

Chapter 12

I met Poppy at the Bunch of Grapes the following day, the weather had improved. We had a drink each and then moved on to a nearby French bistro as the pub's Saturday lunch time fare was distinctly limited, ham or cheese sandwiches, pickled onions kept in a huge glass container on the pub's counter and looking like so many eyeballs, and Scotch eggs arrayed in a translucent plastic bread bin.

We talked about our respective sets of parents. Me recalling how I loved to visit her beautiful house as a child in Singapore; she remembering how welcoming my parents had been to her when we stayed with them in their Spanish home the previous year. We were careful not to say a word about our week's work of trying to discover the catalyst for turning people into traitors. But I did tell her that our trip to Norfolk had all been carefully organized by Susan Anderson and that I would pick her up at the Hendon Police College at about 10 am on Monday morning.

Coffee ended our light, but excellent, lunch at around 2 pm. I paid the bill, using some of the money given me by Susan, allowing somewhat dubiously that the meal was an allowable expense.

'What now?' Poppy asked. 'I've nothing on for the reminder of the day. I'd like to see where I used to live, your place.'

I expected this hint, almost an expectation on her part, and had decided to play hard to get.

'Well let's see how things turn out. Something else first, I would like to go to the Natural History Museum in South Kensington. There is a new exhibition there that I would like to see and it's halfway to my place from here, just a couple of stops on the bus.

We left the museum when it closed at four just as the winter dusk was gathering. I loved going there. It reminded me of the times my father took me there as a young schoolboy after we had returned from Singapore. Apart from the awe-inspiring exhibitions, there was an air of scholarliness and an aura of mustiness. Poppy and I had stood close together as we gazed at the animal filled dioramas. Twice I felt her fingers reach for mine, and both times I dropped my hand away from hers. I had determined that I was never going to get involved with her again, as an antidote to her advances I thought of Susan seated on my sofa the previous evening.

Regarding myself as now being in control of my relationship with Poppy, I no longer had a problem in agreeing to her request to see her old London home. We walked for half an hour through the well-lit South Kensington streets, Poppy recalling out loud all the places that she remembered, which were many. I told her that is was far too early to go into The Zetland, one of our old stomping grounds, when she pulled my arm towards its door, but I added that we could go later on when it opened at 6 pm if she liked.

We reached my apartment and passed through the gate which led off the street. Instead of going straight up to my front door, she started to descend the stone steps towards the basement's door, behind which was the one bedroom studio in which she had lived for all of 1966.

'I don't carry round a front door key to the studio,' I told her. 'You will have to come in through my door and go down those internal stairs if you want to see how your old place looks. It's not changed at all, just a few more of my parents' things spread around, they have only used it twice since you left last Christmas.'

I made a pot of tea while Poppy walked around my apartment. 'This hasn't changed at all, no flowers, no fruit in a bowl, typical bachelor apartment I imagine, and a near empty fridge I expect.'

I looked at her. She was looking towards my bedroom and her face suddenly collapsed in sadness and I saw a tear or two roll down her cheek which she quickly dabbed away. 'No Lucy,' she said hoarsely.

'No Lucy,' I echoed. 'We were happy here together, you know.'

'You and Lucy?'

'Yes,'

'All three of us, in our way.'

'Yes, all of us.'

I guided her towards the sofa and set a cup of black tea, she never took milk I remembered, on the table nearby, the same one used by Susan the previous evening for her wine.

I collected the things that Susan had brought me the previous evening from the desk by the bow window facing the street. Sitting beside each other on the sofa, I told her of arrangements Susan had made for us for our trip the following Monday.

'Nice girl,' Poppy commented.

'Clever too,' I replied

We went through the maps and, although we agreed that I would pay the bills so taking on the typical role of the 1960's husband, I pressed 50 pounds into her hand to cover anything she might need during our trip. She put the money inside her handbag.

'You said earlier that you would pick me up on Monday at 10 from Hendon. Have you got a car now?'

'Yes, almost new, very nice. A Rover 2000, bright blue.'

'And Hendon is on the way?'

'It's practically on our route, due North up the Edgware Road, the other side of Hyde Park. Oh! One thing I haven't told you, we are sharing a room, separate beds of course. Susan said we had to act like man and wife.'

'Not entirely.'

We slowly drank our tea and let our thoughts stray. Poppy drifted off to sleep against the back of the sofa. I returned to my chair and also closed my eyes. I was woken by her getting up and going to the bathroom.

'Just freshening myself up,' she said. 'Then let's go out to the Zetland. Annie's Bar upstairs is where we used to go, isn't it?'

'Yes,' I answered. 'We can collect my car from its garage, in a mews just around the corner, and use it to go out to the pub. Then you can come back here and I'll cook you something to eat. Contrary to what you thought, the larder and fridge are well stocked now.'

'You were good at pasta and grilled meat, but not much else.'

'That hasn't changed, so it will be Spaghetti Bolognaise tonight.'

'Good,' she offered as she closed the bathroom door.

I went down the internal staircase leading from the back of my entrance hall, through the dividing door and into the small bathroom in the studio for my own freshening up.

Poppy was standing at the top of the stairs as I started to climb back up them. 'Can I take a look around my old place? I won't be more than five minutes.'

'Yes,' I replied and reversed back into the studio.

'Without you, please.'

I clambered past her back into my apartment.

---///---

We spent nearly two hours in Annie's Bar. Several of the men drinking in the upstairs bar recognized Poppy, I used to call them her fan club, and she moved into top gear. Her beautiful face was radiant with pleasure as she talked charismatically about her time in Hong Kong, spontaneously relating an almost entirely fictitious tale. But I knew that she would eventually grow tired of all the flattering attention. I recognized her covert signal of 'get me out of here' when it came and we made our excuses that we had to move on to a dinner party.

She had at least three glasses of something masquerading as champagne in the pub and I'd had a couple of pints of beer, so our talk when back at the apartment flowed quite freely as I busied myself with the pasta and minced meat, while she laid the table and opened a bottle of red wine.

'How was your date last night, the physical exercise instructor didn't you say?'

He is a bit more than that. In addition to his work at Hendon where he carries the rank of Sergeant but he is not really an on-the beat policeman, he helps train the British Olympic Judo team. His name is Stephen. He is very nice and very good looking.'

'And?'

'He took me to one of those new wine bars. We spent a pleasant evening with just a very few drinks, he is very fitness conscious, and ate the Hendon equivalent of Spanish tapas.

I told him about my childhood in Singapore and how you and I had bonded there. I also told him that I was an orphan, nothing said about my father and mother, and had attended a convent school with you. He found that rather amusing. In turn, he told me about his three years in the Army as a fitness instructor before becoming part of the Hendon staff. He saw me to the door of my residence block, and I gave him a light kiss on the cheek.'

'Will you stay celibate with him?'

'Certainly, for the time being. Later? Well, we will just have to see how things go between us.'

'He is a very lucky man.'

'I'll try not to cause him as much grief as I did you. And in reply to your unspoken question, I am no longer a virgin.'

Thank God for that. I thought to myself. 'Who was the lucky, or otherwise, guy?'

'You are not on the need to know list for that information. Let's just say that I played my part in Hong Kong as a dubious character. Now let's drop the subject of our respective sex lives.'

'You started that part of the conversation.' I said as I put our dinner on the table.

Later, when we had had coffee and tidied up the kitchen, I told her that it was time for me to drive her back to Hendon. 'It will take at least half an hour, possibly longer if we run into the late Saturday night rush hour.'

'Can't I stay here, in my old bedroom downstairs? I really can't face my military barrack's bed-sitter tonight.'

I started to say no, but the imploring look on her face stifled the word before it could leave my lips. 'The bed downstairs isn't made up and I'd have to find the linen and pillows from wherever my mother has stashed them. I really don't go down there at all these days. Too many memories. And it will be cold.'

136

'So, no?'

'Not at all. You can use my spare bedroom, it's all set up.'

'Are you sure?'

'Oh for goodness sake! We will be sleeping in the same bedroom in Norfolk for much of next week. I promise I'll keep my hands off you now and then, if you do the same.'

'Of course. It's past ten, I think I'll turn in now; I'll take first go in your bathroom.'

---///---

I heard her get up and use the bathroom early the next morning. I stayed firmly in bed. Sunday morning was the time for a lie-in. At about 8 am she stuck her head around my bedroom door. 'I'm off. I had some cereal for breakfast. I've left the packet and a bowl for you on the kitchen table. I'll get back to Hendon by tube, tidy myself up and then seek out Stephen for a day together while you go to your rugby.'

'Stephen is it?'

'Stephen Lowry and as I told you, very nice, so far at least. Bye, thanks for a lovely day yesterday. You are still my best man friend. See you tomorrow morning as planned.'

Chapter 13

Poppy must have been watching out for my Rover as I drew up outside the main entrance to the Hendon Police College at a few minutes past ten, I had barely stopped the car before she opened the passenger door and climbed in beside me.

'Good morning,' she said. 'I remembered the colour of your car from Saturday night, so I knew what to look out for.'

'How was your date with Stephen?' I asked as I turned the car back onto the North Circular Road and headed east towards its junction with the A11, the main road leading out of London to the heart of East Anglia.

'Very good! Among other things, we practised Judo and some unarmed combat moves. He says I'm rather good. That comes from the lessons I took while in Hong Kong. Now, that's all that I'm going to say about Stephen for this whole trip of ours.'

'You practised unarmed combat in Hong Kong?' I asked with some disbelief.

'Yes, Lucy's grandfather was an expert in Karate and took me along for some beginner's lessons.'

'You continually surprise me, but you always have.'

'Actually, the Hong Kong police thought it rather a good thing that I should have some idea of how to defend myself.'

The A11 headed directly north. We drove past the rather depressing straggles of London's suburbia and then bypassed commuter towns, some with tall blocks of flats looking like the workers' paradises of the Iron Curtain. Poppy found the road map given me by Susan in the pocket of her door and began to follow our marked route.

The scenery improved, although generally devoid of any serious hills or undulations of any significance, as we headed to Cambridge. We stopped for petrol and after paying for it I asked Poppy to take over the role of quartermaster for the trip, mainly because the money given me by Susan was very bulky and Poppy's handbag was much larger than my wallet.

'Beginning to trust me now?' she asked.

'Never completely.'

'The famous Cambridge,' Poppy remarked, taking the money but changing the subject. 'I would love to go there sometime. Do you know that the whole time that I was in London last year I never went beyond its bounds? This is my first sight-seeing trip in England and I'm going to enjoy looking out at everything that we pass. Rather flat though it seems.'

'I think the countryside will get even flatter once we get into Norfolk. It will be new to me too. I've never been to East Anglia before.'

'East Anglia?'

'That's what Norfolk and Suffolk together are called. It's a big chunk of England, sort of stuck out by itself jutting into the North Sea. The whole area used to be ruled by the Vikings. Their area stretched all up the right side of England through Lincolnshire and much of Yorkshire.'

'It's funny, but as you said that I remembered it. The Australian Nuns in their wisdom taught British history to their Singapore students.'

'Typical colonisation.'

'Yes, but useful to us in those days because we took British school exams.'

'Really?

'Yes, we took General Certificate of Education exams when we were 16.'

'GCEs? That's what I took too.'

'Then you were colonising yourselves,' she laughed.

We passed through Barton Mills. 'A few miles further and we will be in Norfolk,' I commented and as I did so the road began to narrow. Shortly afterwards we entered the market town of Thetford and stopped at a coaching inn near its centre for lunch. Poppy was studying the road map as I started driving again.

'There is a road leading off the A11 to our left which could take us directly to Holt,' she said. 'It's coloured red to begin with, then changes to yellow and finally to white. What does that mean?'

'It means that the road gets narrower and narrower. It will be a minor road after the red stretch. The road we are on is the biggest road into Norfolk and look how narrow it has become. I think we will stick with Susan's marked route.'

'We are going to go through a town spelt W-y-m-o-n-d-h-a-m; I've no idea how to pronounce that 'Why -mond – ham' is it?'

'No, Susan pointed out that name when we went over the route. It's pronounced Windham apparently.'

'Probably something to do with the Vikings.'

'Probably.'

I saw Poppy run a finger over the map. 'Goodness,' she exclaimed. 'So many of the towns and villages end in ham, in addition to Wymondham that is. Did I say that right?'

'Yes,' I nodded.

'There's Dereham, Fakenham and Swaffham marked as towns and a myriad of villages, some just specks on the map. Cressingham, Raynham and so on and so on. Dozens of them, literally. Is ham a Viking word?'

'Well, I imagine its short for Hamlet. You know, like a small village, something like that kampong near where we used to live in Singapore. But it may well be Viking talk. In other parts of England the ending is, ton. Short for town, like Southampton and Taunton.'

We drove straight through the picturesque market town of Wymondham and on into the centre of Norwich, although we could have used a road around the city I wanted to pass the cathedral and the castle which I knew were in its medieval centre.

Poppy remarked how attractive the centre was. 'This is another place I would like to spend some time exploring. Perhaps we could stop on our way back?'

'Like Cambridge. Perhaps we could.'

From Norwich we headed directly north to the coast and the seaside resort of Cromer. The countryside was generally flat, although punctuated by occasional small hills, and divided up into rather dreary looking fields most, it being winter, without a trace of greenery. The construction of many of the houses we saw changed from brick to small, neatly faced flint. We avoided the sea front of Cromer and then, by-passing Sheringham, took the sign-posted road to Holt. Fifteen minutes later we were on its outskirts with large school buildings surrounded by playing fields on either side of the road.

We drove slowly along the last mile into Holt in the fast gathering gloom of a late November East Anglian afternoon. We saw a few schoolboys of various ages walking along the pavement in small orderly groups, others were cycling singly or in pairs. They were all dressed in grey long trousers and navy-blue blazers.

'They don't have caps on their heads,' commented Poppy. 'I thought all schoolboys wore those rather silly looking peak caps with a crest of some sort at the front.'

'Evidently they don't at Gresham's. And some schools like Eton wear top hats, others sport boaters or go about bare-headed. It's getting dark and we will have lots of time to look around the school site over the next couple of days. Let's get to the hotel and settle in.'

'Into our shared room.'

'Yes,' I closed that conversation. 'And don't forget that we are husband and wife so behave accordingly.'

'While in the public view?'

I didn't deign to reply.

We entered the centre of Holt after making a sharp left turn by a modern looking Post Office and found ourselves in Market Street right outside the Feathers Hotel. Susan's description of it being an old coaching inn had been accurate. The frontage was a long, two storied building with undulating tiled roofs I drove the car thorough an entrance at the hotel's side to reach the stables area and parked on the cobblestoned courtyard, surely the same route that the stage coaches would have used perhaps a hundred and more years previously. The time was approaching 5 pm.

Ted, a man of about my age, greeted Poppy and me inside what passed for the hotel's lobby. He showed us around the ground floor pointing out the dining room, the residents bar and a much larger public bar; the place seemed deserted. Ted told us that the bars and dining room didn't open until 6 pm and that, it being a winter Monday, there were only three other guests staying, all commercial travellers. 'I've given you one of our largest and best rooms. Two double beds as requested by a very efficient lady called Susan. Your secretary Mr Shawyer?'

'No,' I replied. 'More like my employer actually.'

'The room doesn't have its own bathroom, *en-suite* is the expression used I believe. But there is nice one next door and you won't have to share it as there are no other guests in your corridor. I'll take you to your room now. Would you like me to carry that suitcase Mrs Shawyer?'

'I'm fine with it, but thank you anyway,' replied Poppy.

We climbed up a narrow, twisting flight of stairs which echoed the structure and ambience of the whole antique interior of the hotel. The bedroom chosen for us was large, freshly and tastefully decorated in a somewhat chintzy style – the floral wallpaper at least. The two double beds were spaced across the floor so that Poppy and I were to have plenty of room to move around without tripping over each other.

'Will this suit the two of you?' Ted asked.

'Yes, fine,' we replied in unison.

'The bathroom is just next door, but the towels for you are on the beds. I will be downstairs if you need me. Will you be eating with us? Dinner will be served from seven.'

I looked at Poppy, she nodded back at me.

'Yes,' I said. 'But we will be down for pre-dinner drinks before that.'

Ted left, and Poppy put her bag onto the bed nearer the door. 'This is mine, next to the bathroom. Now I'm going to strip off as far as is decent then have a shower.'

'Do you think there is a shower in this old hotel? The bath is probably a zinc tub.'

Poppy hurried out of the bedroom and was back within two minutes.

'No shower as such, but a hand-held hose thing attached to the bath taps. And the bath looks new as does everything else, so no problem for me.'

She stripped down to a silk slip, quite opaque, but with a low neck line and in the upper area of her décolletage was the little ivory tiger's head hanging on a gold chain that I had given to her on her eight birthday. She saw me staring at it, placed it between thumb and forefinger and gently caressed it.

'Yes, David, as always it is never away from guarding my body. Now stop looking at my little tits. You've seen them before in their full brazenness but they are off limits now despite that scrap of marriage certificate declaring otherwise.'

She wrapped her raincoat around her shoulders and carried her sponge bag out to the bathroom. I lay down on the bed she had allocated to me and fell into a light sleep.

She woke me as she returned to the room some three-quarters of an hour later.

'Sorry I've been so long. I decided to have a bath and dozed off – it looks like you have been having your eyes shut as well. If you'd like to use the bathroom now, I'll change for the evening.

---///---

She looked glorious in a knee length, florally patterned dress in shades of green broken by white as we entered the resident's bar at a few minutes after six. Her clever use of light make up had made her look more oriental and exotic than usual, disguising her normally quite apparent part Caucasian heritage. She could have been auditioning for a role in *The World of Suzie Wong*. Ted was acting as bar tender and, from the way he kept glancing into the dining room behind him, also as Maître d. He also took a long and admiring look at Poppy.

Poppy asked for a gin and tonic, I for a pint of bitter.

'The draft beer is all in the public bar,' Ted said in reply to my request. 'I'll go and fetch you one if you like, but if you are into draft beer you might find the other bar more convenient and convivial. People will be starting to drift in there now. This so-called Residents Bar is really only set up for guests taking a drink with them into the dining room or ordering a bottle of wine for their table.'

'Then we will go into the public bar,' I said, looking to Poppy for confirmation. She nodded with a beatific smile directed at Ted who immediately looked away to busy himself with mixing her gin and tonic. I could see a flush enveloping his rather protruding ears.

'I'll bring the lady's drink into the other bar then,' he mumbled.

I could see that the public bar room could clearly hold a lot of roistering locals, but there was only one other customer in it as we entered. A man in his fifties perhaps, dressed in a worn tweed jacket, grey trousers and a light pink shirt adorned with a slightly crooked floral bow tie. He was seated on a bar stool at one end of the bar. He nodded at Poppy and me, then raised a finger to Ted as he appeared behind the bar with Poppy's drink.

Pulling one of the three hand pumps set into the top of the bar counter, Ted poured what I thought was to be my glass of beer. Instead, he handed it wordlessly to the man at the end of the bar who laid some coins on the counter which were immediately scooped up and put into the till by Ted. My pint of beer was poured next.

'Cheers,' said Poppy, clinking her glass against mine. 'Here's to success'. The man at the end of the bar echoed

'Cheers' softly, then began to scan a newspaper which he drew from his pocket.

'So what brings you to this part of the world?' Ted asked.

Poppy had clearly anticipated this sort of question. I hadn't.

'We are on a sort of journalistic fact-finding mission,' was the start of her reply, and I realized she was going to put on one of her charismatic acts. Her eyes sparkled and crinkled to match the smile bursting from her lips.

'Really,' stuttered Ted, completely mesmerized by this exotic oriental beauty who, it seemed to him, was giving him her full attention.

'Yes, you have probably guessed that I'm not really an Anglo-Saxon, although I do have, or rather had, a Scottish grandfather. My home is really Singapore where I met my darling husband.' She gently caressed the nape of my neck. 'And we do spend time in Hong Kong also.'

All true so far, I thought. But, as ever with Poppy, never the whole truth.

'There are now many wealthy people in both of those places who want nothing better for their sons than for them to have an education in the English public school system. Yes, almost entirely sons at present, but I'm sure that will change. Perhaps with my, and of course David's, help.'

Again, a caress of my neck.

'Now these fond parents can read the brochures that schools, like Gresham's, produce. The grounds, the ethos, the education and recreation facilities and the histories. But what they don't have is the soft knowledge. Stories about the pupils. Who they were, what they achieved while at the school, the scrapes they got into, the things and the people that helped form their characters. That is what David and I are looking for, material that we can publish as a guide for the Far Eastern parents.'

'So how are you going to find out about all that sort of stuff?' Ted asked.

'Well, Gresham's is by no means the first school we have investigated, in fact it is one of the last. We did Oundle and Uppingham, both not too far from here, only last week.'

A lie of course, but credible, and she had obviously been doing some homework unknown to me.

'We have become fairly expert at getting what we want,' she concluded her pitch.

'Good evening' the man at corner of the bar called out. 'That sounds an interesting mission of yours, we do have several boys from foreign parts of different ethnic backgrounds at the school.'

Poppy and I turned our attention to this middle aged and rather stout man.

It was my turn to speak. 'Are you on the school staff then?'

'Yes, yes I am. I teach art, thus I am the art master. Stuart Webster.'

Poppy and I introduced ourselves to Stuart.

'You can call me, Webby, if you like. But not, Beaver, that's what the boys call me. Perhaps on account of this.' He ran his index finger over a bushy but neatly trimmed moustache. 'Possibly in combination with my girth.' He chuckled as he spoke and finished with a brief laugh. He was now on his feet and I saw he was short as well as stout, a configuration that seemed to entirely suit his obviously jovial personality.

We chatted with him for an hour while waiting for our dinner table to be ready. He consumed three pints of beer in that time while Poppy and I had had our glasses recharged just once. Other people came into the Public Bar as the three of us chatted together. All locals, I surmised, by the way Stuart Webster greeted each of them.

Stuart came up with a wealth of stories about Gresham's school and its pupils with very little prompting from either me or Poppy. We reacted delightedly to each to encourage him to continue.

'I'm not sure of the exact date, but sometime in the fifties, prefects from Howson's, that's the headmaster's house opposite the library where my art department is managed to get the matron's 1935 Austin Seven car onto the roof of the building. They probably used some technique they had learned from the Handicrafts Master, Scruffy Burroughs, or from the CCF.'

'CCF?' queried Poppy.

'That's the School's Army organisation that all boys have to join,' replied Stuart. 'Unless they or their parents' dissent, in which case they have to do something socially beneficial during the times that the CCF parades. Anyway, it was lowered safely but the matron, who was very popular, never let those prefects use the car again for their late-night jaunts to one of the pubs a few miles away from Holt.

'The large and very heavy wrought iron gates that embellish the school entrance have a habit of ending up on Kelling Heath at the end of the summer terms as part of the school leavers celebrations.

'Then there was the boy, whose name I won't reveal, who distilled gin on a near industrial scale in a disused public toilet near the centre of town. He used the original gas lighting to power the still and was operating quietly selling the brew around the school in pop-bottles until he went onto the open market. The town became full of policemen and reporters from London.'

'What happened to the unnamed boy?' asked Poppy.

'Oh, he was expelled. Probably went straight onto the board of his father's drinks company. Another boy found a Second World War hand grenade on the local rubbish dump of all places. He was looking for slow worms I suppose which he would keep under the lapels of his school blazer for a few days to show his mates and then release back to the wilds. Anyway, he decided to let the grenade off in one of the ponds hidden deep in the school woods. Lots of dead fish, but nobody admitted to the deed.'

Entertaining as these anecdotes were, they were not the sort of information that Poppy and I were seeking so we took our leave of Stuart the art master as soon as Ted said that our table was ready in the dining room. Stuart added that it was also time for him to go to his home.

The menu was short and confined to well-known British dishes. Our tomato soups followed by a steak for me and gammon with pineapple for Poppy. The meals were nicely presented and cooked with care. A bottle of Côte de Rhone graced our table and satisfied our thirst.

Poppy began. 'A bit like Mister Pickwick?'

'Yes,' I replied, 'but entertaining.'

'But not what we want, is he?'

'No, firstly because we were told not to approach the school teaching staff.'

'He approached us,' said Poppy.

'Agreed, but his stories all emanate from after the war. What we want is information dating from the late nineteen twenties and not those sort of stories either.'

'So?'

'So we tap Ted, very guardedly, for other, earlier sources.'

We returned to the Public Bar after we had finished our meals and asked Ted for a brandy each as our night caps. By then there were only three people other than us in the bar and they were seated well away from where we were placing our drinks orders. I was going to let Poppy do the talking to Ted who, I assumed, was still agog with admiration of her, but he provided the opening we needed.

'Did you find out anything useful from Webby?' he asked.

'Certainly very interesting and amusing,' answered Poppy rather uncommitted. 'Although our prospective Far Eastern clients are quite conservative shall we say, and might be a little dismayed at some of the schoolboy antics he described.'

'Oh, he probably concentrated on the few and far between stories that spark his sense of humour. In the main, the Gresham's boys are very well behaved and rather conservative themselves.'

'Well, that remark of yours we can certainly use, and coming as it does not from a member of the school staff but a local observer carries much more weight.' Poppy's words almost stroked Ted who beamed with pleasure.

'Yes,' I interjected. 'We need more opinions from persons such as you, people without an axe to grind but have intimate and long standing connections with the school. Just as you must have running the town's principal hotel.'

Ted's countenance was becoming more and more like Alice's grinning Cheshire Cat. He leant over the bar counter conspiratorially towards Poppy and me, and lowered his voice.

'Webby is a creature of habit and won't be back in here until Friday, I expect. But tomorrow, as with every Tuesday evening, as soon as we open, two old guys called Fred and Bert will be here. They were groundsmen or did the maintenance of the school buildings, or something like that, for years and years. They will know lots about the school, but they will probably need lubricating with pots of beer. They have prodigious thirsts especially when someone else is buying. Although I suppose their stories will be mostly from before the school moved to Newquay.'

'The school moved?' I asked.

'Oh yes. During the war the school buildings in Holt were all requisitioned by the Army so the school moved lock, stock and barrel down to Cornwall. Fred and Bert retired because they were not going to move down to the South West of England. I doubt that they have ever been to Norwich more than a couple of times. I suppose what they may tell you will be very out of date.'

Poppy gave my ankle a little kick then smiled at Ted, moved her face close to his and said, 'Thank you Ted, your idea of meeting with Fred and Bert sounds just what we need. Historical recollections are exactly what we are seeking, they will frame the character of the school and its ethos for us. We will come here at six sharp and sit at that table in the corner over there so we can talk to the two men without being overheard. Can you arrange that?'

As if he had received a command from an angel, Ted replied, 'Certainly, yes, yes; of course I can, and I will.'

We took our brandies to the table that had just been selected by Poppy and sipped them slowly.

'That was a masterly performance,' I commented with admiration.

She gave a little smile but didn't respond to my flattery, then she turned serious.

'It seems to me that these two locals of Ted's may be our best chance. They have been here for years, perhaps their whole working life, with their world centred around Holt and the school. They surely would have knowledge of some sort of whom might have influenced MacLean and his contemporaries before they went up to Cambridge or wherever. But being the best chance may also mean being the only chance; if we foul-up our approach to them then our cover, if that is the right word, will be blown and probably spread all over town. We have to do some strategizing right now.'

Chapter 14

We climbed the narrow, winding stairs back up to our bedroom at about 10 pm, satisfied that we knew how to handle Fred and Bert the following evening and satisfied by the two brandies that we had each slowly sipped. I was uncertain how Poppy was going to handle our first night of sharing a bedroom since we had separated in Australia; however, she took control of things immediately after we closed the door behind us.

'You go and brush your teeth and whatever, David, while I get into my nighty and raincoat. Then you can tuck yourself in for the night while I'm in the bathroom doing my thing.'

When I returned the floor length window curtains were drawn, the two bedside lamps were on and the room's main central pendant light was off. The room looked cosy and was being warmed by a radiator along one wall. Poppy was enveloped in her raincoat as she replaced me in the bathroom. I was in my bed reading a copy of the Eastern Daily Press, the daily newspaper for East Anglia that I had removed from the bar, when she returned.

After she had deftly slipped out of the raincoat and into the bedclothes, she called out, 'Goodnight,' then she immediately turned off her lamp and rolled over on her side to face away from me.

'Goodnight,' I replied and switched off my own lamp. Streetlight from the marketplace beneath the window filtered through the curtains. I lay on my back, eyes wide open, wondering how difficult it might be for sleep to come in the proximity of a body of which I knew every nook and cranny, and a mind which I probably understood better than anyone yet hardly understood at all.'

Five minutes passed. 'Go to sleep,' she called out.

'I'm trying,'

Time dragged through another ten minutes, so the illuminated hands of my watch told me.'

'Do you need a cuddle to get to sleep?' her voice barely above a whisper.

Even if she had not intended that question as a test for me, I treated it as so, and I had an antidote.

'No,' I replied, holding in my mind the image of Susan Anderson smiling at me as we sat together in my apartment. 'Not now.'

'Or ever?'

'Not ever,' I said, but with our history together I couldn't be quite certain.

---///---

By 8 am the following morning, we were both up and dressed after having reversed the previous evening's process for using the bathroom and modestly donning our clothes.

We were treated to traditional cooked breakfasts in the dining room which contained three other men, each seated alone, presumably the commercial travellers that Ted had mentioned. We lingered at our table: me reading the morning paper and Poppy pouring over a tourist brochure for the surrounding area of northern East Anglia.

'It looks like a nice day outside so let's do a bit of touring today,' she suggested. 'But first we have got to walk around the school premises, as we agreed last night. They seem to be spread out all about the town so it will probably take most of the morning to cover on foot, but afterwards we could drive to the coast for lunch. It doesn't look more than five miles away. There is a place called Blakeney by a harbour, some walks over what are called salt marshes, whatever they are, and a nice looking hotel where we could have lunch. We really have nothing else to do here today until we meet up with our two local characters in the bar this evening.'

It was as good idea as any to pass the day. 'Let's do it,' I said.

We took some instructions from Ted who produced a small map of the town and ringed in pencil the principal buildings of Gresham's School. We wrapped up well because although the sun was shining it was not in the early morning producing much in the way of heat. We set out briskly to pace around the conurbation of Holt and soon found the original school building now called, Old School House and one of the five principal boarding houses comprising the school's accommodation. On a small road along one side of Old School House there was a small, flat roofed, rectangular building with no windows and pad-locked doors. Poppy and I looked at each other and simultaneously said, 'Gin distillery.'

Further along the same road we came to a sports field laid out with two rugby pitches.

'Ugh! Rugger!' exclaimed Poppy in her usual way. 'Is this the sort of place where you learned that dreadful so-called sport?'

'Just so,' I replied. 'This time of year is called the Michaelmas term because we are coming up to Christmas, and it is when most schools, at least the private ones, the ones we curiously called Public, play rugby. Then after Christmas and coming up to Easter is the Lent term when the sport is hockey.'

'I like hockey,' said Poppy. 'And I suppose the next term in the summer is called Solstice or something like that, when cricket is played.'

'It's called the Summer term and yes, it is the time for cricket as well as swimming and athletics I would expect.'

We walked back into the town and then out along the road towards Sheringham that had brought us to Holt to previous evening. After ten minutes we found ourselves at a fork in the road. The left branch was signposted to Blakeney.

'That's the route for us later on,' commented Poppy.

The main road continued as the right branch of the junction. There were two large houses either side of the fork. One advertised itself as, Kenwyn and the other as Crossways. Both were marked on Ted's map as the junior houses of the school, but we saw no schoolboys around them.

Another ten minutes of walking towards Sheringham brought us to the main buildings of the school. Woodlands house on the left, followed by Howson's and the rather Gothic main classrooms building framed by the large and sometimes wandering wrought iron gates. A footbridge crossed the road leading to the more modern library building housing Stuart Webster's art classrooms with Tallis house nearby. We started to see boys of all ages walking purposely in groups from place to place around the main buildings. Some were crossing the large parade ground which led to a cluster of low thatched-roof buildings. Beyond the far side of the parade ground stood an imposing looking chapel built, it seemed from our quite distant vantage point, of flint like many of the houses we had passed while leaving the town. Behind most of these buildings stretched extensive sports fields.

'Pretty impressive place,' commented Poppy.

'Fairly typical public school,' I replied.

We walked on, past the entrance to another large building labelled as Farfield, the last of the five houses comprising the Senior School.

'Is that it?' she asked.

'Not quite yet,' I answered after consulting Ted's little map.

A few more minutes of walking and we reached the last of the school's buildings; a modern single story construction that clearly matched the notice board at the entrance to its drive, Sanatorium.

'It's obviously a place of privilege,' Poppy remarked as we retraced our route back to the Feathers Hotel. 'Although I read in that tourist brochure that there are scholarships, based on social rather than academic factors, that enable local boys to attend for very low fees.'

We had seen enough of Gresham's school. Those buildings were not going to provide any help in explaining its penchant for producing Communists in the 1920s and by 11 am we were in my car heading to the coast. The day was remaining cold but bright.

We passed through neat little communities, not much more than hamlets, with most houses built in the attractive flint with which we were now familiar. Reaching the coast, we turned northwards towards Blakeney and parked by its harbour almost outside the hotel that Poppy had suggested for lunch. The journey from Holt had taken less than 20 minutes and we were not ready for food. There was, however, a basic refreshment stall on the harbour quay to provide for the local workers and passing trade. There we drank innocuous coffee and shared a chocolate bar before setting out for a sign-posted walk across the salt marshes. In the near distance, almost on the marshes, was a splendid looking windmill equipped with what looked like working sails which, however, were not turning.

The tide was fully out leaving yachts and fishing smacks leaned over on their sides on the wet muddy ooze of the harbour's bottom This also meant that the marshes were clear of water in the multitude of narrow channels that divided the whole area into a network of tiny inter-connected islands; were we to have slipped off the indistinct path we would have landed in the muddy ooze rather than flounder in several feet of water. Our chosen route roughly followed the main harbour channel until we came to a large, peninsular shaped beach comprised of sand, clumps of scraggy grass and a tall, flint shingle bank. Signs told us of the birds that lived and passed through the Blakeney marshes and warned us off their nesting areas.

By the time we were back at the harbour, our shoes scoured of mud as best we could against grass tufts, it was past 1 pm and we were ready for something to eat. We went into the hotel, ordered a beer each and plates of the house's famous speciality, it claimed, fish and chips. There was a handful of other people drinking and eating in the bar-cum-dining room of what was clearly an old building although not nearly as ancient as the Feathers in Holt. There was a portly, bald, middle-aged man serving the drinks and taking the food orders. He introduced himself as Harold and promptly enquired what Poppy and I, as obvious tourists, were doing in Blakeney in November.

Always one to size up an opportunity quickly, Poppy came out with a similar story to the one she had woven to Ted the previous evening. As usual, for her, it worked.

'I went to Gresham's,' said Harold and with some pride added 'I was a local scholarship boy.'

Because of brains or lack of family money? I wondered, anticipating that Poppy would be asking herself the same question.

'Really,' she said, the siren-like part of her personality taking over. 'And when was that, before the war?'

''Oh well before,' Harold answered.

'Surely not,' cooed Poppy. You look too young, unless it was in the 1930s.'

'1927 to 1929. I had to leave when I turned sixteen to help my father on the farm.'

I saw Poppy direct an eyebrow flicker towards me.

'Otherwise I suppose I could have gone to university, Cambridge perhaps, some of my contemporaries went there.'

Poppy flicked her other eyebrow at me. I took her signal not only of the importance of what he had said which I, of course, had already realised myself, but that I should take over the conversation for a while.

'That must have been a really interesting time at the school.' I asked. 'I mean, did you know Benjamin Britten?'

'Oh yes,' Harold answered.

'I mean, did you know him well, like a pal?'

Harold looked a little uncomfortable. 'Well, he wasn't really in my set. He sort of kept himself to himself. He wasn't there that long. A bit stand-offish really. Did his own thing, all tied up with his music.'

'But you knew him?'

'Oh, yes, I knew him okay.'

'Fascinating,' chimed in Poppy. 'I mean, to have been a friend of someone really talented and famous like that.'

I wasn't going to let her back into the lead so easily. 'And there must have been lots of clever and famous people going through Gresham's at that time. Look at you, you won a scholarship and could have gone to Cambridge. My wife and I never went to university.'

With those stroking words of mine, Harold regained his self-assurance. It was time to cast the bait. 'And what about Donald Maclean, the spy, were you with him as well?'

'Yes, yes. We were in the same class for a while. Fantastically clever and a good sportsman. He and I were great friends.'

That really didn't ring true for me. I just couldn't imagine Maclean being a great friend of Harold the farmer's son. Two completely different social backgrounds, and Maclean was nothing if not a snob, or so I imagined.

I hammered on. 'So you must know why he became a communist and spy against his own country. You could be the key to a great mystery. Goodness, did the police ever interview you or anything like that?'

Harold started to look uncomfortable again. 'No, certainly not. Maclean's downfall happened a lot later, after he left school, at Cambridge so the papers said. I only knew him at school.'

Poppy took over with words of encouragement. 'Apart from being clever and athletic, did he not have anything that might have made you suspicious of him? Knowing what you know now of course.'

'Well … he had his own group of friends, they talked about politics a lot and something they called, the World Order.'

'And you joined in,' Poppy looked at him with a smile and a look of intense interest, all put on, I knew. 'You were his friend, you must have known what his view of the world was? What he wanted to change perhaps?'

Harold was starting to squirm, perhaps he thought that Poppy and I were some sort of police or newspaper reporters. 'Now I come to think of it, perhaps we weren't really that close, just in the same form and only for one year I think.'

Poppy wasn't done. 'I've a sort of uncle that was at Gresham's at about that time. Not a blood relative but connected to my side of the family through a second marriage. A very clever man in his own way. Klugman. Jimmy or James, was he there with you?'

'There was a Klugman. I don't know what his Christian name was, they are not much used at Gresham's, sort of frowned on. Klugman was one of Maclean's set of friends, but not in my form.'

Poppy took the gamble that I would have baulked at, but that was her and she had the figure and face to pull it off on some poor males. 'I've heard Jimmy Klugman, we see him for Christmas sometimes, talk of two boys called Simon. That's their surname. Two Lords I think, brothers. Did you know them?'

Harold, it seemed, could not resist Poppy, few men could. 'There was a Simon Major and a Simon Minor, and their father did have some sort of title I think.'

Poppy closed the loop. 'So, being friends of my uncle put them in Maclean's circle of friends rather than your own pals?'

With a distinct edge of bitterness, Harold replied, 'Yes they were all in his group, pseudo-intellectuals all of them. I'm surprised that they didn't all come to a bad end like Maclean.'

Just then the two plates of fish and chips arrived to relieve Harold's building tension. Poppy and I carried them to a table well away from the bar.

'A busted flush,' I offered. 'A line shooter.'

'Not really. We now know, as we suspected, that all those names of ours were in some sort of cabal at school.'

'That's just what he says. I've been taught to be wary of what witnesses say that they think they know. There is a distinct odour of envy about Harold's description of his school experience. But you are right, it doesn't discredit our theory in any way. You did a great job of drawing him out, but I'm very glad that you didn't go on to ask if those pseudo-intellectuals of his, which they certainly were not, had an influential teacher. He would have clammed up and spread the word that we were police or reporters for some newspaper.'

'So our hopes hang on Fred and Bert this evening?'

'Yes,' I replied. 'These fish and chips are really good, just like the sign outside says.'

After lunch we returned to Holt by a round-about route, hugging the coast, through the delightful village of Wells-next-the-Sea to look at the majestic Holkham Hall over the heads of grazing deer, then inland to Fakenham and finally up the steep Letheringsett Hill to The Feathers where we collapsed onto our beds, reading and dozing until it was time to freshen up and meet our next candidates in the Public Bar.

---///---

We entered the bar at a few minutes past six. Two very rustic looking men were sitting at the table Ted had been asked to reserve for us. They looked about the same age, well into their seventies I thought, although their faces were so weather-beaten and their noses so long, cratered and red that they could have been of any old-aged decade. Their hands were huge, red like their noses, and semi-curled with arthritis, the fruit of years of hard, manual work outside in all weathers, I was sure. Poppy and I approached the table.

'Fred and Bert?' I asked.

'Fred,' answered the taller one, raising the index finger of his right hand.

'He's Fred, I'm Bert,' replied the other, raising the index finger of his left hand.

'I'm David Shawyer,' I said advancing my right arm for a hand shake, but neither of the two men reciprocated. 'And this is my wife, Poppy,' I added, dropping my outstretched arm to my side.

'May we join you,' asked Poppy with her sweetest smile which evinced no response of any sort on the faces of the men.'

'We've been expecting you,' drawled Fred with a very distinct Norfolk accent but no welcome evident on his face, Bert's expression was equally impassive.

'Expecting you,' echoed Bert in an identical voice.

Poppy sat down on the third of the four chairs surrounding the table, facing Fred and Bert and still smiling for them. 'Can I get you both a drink?' I asked.

'Bitter, best, pint of, with handle,' replied Fred.

'Pint of best bitter, glass with a handle,' offered Bert as if he was trying to explain his companion's request.

'Right, got that. And what about you my love?'

'Half of bitter, no handle,' was Poppy's way of teasing me.

I gave the order, mine included for the third pint of best bitter, with handle, to Ted at the bar. 'I'll bring them all over to you. Bit hard to begin with is it?'

'Haven't broken the ice yet.'

'Wait until they are well into their second pints, they will loosen up then.'

By the time I regained the table and sat down on the remaining chair, Poppy was describing our walk across the Blakeney salt marshes to a seemingly unenthusiastic audience.

'Beer coming, is it?' asked Fred.

'Coming is it?' added Bert.

Like manna from heaven, Ted lay the pints of beer in glasses with handles in front of the two men saying, 'I'll be back in a moment with yours, Mr and Mrs Shawyer.'

Without a word, both men raised their glasses and in four great slurps, I counted them, drained the glasses in the two minutes that it took Ted to bring Poppy and my beers.

Ted looked quizzically at me. 'Would you both like another beer? I asked Fred and Bert.

'Aye,' they said in unison.

Poppy completed her story about our walk at Blakeney to the bird sanctuary.

'Don't go there much, got no car,' said Fred.

'No car,' said Bert.

I became apprehensive that Poppy might start talking about Harold of the Blakeney hotel bar, so decided to take the initiative myself.

'Ted tells me that you worked for many years at the school.'

'And know most of its stories and secrets,' Poppy butted in. 'We are hoping you might tell us some.'

'Stories? Yes, started there after the war,' said Fred.

'After the war, so we know secrets,' said Bert. *'Ted told us about you, how you are writing some sort of history of the school.*

'Yes,' said Poppy. 'We want to learn the untold stories of the school.'

Ted brought two more pints of beer and whispered to me 'All being taken care of, on your account, Mr Shawyer.'

The two men promptly drained their new glasses half empty and, like a stage act, together wiped foam off the lips on to the back of their hands with grunts of satisfaction. Something like smiles flitted across their wrinkled lips.

'But only after the war, so you were working there since about 1945, after the school moved back from Cornwall?'

'No, no,' answered Fred as if Poppy was mentally deficient.

'The Great War,' added Bert. *'We was in it, stretcher bearers.'*

'Stretcher bearers, in the Norfolk's.'

'From 1916, when we was just seventeen. The Royal Norfolk's they are called now.'

I had lost track with which of the two were speaking what words, so fast were they now talking. The beer was obviously working on their moods and tongues.

'We saw it all.'

'Terrible things.'

'Got medals to prove it.'

'But never a scratch.'

'Plenty of the trots though.'

'Lots of them.'

'Trots?' asked Poppy.

'The runs. Dysentery,' replied Fred.

'So when did you start at the school?' I asked

'On discharge in 1918,' replied Bert.'

'And when did you finish there?' asked Poppy.

'We finished working for Gresham's in 1940, when the whole school moved down south.'

'But we didn't finish at the school.'

'I don't understand,' I said.

'We were kept on looking after them buildings by the Army until 1944 when they left the place.'

'But you stopped working then?'

'At the school, yes.'

'But we got took on by the gasworks.'

'The gasworks. Stoking the boilers until we made 65.'

'For the pension.'

'The pension, yeah.'

'A year or so ago.'

'Yeah.'

'Yeah.'

That told me that they were not as ancient as the hard, out-door work had rendered them. During this back, forth and sideways chit-chat, we had all finished the drinks in front of us. Fred and Bert were staring in the gloomy depths of their empty glasses when Ted again silently appeared by my side. 'Same again all round?' he asked.

Big nods from Fred and Bert greeted this question. Poppy asked for a gin and tonic.

'So same again except for Poppy, thanks Ted,' I replied.

'How about some food? The kitchen could make a large plate of various sandwiches for you all to share,' suggested Ted.

Smiles and more nods from Fred and Bert.

'That will do us all very well, thank you Ted,' said Poppy.

While we were waiting for the next round of drinks to appear, Poppy asked the two men, who were of very similar appearance, if they were related at all, even perhaps brothers.

'No, not at all,' said Fred.'

'It was our mothers' that were related. They were half-sisters,'

'Same dad, different wives.'

'So not related?' I queried.

'No, not at all.'

'Except, of course the wives were cousins.'

'First cousins.'

'Yeah.'

Mercifully, Ted arrived at that point with the drinks. 'Kitchen says you will have the sandwiches in about ten minutes,' he offered.

The first pulls of the men's third pints, all conducted in silence, reduced the glasses' contents by a third. I thought the silence might continue until, once more, Poppy and I would be looking at empty glasses on the other side of the table, but she stepped in in typical Poppy fashion.

'We had lunch in the Blakeney Hotel today and met a man called Harold. He says he went to Gresham's in the late 1920s. I wonder whether you knew him?'

'Harold who?' asked Fred.

'He didn't tell us his surname, but he was a day boy, had a scholarship but left school at 16 to work on his father's farm.'

'Harold Williams,' said Fred and Bert in unison.

'Came to a bad end.'

'Bad end. Expelled.'

'Expelled, that's why he left.'

'Nothing to do with working on his dad's farm.'

'Expelled!' exclaimed Poppy. 'He seemed such a nice helpful man.'

'That's what she would have thought,' said Fred.

'Yes, she would have thought that. To begin with,' added Bert.

'She?' I asked.

'The girl what got pregnant.'

'By him.'

'Or so she said.'

'Harold got a girl pregnant, but what business was that of the school, to expel him? Oh! Something to do with the school's reputation I suppose.' I asked.

'That, yes. But more to do with the girl being a kitchen maid in Harold's house,' said Fred.

'Kitchen maid,' added Bert. *'Absolutely forbidden to muck about with those young girls, though three or four have fallen over the years. Last one in 1960.'*

'So what happened to Harold Williams after he left school?' Poppy asked.

'He went to work on the family farm, about ten miles away towards Norwich. His dad made him marry the girl,' replied Bert.

'At sixteen?' I asked.

'No,' replied Fred. 'When they both got to eighteen, and had a little boy to show for it.'

'But if he worked the farm, why was he behind the bar at the Blakeney Hotel at lunchtime today?'

'He didn't get the farm when his dad died,' answered Fred

'No, his elder brother got it,' said Bert. *'But then Harold got wounded in the Second War and couldn't do the heavy work on the farm so he became a part-time representative for a fertilizer company.'*

'But that's only part time, so as to keep the family going he has to fill in as a barman when needed,' added Fred.

'He also gets a war pension.'

'Yes, he gets that, but that ain't much, so he has to fill in with the fertilizer and bar work.'

'The family is still going strong then, because he sells fertilizer and works in the Blakeney Hotel. That's pretty good dedication, when he's got a war wound as well,' Poppy commented.

'Yes, turned into a real family man. Three kids and same wife, and still living in one of the farm cottages.'

'All done up now.'

'All done up and modern like.'

A huge plate of sandwiches arrived along with four smaller plates and a pile of paper serviettes, brought by a smiling lady from the kitchen.

The two men tucked in voraciously, Poppy and I emulated them but rather more slowly. I ordered two more pints of beer for them which Ted brought over almost instantly; he had probably been tracking the emptying process of their glasses. The men were fed, well lubricated and becoming garrulous. It was time to activate the final bit of the process hatched by Poppy and me the previous evening, but now modified by the inclusion of Harold. I had the lead.

'We were talking to Harold about Donald Maclean. Did either of you know him when you worked at Gresham's, nearly 40 years ago I suppose it is now.'

'We knew of him. Should have been shot.'

'Shot, yes. That's what they did to cowards and traitors in our war.'

'Except that he wasn't caught,' I said.

'But should have been.'

'Yes, would have been if it hadn't been for the others.'

'They should have been caught and shot too.'

'All of them, together, shot. He had brothers at the school. Two or was it three?'

'Two or three, all spaced out. But I don't really remember them.'

'Me neither. But that Donald should have been shot.'

The mention of brothers was news to me. I couldn't remember seeing anything about them in any of the files we had been pouring through in London. I made a mental note to discuss that omission with Poppy later. However, with the two men's opinion of Donald Maclean now well established, I felt confident in sailing on. 'Harold told us that he belonged to a group of similar young men, Gresham's schoolboys. Can you remember their names, Poppy?'

'There were two brothers, name of Simon. Simon Major and Simon Minor. Oh! And another boy with a rather foreign sounding name .. Kluger? No, Klugman.'

'That's right,' I added. 'But I have never heard of them becoming spies or traitors, never heard of them at all before today in fact, although Harold said that they were very clever.'

'I remember those boys. All part of one group,' said Fred.

'Yes, snobbish lot,' Bert added.

'Yet one became a traitor, and the others didn't. Perhaps they were all against the British Government but maybe one of the school masters talked them out of it, all except Maclean that is?' I wondered aloud.

'If he did that then he would be some sort of hero, wouldn't he?' Poppy chimed in trying to make the remark sound completely innocent. 'What do you think Fred?' She fixed Fred with a beatific smile, who promptly buried his face into his pint glass, while Bert provided the reply.

'Well, it could have been some master like you say Miss, but it could also have been someone else, couldn't it Fred?'

'Aye,' said Fred, sounding a little guarded.

But after four pints of beer, Bert was not to be stopped now. *There was a man, he may have been foreign. He wasn't a proper master at the school. He gave private lessons to help some boys get into university, especially Oxford or Cambridge.'*

Fred returned to the conversation from the depths of his now near empty glass, and was not going to be outdone by his friend. 'Gave them special tuition to pass some special university entrance exam and get through the interviews.'

'Did it in the evenings in a house he rented in the town.' Bert was now in full flow.

'Do you remember the name of this possible hero?' I asked with what could only have been my final card.

'Seb Miller,' they replied together

'Seb Miller,' repeated Poppy.

'Aye,' they chorused again.

'That name, Seb, what was it short for. Sebastian?'

'Don't know, everyone knew him as Seb.'

'Could have been Sebastian, could have been a lot of things, but always Seb to everyone here.'

'Used to drink in this pub sometimes.'

'That's how we know.'

I shot a look at Poppy to close down the conversation which she ignored, correctly as it turned out.

'I wonder what happened to him, to Seb Miller?' Again the tone of innocent wonder from Poppy. 'Did he go down south with the school during the Second World War? Goodness! Is he still here?'

'He left here well before that war.'

'Said he was going to Canada.'

'That's what he said.'

'Then suddenly he was gone, no goodbyes.'

'Gone, then nothing.'

I pressed my foot hard on Poppy's open toed shoe and saw her wince, but she got my message.

'Well, that was all quite interesting,' she said. 'But what we really want to hear is some funny stories about your days working at the school.

'We'll need to go and ease our springs before then,' said Fred.

Book 3

The SINKER at the
far end of the line

Chapter 15

The two men, our guests and seemingly confidants, told tales to us about the school for another half hour and another pint of beer each before they said that it was time for them to walk home to '*the missus's*'. Most of the stories were similar to those related by Stuart Webster the night before but one, the last of the evening, caused them great mirth in the telling. It was connected with school because the presiding senior magistrate was a very upright and old-fashioned Gresham's schoolmaster. The case before him involved the whole of a local pub's darts team being caught servicing in turn, or more likely, the other way around, a willing and financially ambitious girl behind the pub's woodshed. The public gallery of the Holt magistrates court was packed with pupils anxious to learn about life in the raw.

Poppy and I finished the evening with a whisky each and turned in before 10 pm. But before then I asked her if she had seen any mention of Donald Maclean's brothers attending Gresham's in her files. It was as much news to her as it had been to me so we agreed to ask our London puppeteers about the omission. While we sipped our nightcaps, we also decided that we would return to London the following day and there try to find out, with the help of Jean, Susan and whoever else they might rope in, more about Seb Miller.

After finishing breakfast on Wednesday morning, we checked out of The Feathers Hotel for a leisurely drive back to London. Poppy paid our bill using the cash given us by Susan as she had for our lunch the day before in Blakeney. We needed to call Jean but there was no phone in our bedroom, and we could not use the phone in the hotel's lobby in case we were overheard, as we surely would have been by Ted who had taken to hovering around us whenever we were in the hotel's public rooms – the 'Poppy' effect of course. We said our goodbyes to him, thanking him for a pleasant stay and for his pointers to the people with whom we had talked.

'We will probably be able to pick out sufficient material for our article from the many stories we were told, but if not then we may come back,' I told him in reply to his question.

We stopped the car by a roadside public telephone booth just outside Sheringham. We crammed ourselves into the tiny cubicle and spread all the coins we had onto the small shelf by the side of the telephone's black cradle-cum-cash box; we had more than enough to make the long-distance call to Jean in London. Poppy found the number in her purse and took possession of the handset; my part was to feed more coins into the cash box whenever she indicated.

Jean answered the call straight away and, as best I could tell by keeping an ear close to the handset as Poppy tried to shoo me away, hardly spoke as Poppy related what we had found out about the man known as Seb Miller. Eventually I heard the phrase, good work, from Jean before I surrendered to Poppy's elbow in my ribs while she listened intently to instructions. We gathered up the unused change all of which went into Poppy's purse and eased ourselves out of the booth.

'Well? I asked impatiently.

'We are to turn up in our office at the usual time tomorrow morning when Jean, and perhaps Susan Anderson will meet us. In the meantime she, Jean that is, will try and discover whatever she can about Mr Miller.'

We stopped in Cambridge and wandered around the colleges' precincts for three hours, taking lunch at old pub. Poppy was enraptured by what she saw and determinedly linked her arm with mine as we walked the narrow streets. I dropped her at Hendon Police College and was back in my apartment, with the car tucked away in its garage, just as the late afternoon London rush hour traffic was starting.

---///---

As usual, Poppy beat me into our Old Air Ministry office by a few minutes on the Thursday morning and at 9:15 am I answered door knocks to admit both Jean Hathaway and Susan Anderson.

We sat around the large central table and Jean asked us to recall what had happened while in Norfolk. I covered the conversations with Stuart Webster and Harold Williams. Poppy those with Fred and Bert. She managed to mimic the speech patterns of the two men rather well. When we had finished and replied to a few questions from our two visitors, Jean started to speak in very measured tones.

'Your story, as it stands, is really not much to go on except, as you pointed out Poppy, it in no way contradicts your theory of some malign entity at Gresham's in the late 1920s.'

I saw Poppy's face fall.

'Until,' Jean continued, 'one takes account of what I have found out since your phone call yesterday. When you first proposed your schooldays theory to me, Mr Noakes and Mr Russel, I think I told you that I have a nephew that goes to Gresham's. He is sixteen, took his GCE 'O' Levels last summer and passed all eight. He is my sister's son. Her husband's elder brother, Joshua, went to Gresham's in the 1930s, after Maclean and his contemporaries had left, of course. Thus, he is one of my nephew's uncles and probably the main reason that said nephew was sent to Gresham's. Joshua is very much part of what I regard as my family and I've been in contact with him, in fact we shared a couple of drinks together last evening. He is a civil servant in the tax office, quite senior, works not too far from me, and he remembers Seb Miller.'

Jean paused to look at our reactions, which probably registered anticipation, and then she continued. 'Well, he actually remembers Mr Miller because that is what the boys had to call him. He has no idea if his Christian name was Seb, Sebastian or anything else. Joshua remembers Miller because he gave Joshua evening tuition, along with two other boys, to help him pass the Civil Service entrance exam in 1935, which he duly did. He thinks he received the tuition for two hours each week, a total of four or five sessions. The tuition was conducted in the downstairs lounge of a rather old, small but elegant house in the centre of Holt. He thinks that Miller rented the whole house; there was no wife around but a younger man perhaps a lodger, or servant even appeared at times.

So we know that Seb Miller existed and worked in much the way that your two friends, Fred and Bert, described. We also know, thanks to Joshua, that he had rather 'liberal' views which today would be regarded as very Left Wing according to Joshua. Apparently he could make the type of world he envisaged very attractive to young minds. Joshua clearly remembers that he was ferociously anti-Franco and hoped that his defeat would lead to socialism being adopted all over Europe. Joshua believes that these views caused Gresham's to stop using him as a tutor in reaction to complaints from the parents of some schoolboys, not his I'm pleased to say. He says that Miller departed soon after his tuition. He also remembers Miller telling him that he would like to start his own school somewhere in Canada where, he said, he had friends and family.'

'Wow!' exclaimed Poppy. 'Things are beginning to join up.'

'They certainly are,' said Susan, the first words she had uttered since first entering the room and greeting Poppy and me. Her eyes were glowing and she directed a smile at me and to me alone.

'One thing,' I asked of Jean. 'Did Uncle Joshua say anything about a foreign accent?'

'I asked him that. He said that although Miller spoke excellent and elegant English there was a very slight trace of an accent. He thought, because of the Canadian connection, that his childhood language might have been French and learned in Quebec.'

'That's plausible,' commented Susan.

'So what now?' asked Poppy with excited enthusiasm as a general question to all of us, but I interrupted before she got an answer.

'Jean,' I began. 'Before we go any further, Poppy and I want to know why in all those files given to us by you in this office there was no mention of Donald Maclean having brothers at Gresham' School? Such knowledge might have sent us speculating a different theory to the one we have all been working on.'

Jean didn't miss a beat. 'You have a point David, but the answer can only be given by Mr Russel himself although I can assure you that the reason for the omission of their names has not in any way affected the course we are currently following. Now, returning to your question Poppy, we find Seb Miller. Susan has already started people looking through various government data records. But if he left Britain in 1935, well before the war started, and then moved to Canada, it would be very lucky if anything significant were to turn up here. So in the meantime, Susan and the two of you are going to the Canadian High Commission to look at phone books. The story is that we are trying to trace Mr Miller, formerly of the UK but now believed to be living in Canada, so that we can give him a medal and pension from the First World War. By the way, Joshua thinks that Miller would be well over 70 years of age now, so he could be dead, in which circumstances the whole exercise would be Case Closed. I have to get back to my office now. I suggest you three take an early lunch then make your way to Canada House. They have already been warned of what you are trying to do.'

---///---

We arrived at Canada House, with its impressive colonnaded portal looking as if it should be overlooking Athens rather than Trafalgar Square, at exactly midday. We had eaten sandwiches in a café down a nearby side street that had been recommended by our taxi driver. Susan was firmly in charge of our little party. She spoke first to an usher at the entrance to the building who immediately admitted us to a very large lobby, decked with Canadian pictures and framed with marble columns which reminded me of the entrance to a temple. There we were met by a lady who appeared to be acting as a receptionist. This lady was prepared for our arrival and led us into a small conference room just off the lobby, the table at its centre was laden with telephone directories.

'Each pile of directories comprises the telephone numbers of one Canadian province, territory or major city,' the lady said in a pleasant Canadian accent. 'I don't envy you your task searching for just one name among all those, talk about a needle in a haystack. Still, if the man is due a medal and some money then I wish you the best of luck. There is a toilet behind my desk outside and a water fountain. If you need anything else just come and ask. I'll be here until five when you will have to leave the building, but you can always come back tomorrow.'

She left us staring at the piles of book.

Poppy grabbed the top directory from the pile nearest to her and started to thumb through it.

'Stop!' said Susan, quite sternly. 'We have to have a plan and a process for what we are trying to do. That's my expertise, I know how to tease out information from collections of miscellaneous data. So, question number one for you to answer and us all to agree upon is what are we looking for?'

Poppy, as I knew, had an aversion to being instructed or interrogated and answered rather testily, 'Seb Miller'.

'And if we find that name and a telephoned number buried in these pages, then what?'

'The number will be traceable to a place in Canada, and we will go and find him,' Poppy said and made it sound so simple, but her reply made me remember one of the maxims quoted during my Farnborough course; To every problem there is an answer that is simple, plausible ... and wrong. I believe it was penned by Frank Whittle, the man attributed by the British for the invention of the jet engine. Poppy was about to be proved wrong by Susan, I knew, and that was such a rare occurrence that I anticipated enjoying the coming put-down.

Susan took the directory from Poppy' hands. 'This is for the Toronto metropolitan area, covering a million people I would guess, although I don't really know.' She flipped through the pages. 'Here is the section for the Ms.' She turned over a few more pages. 'And here is where the first Miller appears. About 20 Millers on this page alone of which I can see five with an 'S' in the initials. Some of the entries include first names, but I can't see any Sebastians among this lot.' She turned over the page. 'Oh! And a lot more Millers on the next page.'

'All right,' Poppy cried. 'I'm sorry. A silly answer on my part. There are probably hundreds of Millers listed in all those telephone directories, and many could have S as an initial. We obviously can't visit them all.'

'No harm done,' said Susan consolingly. 'And I'm sorry that I came on a bit strong, but I'm excited in what you have achieved so far and I want us to have the very best chance of success. What we need is some sort filter or correlation for the S. Millers, and I have an idea for that.'

'Go on,' I said. 'Our best chance is to follow your lead, I'm sure.'

'Thank you,' replied Susan. 'We have another clue that we haven't yet considered.' She looked at Poppy and me but received no signs from us of knowing what the clue might be.

'We have been told, by two different sources, three if you differentiate between your Fred and Bert, that Miller was going to start a school. Now, if you are going to start a school, from scratch that is, you need to name it. We have to guess what that name might be, find a telephone number for it and match that number to that of an S. Miller.

Polly had switched right on again. 'It seems to me that the name might in some way reflect Gresham's. It could be 'Holt Hall' for instance.'

'That's the right track,' said Susan, although I suspected that she had already conjured up that name by herself. Then my brain started to work.

'Or something more esoteric like, Holtham.'

'What?' exclaimed Poppy.

'Holt for where Gresham's is and ham because of all those Norfolk town names, Dereham, Fakenham, Swaffham. The ones you read out when we were driving up there. Even Gresh-ham perhaps.'

'What about something based on his name?' asked Poppy.

'Could be,' replied Susan. 'Well, I think that we now have a process to follow. We have a filter or filters. A school that starts with either, H or G and is redolent of either Holt or Gresham's, or has Miller as part of the name. We have enough to make a start I think.'

Susan reached inside her capacious handbag and pulled out pencils and pads of paper.

'Poppy and David, you start on finding the S. Millers. I suggest that you start with the big cities. You, David, take the ones in the west, that is Vancouver across to Winnipeg. You, Poppy, Toronto to Montreal, and those in the Maritime Provinces, that is Atlantic Canada. After that look at the provinces and territories – David those in the west and Poppy those to the east. Just noting the last four digits of each telephone number will be sufficient. For my part, I'm going to look for the schools. If you use a different sheet of paper for every directory and identify it to its source, it will make it easier for me to check for correlation with the schools I find, if I find any, that is.'

She pulled out a folded map from her bag. 'And just in case geography is not one of your strong subjects, here is a complete map of Canada.'

Apart from comfort and thirst breaks, we worked continuously and in near silence until well into the afternoon. Susan was conjuring with possible school names and then trying to find such places in the directories. If she struck lucky, which was infrequently, she would check the telephone number she had found against those on the lists that Poppy and I had already completed and then search the directories that we had not yet opened. As the hours passed, her face became determined with her chin set almost aggressively as she scurried between her lists, Poppy's lists, my lists and the directories.

Then, at about 3 pm, she called out 'I've got something promising, a school called Millhouse College, on Vancouver Island, in British Columbia. I'm surprised that you didn't see it, David, when you were looking at the Vancouver Island Directory.'

'I haven't looked at the Vancouver Island directory yet,' I said.

'But the bad news is that I couldn't find a suitable Miller in that directory when I discovered the school,' continued Susan. 'So let's all look at it again together. Three pairs of eyes.'

We found half a dozen Millers with S as an initial but no 'Sebastian' and none with a number matching that of Millhouse College. Poppy pointed out that the school might have its own telephone line independent to that of S. Miller but, by studying the map, we saw that none of the latter named came from the area, Qualicum Beach, given in the directory as the location of the school.

We sat in silence for a while, contemplating the defeat of our efforts, then Susan spoke quietly and very deliberately with a hand placed firmly on the closed Vancouver Island directory

'Wasn't there some indication from Jean and the characters in the Holt bar that Miller may have had a foreign accent?'

'A very slight one,' I replied. 'Possibly French, because of his affinity for Canada.'

'But suppose it wasn't French,' Susan continued, slowly, softly and very deliberately. 'Suppose it was German. I travelled for a summer throughout Germany, Austria and Switzerland and speak pretty good German, in which case his birth name could be Müller. The spelling would be like this.' She wrote the German spelling on one of the pads and showed it to Poppy and me. 'Or possibly without the umlaut and a variation.' She wrote down Muehler and Mueler and Muler.

'So now we look for something that matches one of those?' I asked. 'That might make sense remembering that the young Philby was much influenced by German friends and his Austrian wife.'

'Well, yes. We do that but look for a J initial too.'

'J,' queried Poppy.

'Yes.' Susan started to get animated and said excitedly, 'Suppose his shortened first name was not Seb but Sep. That's a very common colloquial shortening of Joseph in parts of Germany and Austria. So we look for that name or a J.

She flipped open the directory in front of her. It took her less than 30 seconds to exclaim 'Here! Here it is, Joseph Muhler of Qualicum Beach. Qualicum Beach where Millhouse School is!' She spelled out the letters of his name and accented the difference between the pronunciation of the surname variants. 'Although, as predicted by you Poppy, the telephone number is not quite the same.'

We copied down the full telephone numbers of the school and of Muhler as she read them out.

Poppy and I gave a small burst of applause.

'It's too early for us to go and celebrate in a bar somewhere, and I have to get back to Jean and hopefully Mr Noakes,' said Susan. 'So let's tidy up, thank the lady outside and meet in our Defence building den tomorrow morning to decide what to do with this information.'

It was still only mid-afternoon as we climbed into our individual taxis. Susan to wherever she called her office, me to my home and then to Questors theatre for an evening of set construction, and Poppy to Hendon for an evening, I supposed, with her Judo instructor Stephen.

---///---

Much like the previous morning, Poppy and I were waiting in our room in the old Air Ministry building when Susan, Jean and Mr Noakes arrived. He took the chair at the head of our conference table while the remainder of us distributed ourselves around him. He started to speak.

'We, that is you, seem to have make some sort of break though. We have been in touch with our Consul in Vancouver who has confirmed that Joseph Muhler, we'll continue to call him Miller, I can't do umlauts in my mind or tongue, is the owner and principal of Millhouse School at Qualicum Beach, a small town half way up Vancouver Island. Except that the school no longer seems to be functioning although Miller is still alive and living in the building. It was started in 1936 and apparently was a well-known and respected small, senior boarding high school for boys;. That is until the sixties when another private school on the Island gained some very prestigious students and became the place for the sons of the wealthy and the posers. So the question is, what is to be done with this knowledge?'

'We know who might have planted the seeds of treachery in Donald Maclean's young mind,' I offered.

'Yes, but so what?' Noakes commented. 'Maclean's case is all done and dusted, and he is safe in Moscow, his dirty work all completed. No, we have to go back to where we all started out not so many days ago. What we, as Eugene

184

Russel's little gang is tasked to do is to find out, right under MI6's noses and totally concealed from them, if Miller has influenced other young minds to treachery either in or out of school, a mind that even now might be buried within MI6 itself.'

He paused for a moment then looked very hard at Poppy and me.

'We, that is you again, David and Poppy, have to get out there and talk to him. Persuade him, bully him, threaten extradition, anything to extract other names from him. I have to get things agreed with Eugene Russell who was not available last night or this morning, but I will be seeing him later on today along with Jean. There are things that have to be done to get you to and from Canada, and to ease your task once there. So take the rest of today off. Tidy up your lives so that you can travel to Vancouver Island for an indeterminate length of time and meet back here tomorrow, Saturday morning at, let's say ten as Eugene Russel may like to be here and he is not an early riser. Oh, and make certain you bring your passports with you. The ones you used to get back from Hong Kong. Your married ones.'

With those final words Mr Noakes and Jean departed.

'I'm going shopping for some warm clothes,' said Poppy. 'Canada in winter, brrrr!'

'Actually,' Susan countered. 'Vancouver Island has quite a mild climate I believe, not like the Canadian interior.'

'All the same, I'm going shopping,' Poppy said with finality, and handed me the keys of the room, 'So your turn to lock up again, David.' She was gone before I could reply.

Susan turned to me. 'Shopping? Is that what you are also going to do?'

'No,' I replied. 'I've got enough warm stuff, but Poppy came here from the Far East and was not well equipped for

Britain's November, although she had a huge buy-up last week which I would have thought would have been enough.'

'But she lived in London throughout last year, didn't she?'

'Yes,' I replied, hoping that the next question was not to be about where she had been living. I changed the subject: 'I expect she has a date this evening, some guy she has met at Hendon Police College where she is living.'

'Would you like a date this evening, ' Susan asked, gazing steadily at my face which I knew clearly portrayed my inner shout of YES!

'Then meet me at the Green Man at the top of Putney Hill, do you know where I mean? At seven say?

'Yes, at seven. I know the place, not too far from where you live, supposed to be an old highwayman's haunt.'

She walked to the nearest tube station to catch a train home. I caught a bus back to Earls Court and went into my local bank to move some money between accounts, pay utility bills and draw some Canadian dollars.

---///---

I took my car out of its garage and drove the ten minutes from Earls Court, through Fulham, across Putney Bridge, up the Putney High Street and over the junction with the Upper Richmond Road. I knew that Susan's flat was close to that junction but I pressed on up Putney Hill to Tibbets Corner and arrived at the Green Man pub. The illuminated pub sign appeared to be that of an early Briton dressed entirely in green shrubbery. I parked the car on the common opposite and walked into the bar, scanning for Susan through the throng of businessmen, all supposedly on their way home. I was ten minutes early for my date but I had guessed that Susan was not a person that would be late.

I decided to wait by the open doorway by the pub's entrance where Susan would be able to clearly see me, rather than lose my way in the crowd stacked by the bar as I jostled for an early drink. She stepped into view at exactly 7 pm dressed in a full length coat of a stunning burgundy colour. The warm light above the doorway momentarily bathed her face and her friendly smile signalled that she was genuinely pleased to see me. It also showed the slight shadowing of her facial bone structure, not masked by her usual glasses and confirmed what I had already suspected, she was beautiful. Not in the exotic quasi-oriental sense of Poppy whose face had near driven me to distraction, but in her strong Celtic features.

After greeting her, I asked 'No glasses?'

'Contacts,' she replied. 'I've only just started to use them and I'm not sure how I'm going to get on with the wretched things. Taking them in and out, and sterilizing them all the time is a pain. Still, on a first date I want to look by best. Afterwards you will probably have to put up with my glasses.'

'It's very crowded here,' I said. 'Do you want to go somewhere else or straight to a restaurant?'

'Here is fine. It's always crowded here at this time in the evening with after-work swillers, even worse on Fridays. But this is one of my favourite pubs. They know me here and a gap will probably miraculously appear in the crowd if I push through rather than you. First drink is on me, after that it's all down to you this evening. A pint of best bitter for you I guess.'

I nodded and smiled, Susan was pushing all the right buttons with me. I was looking for a table where we might sit, without success, when she returned holding my beer and a gin and tonic for herself. I apologised for there being no place to sit.

'Doesn't bother me,' she said. 'But let's have just the one drink here and head out, we can hardly hear each other over this noise.'

'Do you have any suggestions? I don't know any restaurants around here.'

'There is good Italian one in Wimbledon, hardly five minutes away by car. That's if you came by car?'

'Yes, my car is outside, how did you get up the hill to here? Bus?'

'I walked, hence this thick coat and the boots.' She tapped a black calf-length boot against the wall we were propping up.

This first date with Susan was a delight. The ice had been broken in the Green Man and was further melted by a bottle of Chianti and excellent Italian food. I learned that she was the sole child of a professional couple in Edinburgh, he a judge, she a doctor. She was much loved, and loved much in return. She had been expensively educated which, when coupled with her obvious intelligence, had resulted in a First Class degree from Edinburgh. The Scottish Office had singled her out as a candidate for public service, and after a couple of moves she had found herself working in the office of the Home Secretary in London. I commented that she looked very fit and she told me that she rowed two or three evenings on the River Thames near Putney Bridge except for the four winter months when she swum at Roehampton Baths instead. I told her that I was a swimmer also.

'So, something in common already,' she commented.

I told her about my early life in Singapore and my recruitment into the world of marine insurance. I skirted around the subject of Poppy, saying not much more than that she was a childhood friend with whom I had stayed in touch.

'I have been briefed about you and Poppy,' she said. 'I know the bare bones about your relationship, you don't have to be so coy with me. You are married to each other, after all,' she added with a smile. 'One's first love stays with one, no matter what happens later in life. Don't deny Poppy, she is part of what you are.'

'Sorry,' I replied. 'Yes, she is part of my life, my history, and she is a lot of fun to be with. Very clever too. She can run rings around me when she wants to.'

'And has done, I know.'

'What about you? What part does your first love play in your life?'

'I was 16, he was 18, just out of school. A typical teenage romance and it lasted a whole, happy year. We are still in touch, Christmas and that sort of thing. He's married now with two young children. He was, is, a nice man. He was my first.'

'And now? You have another love now?'

'No, just a few good friends. Do you?'

'No,' I replied. 'Friends, that's all.'

'And Poppy.'

'Just friends,' I emphasised.

I drove her back to Millbrook Court, next to Putney Bridge station on the Upper Richmond Road. I parked the car outside the entrance that led to her flat on the first floor and opened the car door for her.

'Thank you, David, that was a lovely evening,' she said, extending her arm to shake my hand. There was to be no kiss I realised, but I asked the obvious question.

'Can we meet again?'

'Yes, yes of course.'

'This weekend?'

'Let's just take it easy, wait until the pressure is off both of us, wait until your return from Canada.'

'Has that been decided? Poppy and I are going to Canada?'

'It's obvious, isn't it? See you tomorrow.' Then she was gone.

---///---

Saturday morning at the Old Air Ministry building opened as had Friday's, with the addition of Eugene Russell heading the four-member group from the Office of the Home Secretary. And as at Eugene's first meeting there, Susan trailed in pushing a trolley with a tea pot, milk, sugar and numerous biscuits of several sorts. She poured out the tea and placed the milk, sugar and biscuits on the conference table where we all seated ourselves, Eugene taking the chair position.

After congratulating Susan, Poppy and me on what we had achieved so far, he placed me squarely on the spot.

'Before you set off to Canada, David, along with your friend and wife Poppy. Oh! I see from your face that you hadn't received a formal notification of that before now. You can, of course, refuse in which case I suppose that we will have to send Jean instead. But you and Poppy did so well poking around Gresham's School that it would be a pity to break up your team. You will go?'

I said 'Yes.'

'And you Poppy?'

'Of course.'.

'Good, now back to where I started. Before you go I want to be absolutely certain that you, David, understand your task.'

'It is to find Joseph Muhler, or Miller, and ascertain who in addition to the schoolboy Donald Maclean he might have suborned.'

'And you Poppy, do you agree with that interpretation?'

'Yes, that is what we have to do. We are not after Miller per se, but his history. And while we are on the subject of buts, why was there no mention in the files of yours that we scoured of Donald Maclean having brothers at Gresham's school?'

Eugene was unflappable, he moved in political and diplomatic circles in which unpalatable subjects had to be tackled, seemingly unreasonable actions taken, plausible excuses contrived and broadcast. Poppy's question was not going to faze him.

'You can imagine,' he started his reply as if he were educating some junior civil servant. 'Donald Maclean's treasonable behaviour and subsequent decamp to the land of his masters caused a great deal of grief to his four brothers, three of whom went to Gresham's and a much younger one who didn't, and to his sister who was a secretary in MI5. Thankfully his highly respected politician father died in 1932. The youngest of the brothers is the current head of Macmillans Publishers but had to give up a promising diplomatic career when Donald's case opened up. Another brother was, until recently, a very senior Royal Navy Officer. All the living siblings were thoroughly investigated and no trace of any contamination from Donald was found. One brother, Ian, was a pilot killed in the war. There was no reason to further complicate those files you waded through with names of the complete Maclean menagerie; they constituted a rabbit hole down which I had no wish for you to explore. We already knew all that needed to be known about Donald Maclean and his family, except the one thing, the one person who you have succeeded in identifying. So, no more about the Macleans.

'And now,' concluded Eugene with a satisfied smile that split his well-fed face. 'I officially, but covertly, endorse this expedition. And so, Noaksy, will you brief on the mechanics of David's and Poppy's journey, please.'

Mr Noakes stood up to give his briefing. 'On Monday, you will set out by plane from London Heathrow Airport to Vancouver. No first class this time I'm afraid, back of the bus for you both. When you arrive at Vancouver you will be met by a member of the local British Consulate. This person will be your point of contact throughout your time in Canada. If you need to contact us in London always do it through him. We don't want any direct phone calls from you to our office or staff. At a time to be agreed with him, you will set out by car and ferry to Vancouver Island. There you will drive up to an area chosen by him but in the vicinity of Millhouse School and settle into a hotel, again chosen by him. When you have finished your work with Mr Miller, you are immediately to contact this man by public phone, using a special telephone number that he will give you, and tell him everything you have accomplished. So a simple piece of vital advice, make sure you carry plenty of Canadian change for that call. Afterwards you will follow his instructions for your return to Vancouver and hence back to London. Any questions so far?'

Poppy and I replied that everything was clear to us, so far.

'Good,' concluded Noakes as he sat down. 'Now Jean will provide more nitty-gritty.'

Jean Hathaway stood up and started to take things out of her briefcase, laying each item on the table in front of her.

'Firstly,' she began. 'New passports in the names of David and Penelope Parsons. Married couple again, containing a few visas for countries that you have both supposedly visited; read and memorise what those countries are. And inside the back covers of the passports, an embossed, pasted-in page stating that you are members of the British High Commission in Ottawa. To some this would seem to indicate that you have some form of diplomatic accreditation or immunity, but in fact it means virtually bugger-all. Think of a surplus of chain mail worn by a Shakespearian actor that is actually a fisherman's sweater sprayed with silver paint.'

'Why new names?' asked Poppy.

'To completely disassociate you from your trip to Gresham's in case anyone is keeping an eye on you both.'

'This is beginning to sound more like some sort of mission rather than a trip to interview an old man,' Poppy countered Jean's explanation.

'Just sensible precautions,' Noakes said soothingly.

Jean continued. 'And to make sure that there can be no embarrassing muddles, please give me the ones with which you travelled back from Hong Kong.'

Poppy and I passed the passports to Jean who inspected them to ensure that they were the ones she had requested. She continued with her briefing. 'Secondly, money. There is one thousand Canadian dollars in various denominations of notes in this envelope, sorry no coins for telephones, and you can change some of what is left of the Sterling you were given at the airport. Poppy, I believe you act as purser for the two of you, so you take charge of the money.' She slid the envelope across the table to her.

'Next, here are your tickets to Vancouver. You leave Monday morning and change planes in Toronto. The return tickets are open because we can't predict when you will be catching a plane home, but presumably within a week or so of leaving. And finally we have compiled a set of photographs of the school boys at Gresham's that he may have influenced.. Maclean obviously, but also Roger Simon, Brian Simon, James Klugman, Gerald Holtom, who was a day boy, by the way, and Benjamin Britten.'

'I thought those last two were out of the equation, didn't you say that Mr Russell?' I asked with surprise.

Eugene Russel replied, 'Yes, they are of course. But I am persuaded that you need to travel with the full set, so as to speak. You need to know what they all look like so you can, if required, show Miller pictures to jog his memory.'

'We have had a police artist work on the photos we had which are of mature men to make them look more like the schoolboys they were when Miller knew them,' Jean explained before retaking her seat.

'Now,' said Noakes, 'are there any questions?'

'Lots,' replied Poppy with a hint of surliness in her voice. 'But I can't think of how to phrase them at the moment. But how did you manage to get all this done so soon, the new passports and the photos especially?'

Noakes replied. 'The photos have been in preparation for a number of days, since before you went up to Norfolk. And as for the for the passports, let's just say that we have access to very accomplished technicians who worked until late last night.'

'Just call me any time before you go when you have actually composed those questions.' Jean added evenly. 'You have my number and I'll try to help you. Now we really must all be off.'

Susan gathered up the tea things and pushed the trolley out into the corridor. Throughout the meeting her expression gave no hint of our time together the previous evening.

Eugene Russel departed with Jean and Noakes in tow, wishing Poppy and me, 'Good luck.'

We gathered up our new passports, our air tickets and the photos, which Poppy elected to keep along with the Canadian dollars. Poppy skimmed though the pages of her passport. 'Penelope Parsons, Mrs. Apparently I've been to Turkey and Morocco, how about you?'

I looked at mine. 'The same,' I replied.

'Are you a teeny bit suspicious about this journey of ours?' she asked. 'That crowd seemed to have done a lot of homework between yesterday afternoon and now.'

'I think they have preparing a Plan B in case things go wrong, although I can't see how anything could. But that's why they have the Vancouver Consulate exercising some sort of control over us. Let's just go and play it by ear within the rules we have been given. I'm looking forward to visiting Canada, even in the depths of winter.'

'Well, so am I,' agreed Poppy, her doubts seemingly shaken off. 'After all, we did much worse things in Broome.'

'*You* did,' I replied with emphasis. 'It's coming up to eleven. We can tidy up and secure this place against our return, but we have a weekend to fill.' I looked at my airline ticket and accompanying note for the first time. 'It says here that we have to check-in for the flight by 9 am Monday morning. As you may remember, there is still no direct rail line from the centre of London to Heathrow airport. From my place I can get there by taxi or coach, all quite easy. But you are on the other side of London and that's a long and tedious journey into central London and out again.'

'Then I'll take a taxi and use some of the Sterling that we have left. I've still got over 200 pounds I think.'

'You will be travelling right in the Monday morning rush hour. It will take the taxi an eternity and that's if you find a driver willing to take you all that distance.'

'Have you a better suggestion?' she asked, knowing the answer already.

'You can stay with me Sunday evening if you like, then we can both travel together.'

'And that won't interfere with your social life? Miss goody-two-shoes Susan Anderson for example?'

'Nothing planned in that area, and don't be so unkind. She is probably not so meek and mild as you make out. That afternoon at the Canadian High Commission showed how effective she can be, and how she can take charge when necessary.'

'Take charge, really?'

'No less effectively than you so often do. And talking of one's friends, doesn't Mr Judo man–'

'Stephen.'

'Doesn't Stephen expect time with you this weekend?'

'Yes, and he will get it. I'll make my way to your place on Sunday afternoon, late, in case you are out watching rugger with your boozy friends and you can cook me one of your famous pastas. I'll bring the wine.'

'That's fine by me,' I said. 'You can have the spare room upstairs.'

'Not my old place in the basement?'

'No, that's off limits to you.'

We closed up the room, Poppy kept the key, and we made our ways back to our respective homes.

Sunday evening with Poppy was pleasant and, with separate bedrooms, there was none of the intrinsic but suppressed, sexual tension of the shared hotel room at the beginning of the week.

Chapter 16

What with our travelling back through time zones, we arrived in Vancouver late Monday afternoon, British Columbia time, after long and tedious flights above the Atlantic and across the snow strewn landscapes of Canada. We talked a little, given that discussions of our mission were firmly out of bounds, read some, ate, slept and fidgeted in our tightly packed seats. We were very pleased when our aircraft turned over the eastern coast of Vancouver Island, clearly visible from Poppy's window seat, and started its final approach over the sea into Vancouver.

Our new passports, perhaps because of the note inside their rear covers, provided us easy passage through immigration and customs into the baggage collection hall. The airport looked very small and rather neglected after Heathrow and Toronto. A man waiting for us in the arrivals hall looked familiar.

Poppy called out, 'My God, it's Paul.' Before rushing to embrace the man.

Sure enough, it was the same Paul that had chaperoned me in Hong Kong and had tried to protect Poppy and poor

Lucy during the riots there. He shook my hand once he had disengaged himself from Poppy.

'You get around, Paul. How long have you been here?' I asked in astonishment.

'About two days longer than you,' was his reply. 'Sent over to provide assistance to you, for whatever you are up to. Let's talk more in the car, its parked right outside, courtesy of its special number plates.'

Paul took hold of Poppy's suitcase and led us outside the terminal to a black Chevrolet saloon car. He opened the boot, or trunk I supposed given where we were, for our luggage and then asked us to sit in the rear of the car.

'Makes it look like I'm your chauffeur and that you are important somebodies which, judging by the signals and phone calls over the past few days from London, it appears you are.'

As he moved the car out into the airport traffic, he told Poppy and me that he was taking us to an hotel near the airport where we were booked in for two nights, but could stay longer if we wished. 'That's to let you get over the long journey, jet lag I believe it's being called now, and decide in your own time when you want to travel to Vancouver Island. I'm suffering it quite badly myself, the rushed journey from Hong Kong was no picnic. This car is going to be yours for the time you are here. Have either of you ever driven an automatic before?'

'No,' we chorused.

'Well, just watch what I do. It's really very easy, you just have to stop looking for the clutch pedal. Place your foot on the brake, put the car into drive, see this indicator above the steering wheel, release the brake, press the accelerator and off you go. And look, those mountains in the distance, they are north of Vancouver so aim for them and you can't get lost.'

'Why are you here Paul?' I asked.

'Because of Poppy and you, and because of trying to make up for my useless effort to protect your friend Lucy. I'm so sorry for that.'

Poppy leaned forward and gently stroked the back of Paul's head. 'It was no-one's fault. You tried your best and nothing could have prevented what happened. Did you know she was David's lover?'

'No, I didn't. So sorry about what happened, David.'

'Thank you,' I whispered.

We drew up at a monolith of a hotel right by the side of a river. 'The north branch of the Frazer River,' said Paul. 'The south branch is a few kilometres lower down the mainland. There is a picturesque fishing village there, Steveston, you might want to go there to chill out tomorrow. Now, you have been booked in here as Mr and Mrs Parsons by the Consulate, so the hotel should treat you well. Your reservation is initially for tonight and tomorrow night, and the Consulate will pick up the bill for the room along with any expenses like meals and drinks. Because of, shall we say, your ambiguous marital status you have a suite on the top floor with a separate bedroom, a bed-sitting room and a shared bathroom between.

'It sounds like you have been up there to inspect the place,' Poppy commented.

'I've checked it out, certainly,' Paul replied.

While Paul parked the car, Poppy and I registered at the hotel's reception desk where we were told that our luggage would be taken up by hotel staff to what was described as our Junior Suite. Paul returned just as we finished checking in and suggested that we order coffees. He said the tea was not likely to be good and would be served as a kit comprising a pitcher of not too hot water with a tea bag for us to dunk it in ourselves. As we waited for the coffee he filled us in with further advice and instructions for our excursion to find Mr Miller.

'But first,' I asked. 'Please explain more about why it is you that has met us, good though it is to see you, rather than someone from the local Consulate.'

He explained that that, having been born in London during the Blitz to a Canadian soldier father and English mother and stressing that they had been married at the time, and still were, and now both living in Edmonton, he had dual nationality. Educated mainly in Britain, before his father finally managed to persuade his mother to leave England and settle in Canada, he had retained his British accent. He was, in fact, a British Civil Servant associated with policing and for the past few years had been involved in investigating the flow of money of dubious pedigree from Hong Kong to Vancouver in the wake of the burgeoning movement of wealthy Hong Kong Chinese immigrants to Vancouver. Thus, he frequently travelled back and forth between the two cities. While he had no real idea of what Poppy and I were up to, or so he said, he was aware that the need to know perimeter around us was very tight. That perimeter would have had to be considerably expanded if some other person had been chosen to be *your man on the ground*, as he put it.

The coffee arrived. Paul pulled out an envelope from his jacket inside-pocket and extracted a map of Vancouver Island which he lay on the table after moving our coffee cups to the side. Next, he took out a page of typewritten paper. 'I have written some notes on how to use the ferries to get to Vancouver Island. There are two principal ways across, both include ferries which are frequent, so don't bother to book ahead particularly at this time of year. Just turn up on spec and if it's not Friday or Sunday you shouldn't have to wait too long. You can take the terminal 15 miles or so to the south of this hotel, shown on this map here, beyond the south branch of the Fraser River which I told you about earlier. That route will take you to the south end of Vancouver Island about three quarters of an hour's drive from Victoria.' He used his index finger to point out the island ferry terminal and the City of Victoria on the map.

'The alternative is to drive to the north of Vancouver to another ferry terminal, here at Horseshoe Bay, and cross over to the city of Nanaimo. As I've indicated on the map, Nanaimo is a long way north of Victoria and well on the way to your destination of Qualicum Beach. It's up to you to choose which route to use; the Nanaimo route means much less driving on the island but means that you will have to negotiate Vancouver traffic to get to Horseshoe Bay. I don't know how confident you both are at driving on the, to you, wrong side of the road. As I said, the Chevy car is yours to use for the duration. You will find its registration and insurance papers in the glove box.'

He placed a set of car keys on the map.

'How are you going get to wherever you now have to go?' asked Poppy.

'By cab,' was the short answer with no indication of where he was going to. He pulled out another piece of paper from the envelope. 'This is the hotel I have selected for you It's an appropriate distance from your Millhouse School, neither too near nor too far, in a town called, Parksville. I've marked both places on this map. I have provisionally booked you in from Wednesday afternoon for three nights. If you want to change that then give them a ring. It's a motel so will expect payment when you check in. Use cash for everything, I mean everything. Finally, here are two identical business cards. They're blank except for my first name and the number at which you can reach me any time day or night. Always use public telephones located in the open. Canada is well provided with them. Never use a hotel call box.'

Paul shook the envelope and a shower of change cascaded out on the map. 'That's to set you up for your first call to me, which should be as soon as you have settled into your Vancouver Island motel. I'm off now. Welcome to British Columbia.' He glanced through a nearby window, 'and the rain for which it is well known.'

'Do you think,' began Poppy, after Paul had departed. 'That we are in charge of this task of ours, or are we being controlled and being prepared for something that we have not anticipated?.'

'I'm not quite with you, explain some more please.'

Poppy made her points, emphasising each one by rapping her tiny fist onto the centre of the map.

'We have new names, for the second time. I still don't see the necessity of that.

'We have a man on the ground as he put it. He's a minder!

'We have some sort of pseudo diplomatic identities. Is that so we get out of legal difficulties if we get into a scrape of some sort?

'The Vancouver arm of the British Consul General to Canada is providing us cover for what we are supposed to be doing.'

As a prima facie went, her points all seemed valid, but I thought she was over-dramatising. 'We are going to talk to an old man, that's all. But our sponsors in London want a Plan B in case we screw up and precipitate some sort of diplomatic row. The Canadians could claim, perhaps, that they should have been involved in the tracking and interviewing of Miller.'

'It sounds to me that if we do screw up, as you put it, we will be thrown to the wolves.'

'Now you really are being over-dramatic.'

---///---

Poppy and I settled into our spacious Junior Suite. I opted for the bed sitter while she took the bedroom. We took turns in the bathroom to shower and generally freshen up, but by 7 pm fatigue was beginning to hit us. We knew we had to resist collapsing in bed for as long as possible so we pulled ourselves together, had a couple of cocktails each in the hotel bar then moved to the dining room which overlooked the dark stream of the river and ate a light dinner. Back in the room we watched a newscast on television but by 9 pm we had to surrender to sleep.

I lay partially awake for about two hours in the early hours of the following morning with the parameters of our task circulating fruitlessly through my addled brain. I saw 4 am pass on the luminous face of my wrist watch, but then nothing more until Poppy came into my now sun-lit room and whispered, 'Get up sleepy head, it's nine o'clock and I'm bored and hungry.' Then she kissed me on my forehead.

Over breakfast we examined the map that Paul had provided, trying to make our minds up which of the two ferry terminals, north or south of Vancouver, we should use for our crossing to Vancouver Island. We determined that we should confirm our confidence and competence in driving an automatic car on the, to us, wrong side of the road before deciding to brave the Vancouver traffic to reach the north terminal at Horseshoe Bay.

We set out in the Chevrolet, me driving first then Poppy, and headed to Paul's suggestion of the riverside town of Steveston. There was no mistaking that it was a working fishing port. The harbour was stacked with purposeful looking fishing boats and opened into fast-flowing water at the start of the River Frazer's estuary, but it was picturesque and charming in its way. After a fish and chips lunch at a café by the harbour side, we crossed the river at the suggestion of the café's owner and spent the afternoon walking around an island famous for being a stopping-off place for migrating birds. We saw very few birds as it was November and the wrong time of the year. Added to which, the persistent rain tried its unsuccessful best to make us feel miserable.

Returning to our hotel, we collapsed onto our respective beds for the night. When we arose refreshed the next morning we were eager to get on our way to Millhouse School. Driving had not been a problem for either of us, so we saw no problem in making our way through down-town Vancouver to the Horseshoe Bay terminal and hence the direct ferry to Nanaimo. We caught the 7 am ferry after a just thirty minute wait in a vehicle line-up at the uninviting looking terminal. Poppy had asked me to do the driving through the just-waking up Vancouver traffic.

Ninety minutes later, Poppy was driving the Chevrolet off the ferry and onto the quayside in Nanaimo harbour. The winter sun was starting to shine and the temperature not unpleasant. A twenty minute drive northwards took us out of the scruffy Nanaimo suburbs and onto a pretty road that more or less followed the coast line towards Qualicum Beach. We stopped for coffee at a stall in a lay-by from where we could see the coastline of the British Colombian mainland with massive mountains beyond and islands scattered in the narrow sea passage between.

'This place looks like some sort of paradise,' Poppy said softly.

'But with its secrets.'

'Yes, as everywhere.'

We arrived in Parksville at midday. A seaside resort town with a myriad of hotels and motels to cater for the summer holiday makers. A placard by the side of the road proclaimed Parksville to be the sunshine capital of British Columbia. Much of the accommodation appeared to be closed for the winter but the Happy Days motel selected for us by Paul was cheerfully open. It was less than 100 yards from a pristine, sandy beach fringed by a few cafés and the like.

As it was too early for us to check in we took a walk along the near deserted beach and ate sandwiches in a café overlooking the sea front. We checked into the motel in the early afternoon and paid cash for two nights with an option for a third. Then, with Poppy navigating from our map of the island, we headed northwards again for about 8 miles to Qualicum . We stopped at a roadside telephone call box and dialled the number that Paul had given to us. He answered straight away. I simply told him that we had moved into the motel and were about to pay our first visit to the school, he seemed satisfied.

Just after we passed the road sign indicating that we were entering the town area of Qualicum Beach, Poppy, with a finger on the map, told me to slow down and look to the right, towards the sea which had been separated from our road for some miles by thick woodland dotted with occasional houses. Hedges appeared on her side of the car and then a driveway marked by a noticeboard attached to two rickety poles. The words *Millhouse School* were painted at the top of the board in faded back paint, and under these was a pasted-on sign announcing, *Available for hire for weddings and other functions,* along with a phone number.

'That's the same number as the one we found in the Canadian High Commission in London,' exclaimed Poppy.

I drove the car to the right hand side of the road and stopped it across the entrance to the drive. A large, sprawling house could be clearly seen at the end of the drive, set well back from the road and surrounded by grass lawns and trees. I moved the car a few yards past the drive and parked on the hard shoulder of the road. The house was now shielded from our view by the hedge, as was our car from the house.

Neither of us spoke for a moment. Poppy broke the silence. 'Are we going to go in now and announce ourselves, or do you want to leave it until tomorrow?'

'It's not yet three o'clock and I don't think that we should waste any time now that we are here. I think we should to go the house right now to find out if Miller is still alive, state our business in general terms and ask to have a more formal meeting with him tomorrow. Based on the reception we receive today, we can plan our tactics for tomorrow over dinner tonight.'

'Good compromise,' Poppy agreed. 'Let's go!'

I reversed the car back up the road then drove slowly up the tree-lined gravel drive to a large parking area. It too was covered in gravel and appeared to have been raked clear of the late autumn leaves lying red and brown underneath the surrounding trees which shaded extensive lawns.

A wooden, peaked roof portico framed what we took to be the school's main entrance judging by the glass-paned, double doors. The building was two story, brick built, with a framework of black wooden beams. There was a myriad of small, square windows set into the walls facing us. Looking at the configuration of the red tiled, pent roofs gave the impression that the building as a whole was H-shaped. Mock Tudor was my immediate impression, similar to many houses found in the stockbroker belt of the outer London suburbs, but nevertheless handsome and imposing in its setting. A bride and groom would be happy, I imagined, to hold their wedding reception in such surroundings.

Poppy pressed the doorbell button and we heard a loud electrical ring from inside the building. A lady came out of the interior shadows and opened the door to us. She was perhaps fifty years of age, tall, well-built and dressed in a white blouse with matching trousers, like the all-white uniform of a nurse.

'Yes?' she asked in a friendly voice. 'How may I help you?'

I had agreed with Poppy that she would do most of the initial talking as she had proved so effective during our trip to Norfolk.

'My name is Penelope Parsons, and this is my husband David,' she began. 'We were hoping to speak with Mr Muhler,' she used the Germanic pronunciation that the Consul had confirmed. 'That is, if he still lives here?'

'He certainly lives here, this is this house,' came the reply. 'I am Patricia, housekeeper, and I also arrange the functions that we host. Is that why you want to see him? Because if you want to have a wedding reception or something like that then I'm the person you need to talk to. Mr Muhler does not have much to do with that side of things now.'

'No, our visit has nothing to do with arranging a function, although this would have been a lovely place for us to have had our reception, wouldn't it David dear?'

I gave Poppy a mental kick on her ankle, she continued to address Patricia.

'We are from England, as you might have gathered from our accents, and our field is education. We are researching how school children are prepared for life after graduation and we have discovered that Mr Muhler was particularly successful in doing that while working in England. We want to talk to him about that and we would also like to know how he had to amend his methods when he opened this school in Canada. We really want to talk to such a distinguished teacher.'

'I'll go and speak to him,' replied Patricia. 'He is very old now, you know, and not in the best of health, but he likes to talk to people about, what he calls, the old days. Come inside and wait in the reception hall.'

She stood back from the front door to allow us to enter a large open area which spanned the whole width of the building; this area extended into a bright sunroom at its far side giving the effect of a large and airy atrium. The walls were of wood panels and rose to meet the ceiling two floors above; halfway up the far wall was a wooden gallery which led through doors from one side of the room to the other. The flooring was a combination of carpet and parquet. This was where the wedding receptions took place, I assumed, and would also have been the main assembly hall for Millhouse School when it was still functioning.

We stood admiring our surroundings for five minutes, until Patricia emerged from a corridor on our left pushing an elderly man in a wheelchair. He was wearing a thick yellow sweater which ended underneath the brown blanket that covered the lower half of his body. He wore a tartan flat cap on his head while lightly shaded glasses masked his eyes.

'Sep,' she said, 'These are the two people I told you about, Mr and Mrs Parsons, from England. Mr Muhler will speak to you for just a few minutes. He is always tired in the afternoon but much more lively in the morning, aren't you Sep?'

A non-committal grunt emerged from Mr Muhler who extended an arm from underneath his blanket and waved a thin, frail, near translucent hand at some chairs nearby indicating for Poppy and me to sit down. Again I allowed Poppy to open the conversation once it became clear that Muhler was not about to start talking without stimulus from us.

'Mr Muhler,' she began. 'Patricia may have told you that my husband, David, and I, I'm Poppy, have been tasked to examine the way scholars in their final years at high school are prepared for subsequent careers.'

With a quiet voice, hoarse as if with a sore throat and laced with distinct aggression, Muhler asked, 'Who tasked you?'

'A branch of the British Government,' she replied, which had an element of truth, and then continued in an effort to stall too many similar questions. 'We are comparing how such school boys, yes, mainly boys I'm afraid, were prepared in the past for entrance into Oxford or Cambridge or to pass exams for the higher echelons of the Civil Service. Then we will compare what was done in the nineteen twenties and thirties with modern day practices.'

'With what objective?' A slight trace of a middle European accent was detectable in Muhler's question, the aggression also still apparent.

'The objective is to ensure that the British Government's current crop of potential high flyers, politicians, Civil Servants, industrialists and bankers, just to name a few examples, are as capable, preferably more so, than those that led the country through the Second World War. We live in dangerous times again, the Cold War and all that.'

'So what brought you all the way to Canada to see me?'

'There are some other people that we want to see while in Canada, to ask much the same questions. You are the first on our list because Qualicum Beach is the furthest away for us to travel. We will be heading in our homewards direction when we stop in Toronto and Montreal, but more importantly, because we have been told that your coaching at Gresham's School was singularly effective; a number of your pupils have done extremely well in their public lives.'

'Really?' The aggression had gone. *Had Poppy got her preamble right?* I wondered. *And hadn't she mentioned Gresham's School rather earlier than we had agreed?* Mr Muhler pulled himself a little forward in his wheelchair, showing interest in what she was saying.

'Like who?' Muhler asked. I sensed that we were about to enter dangerous territory, but Poppy and I had rehearsed this bit.

'Like Gerald Holtom, for instance.' Poppy replied. 'He is a leading industrial designer, but more importantly helped found the Campaign for Nuclear Disarmament. He is the one that came up with the logo, the one by which the movement is known throughout the world.' She pulled a drawing from her hand bag that she had made with lipstick the previous evening, while we had been planning our tactics.

'I know that symbol, it's famous.' There was admiration in Muhler's voice and a trace of pride. 'So Holtom, I didn't know what his first name was. I'm not certain I tutored him by himself but I certainly knew him by sight because he was friends of some of the boys that I did coach. He was a day boy. I used to see him around town in the holidays with his father.' His voice started to sound tired. 'It was all so long ago, the nineteen twenties. Forty years.'

'Can you remember the other boys from those days?' Poppy persisted.

Muhler looked a little confused. 'Well, there was Britten of course. He was brilliant even then, everyone wanted to be associated with him, schoolmasters that is. But I really wasn't one of the tenured staff and I didn't teach him. I supposed I would have liked to, but I don't think he needed help from the school to achieve what he has.'

Patricia looked at Muhler. 'You are very tired Seppy, and I think you should have a rest now. Build up your strength for supper and your glass of whisky.'

She started to usher Poppy and me towards the front door. Muhler raised a hand as if waving good-bye and said 'Come and see me again soon.'

'We will,' I smiled back at him and returned his wave.

As we reached the door Patricia suggested that we should return on the morrow. 'He is always much livelier in the morning and you seem to have sparked his interest, not many things do these days. Come at about ten thirty and you can have coffee with him.'

'Thank you,' I said. 'We will definitely be here at ten thirty and look forward to continuing our chat. As it's still light now, could we take a walk around the grounds?'

'Certainly,' she replied.

'Do you live in this beautiful place?' asked Poppy

'It is lovely isn't it? But no, I live a few miles away, on the other side of town. I work what you might call office hours here except for when we have a weekend function, then, of course, I have to come in.'

'So who looks after Mr Muhler when you are not here?' was my question.

'He has a live-in companion here that takes care of most of his needs. He is in town doing some shopping at the moment. There is also another man who maintains the grounds and does small maintenance jobs around the house, he comes most days.'

Poppy and I walked slowly around the building itself first, and then extended our tour around the surrounding extensive, and well-kept lawns. At the back of the building the lawns extended from the sunroom all the way to the sea edge with the mountainous coast of the mainland beyond.

A large gazebo stood almost at the sea's edge. 'The centre piece for a wedding reception,' I remarked to Poppy. 'You are right, great place to have it. Too bad we are already married.'

She ignored my little joke but instead started to enthuse about our conversation with Muhler. 'We are getting there, David. We got him talking about his time at Gresham's and even discussed a couple of pupils.'

'Holtom and Britten, two people completely off our radar,' I replied rather dismissively.

'You are not getting it David. It's a good start, a very good start. Tomorrow we can bring up other names of greater relevance to our quest, but we will have to be very careful about mentioning Donald Maclean of course.'

'We shouldn't even think about doing that. What we have to do is to get him, not us, to bring up names; names of people that we haven't heard of. After all, it's all about discovering the identities of people that we know nothing about at this time.'

'We obviously have to strategise, isn't that the word you use? Over dinner this evening.'

'Yes,' I agreed as we returned to our car, with me taking the driver's seat as before.

Chapter 17

The front door of the old school building was ajar when Poppy and I arrived at precisely 10:30 the next morning, Thursday the 23rd of November. As I reached for the doorbell, Patricia appeared in front of us and invited us to come inside.

'Sep will see you in his study,' she said, leading the way through an open doorway at the far left corner of the reception hall. A short corridor gave way to an open area surrounded by four doors and one window through which I could see the gazebo by the sea edge. Three of the doors were closed and one was wide open. The doors were of the same dark, handsome wood which matched the panelling of the corridor walls. The whole effect was rather sombre and old fashioned; it reminded me of one of my grandparent's houses in North London which I used to visit as a child.

Patricia took us through the one open door into a spacious room which had all the trappings of a Headmaster's study, its contents, if not its décor, matching almost exactly that of my own headmaster's at University College School, London. The walls were of wood panelling to picture rail height, matching all that we had seen in the rest of the building. There was a large desk situated almost centrally with three large wooden chairs in front. *Seating for the Headmaster's court or culprits,* I thought. Behind the desk was a closed door flanked by two large floor-to-ceiling bookcases but no chair. The shelves of the bookcases were lined with dusty, tattered looking books punctuated by several small framed photographs.

Patricia made her excuses and left us alone in the study, saying that Mr Muhler would be with us in just a moment. Poppy walked quickly behind the desk and started to peer at the photographs, some of which I could see were of schoolboys. The door behind the desk started to open and Poppy quickly moved back to stand by my side.

Mr Muhler appeared in the doorway, seated in his wheelchair as the previous day. The chair was being pushed by a man dressed in a dark suit, white shirt and dark coloured necktie. As he came more into my view, I could see that he was perhaps in his mid-fifties and of similar height to my six foot. He looked fit and moved easily. His head was completely bald, but as he got nearer I could see from the stubble on his scalp illuminated from a light above the doorway that this was a cultivated appearance that matched my initial impression of him as a nightclub bouncer.

'Good morning,' Muhler greeted us in a stronger and clearer voice than the previous afternoon. 'I'm sorry, I can't remember your names.'

'Mr and Mrs Parsons,' I replied. 'Poppy and David.'

'Poppy and David. Ah! Yes, I remember now. You want to talk about boys I used to teach in the old days, in England.'

'That's right,' said Poppy. 'And your Canadian pupils too.'

The dark-suited man manoeuvred the wheelchair so that Muhler was now in his rightful place sitting behind his desk, a headmaster once more, and spoke for the first time in perfect but heavenly accented English.

'My name is Karel Kosler. I look after Mr Muhler.'

'Hello, Karl,' Poppy said.

'Karel, with an e,' corrected Kosler.'

'Karel, sorry,' apologised Poppy.

'We can give you half an hour, no more,' said Kosler standing very erect beside Muhler in his wheelchair.

'Just half an hour?' Poppy said with disappointment.

'No more. Mr Muhler has a medical procedure at eleven.'

'Are you ill, Mr Muhler?' I asked.

'No more than you see in this chair,' Kosler said without giving Muhler a chance to reply. 'It's a type of massage, limb and joint manipulation. I give it to him twice every day. Now, as time is limited, let us proceed.'

'Please sit down both of you,' Muhler invited. It is uncomfortable for me to have to gaze up into your faces all the time.'

Poppy and I sat down on adjacent chairs, adjusting their positions so that we were facing both Joseph Muhler and Karel Kosler. When we had gotten back to our motel the previous afternoon we had decided that, once again, Poppy would make the running in our conversation with Muhler.

'You were telling us, Mr Muhler, how you successfully tutored boys at Gresham's School to enable them to gain entrance to Oxford, Cambridge and the British Civil Service. We also discussed how some of these pupils of yours went onto become valuable members of the community. We even talked about two of them, Holtom and Britten. We can perhaps talk about Gresham's some more but first, perhaps, how about the boys that went to your school, Millhouse?'

Again Kosler answered for Muhler. 'The school closed six years ago.'

I was annoyed that this answer had come from him, but I decided to try to engage with him rather than repeat the question to Muhler. 'Can you tell me why the school closed?'

'Because another school further down the island began taking the sort of boys we were seeking. Nearer to Victoria and Nanaimo it was easier to get to than here.'

But the question had aroused Muhler too. 'That school is much larger than here, we only ever took 60 boys at our height and therefore they were better equipped. It became a place for boys that were expected to do great things with their lives, not like little Millhouse School. I was getting old and infirm. It wasn't possible for me to fight back.'

'But,' Kosler added. 'When Mr Muhler started Millhouse in 1937 it was the only private high school on the island and probably the only one modelled on the British public school system in the whole of British Columbia. We had great success for at least twenty years, didn't we Sep?'

'Yes, yes we did,' agreed Muhler with a touch of pride. 'The boys were happy here and every one of them graduated. Some went on to university, a few died in the war. There used to be regular reunions, but not now. I expect they all think I'm dead. They are almost right.'

'Nonsense Seppy, nonsense. You've got years yet ahead of you,' soothed Kosler.

'Perhaps, thanks to your care.' Muhler patted Kosler's hand which was placed on his shoulder.

'It sounds, Mr Muhler, as if you were not preparing the Millhouse boys for their futures in the way you did your Gresham's pupils,' Poppy suggested

'No,' he agreed. 'It was quite different at Gresham's. I wasn't a master there you know, not a member of the staff. I gave private tuition in the evenings to a few boys who were intent on particular paths. Mature boys 17 or 18 years of age in their last year at school. They knew what they wanted from

216

life. They knew what they had to learn, and I taught it to them. Exceptional boys, most of them.'

Poppy started to move into dangerous ground. Our allotted time was running out. 'The organisation we work for gave me a list of these exceptional boys.' She pulled out a piece of paper from her bag that looked a little like a shopping list. 'Here are two boys with the same surname, Simon. Do they ring a bell?'

'Oh yes!. I remember them well.' The pride of recollection was clear in Muhler's tone. 'They were brothers, about two years between them. Roger was the elder. I think the father was a lord of some sort. I can't remember the Christian name of the younger. We didn't use first names much at Gresham's. I tutored them both for Cambridge. They both got in and did brilliantly I believe. Yes, they were successes for me.'

I looked at Kosler when Poppy brought up the Simon boys' names. He had an impassive look which did not change during Muhler's remarks about them.

Poppy referred to her list again. 'Then there is somebody called Klugman.'

With a speed that completely belied his size, Kosler put one knee on the desk, stretched his free arm out and snatched the list from Poppy's hand.

'*Ach Gott*!' He exclaimed as he stared at the list of names. 'Listen Seppy, listen to these names, Britten, Holtom, B.Simon, R.Simon, Klugman, Medley, and right at the bottom, Donald Maclean.'

Muhler took the list from Kosler and squinted at it through the lower half of his tinged bifocal glasses. Poppy and I stayed stock still and mute in our chairs, not knowing what would come next but realising that our carefully crafted strategy was blown.

Muhler was the next to speak 'Get them out of here now, Karel,' he snarled.

Kosler came around the desk to face Poppy and I. We stood up, as much to face possible violence as to prepare to exit the building.

'You two arseholes have betrayed our trust. You have spun a story of doing educational research but clearly have a completely different agenda. I guess you are freelance journalists still trying to excavate the past of Donald Maclean and his progressive thinking, idealistic friends. Somehow you have created a link, a fictitious chain, through Gresham's School to Joseph Muhler, my friend, employer and teacher. There is no such connection, you have wasted our time and greatly insulted us. Now go!'

We should have slunk out quietly but Poppy, typically, was not going to leave without a parting shot. 'We are going. We never intended to insult Mr Muhler. But there is a link, as you call it. You both know it and even as we bow out there will be others who will start their own probing sometime in the future.' But most of her words were lost to their intended audience by Kosler spinning Muhler around in his wheelchair and hurrying him out through the doorway by which they had entered the study.

'Damn and bugger, damn and bugger,' Poppy muttered through clenched teeth as we got back to our car. 'You drive, I don't feel capable.'

'Let's go into the town here and get ourselves a big drink each,' I suggested.

'Good idea. But it's not yet eleven. Are licensing hours here like England? If so, the pubs won't be open yet.'

'So let's go back to Parksville then. There should be something open by the time we get there.'

Just a minute into the drive Poppy started to sob bitterly by my side.

'Oh David, I'm so sorry,' she gasped. 'I screwed it up completely. You entrusted me to get it right, but I failed. Failed you, failed everyone.'

I brought the car to a halt by the side of the road and put an arm around her shoulder, drawing her face into my chest. 'You didn't fail. Ours was a lousy plan but it was the one we made together. We didn't know that Muhler had a goon as a carer. I wonder what his story is? He obviously knew about the connection between the people on our list and Donald Maclean. And he seems to be a German or Austrian. Say he is 55 now, that would make him born in 1912. Do you remember those two German, communist, anti-fascist activists that were involved in recruiting Philby to their cause?'

Poppy's brain reactivated, her snivelling stopped and she disengaged herself from my clasp.

'You mean Munzenburg and Deutsch? They were sniffing around Philby and his cronies in about 1934.'

I continued. 'At which time Kosler would have been about twenty-two years old. Suppose he was one of their disciples. Perhaps he was sent by them to watch over Muhler when he moved to Canada. Perhaps he was the person that Jean's uncle Joshua had seen in Muhler's house in Holt?'

'In which case his name might be one that Noakes and Co would be interested in.'

'We have nothing else to offer them, only a story of failure. No additional names for their MI6 dossier,' I concluded flatly.

Poppy turned to face me, despite the tear tracks still glistening down her cheeks, her eyes now sparkled with excitement. 'I've got an idea. Get me to that pub while I mull things over a bit more; I'll tell you what's on my mind when I get the first glass of Canadian Rye in my hand.'

We found a rather run-down looking pub near the centre of Parksville that was located on the wrong side of the main road to permit a view of the beach, but it was opening up just as we arrived. We were the first customers of the day and the barman welcomed us as he attended to the lighting of a large log fire in the corner of the bar. We sat at a table near to the fireplace and after a couple of minutes two glasses of whisky arrived, we had both insisted that we wanted no ice.

'Well?' I asked Poppy after I had swallowed my first sip. 'What is this idea of yours?'

'Did you see those small photos on the bookshelves behind Muhler's desk?'

'Of people I think, they were too far away for me to see clearly. But you were behind that desk when Muhler was pushed in; you were looking at them.'

'Yes, I was. And I had just enough time to see that they were of small groups of schoolboys dressed in school uniform.'

'Gresham's uniform?' I said, my excitement starting to rise as I began to catch Poppy's drift.

'No,' she replied. 'Most of the photos, say six of a total of about eight I think, were of Millhouse School pupils. Definitely not Gresham's boys, the uniform looked very different. But two of the photos probably were because, now I try to recapture what I actually saw in just a fleeting moment, I think one of the boys in one of the two small groups was Donald Maclean.'

'So Muhler keeps a record of the guilty parties on his study shelf?'

'Seems like it.'

'No wonder Kosler was so enraged when he saw your list. Those photos comprise a shrine or icons. Was Muhler himself on the photos?'

'On the Millhouse School ones certainly. But I had only such a very quick glance at the two photos of interest to us that I don't know if he was there or not.'

'I think I see where you are heading with this notion of yours, but go on and I'll try not to interrupt.'

'OK, but first another rye whisky.'

I went up to the bar and collected two more shots. By the time I got back to our table Poppy had spread out the photos given to us by Jean. 'Look,' she said. 'If we could get back into the house tonight–'

I was about to exclaim in disbelief when she leant across the table and put a hand across my mouth. 'Shut it, David,' she said firmly. 'You promised not to interrupt.'

I nodded; she took her hand away. 'We get inside. We compare Muhler's photos with these on this table and we note any we can't recognise. And then we come to the tricky bit. We hope against hope that the names of the boys are written on the back of the photo frames.'

'And if they aren't?' I asked

'If there are no names then we take the photos with us.'

'And give the whole game away?'

'Oh! I think that's happened already. And remember we are not trying to incriminate Muhler. Noakes and Eugene Russel made that very clear to us. We are after the name or names of boys that he might have set up as future spies against Britain. No, even that is rather too strong … it's boys that he may have so influenced that at some time later they may have decided to become spies. So, are you on for this last attempt?'

'Yes, of course,' I replied. 'There is no other action that I can think of. We will break in sometime after midnight, leave our car parked somewhere unsuspicious and walk up to the house. We will need to buy some torches, or as I believe they call them here, flashlights. So, until then?'

'We will try to take our minds off what we are planning to do tonight. Walk, shop, eat, rest.'

Chapter 18

We dodged winter showers as we walked the Parksville beaches, our anoraks bundled tightly around our bodies and our hands encased in the leather gloves which we had bought in the town along with two small torches.

'We must wear these tonight,' said Poppy, stretching her fingers inside her glove. 'No fingerprints to be left by the burglars.'

We tidied up our motel room and told the receptionist that we would be leaving very early the following morning to catch the first ferry back to Vancouver. 'Just leave your room door open when you leave with the key in the lock, you're all paid up. Have a nice evening,' she replied.

---///---

As she had become the de-facto leader of we two, would-be criminals, I suggested to Poppy that she drive the car to Qualicum Beach. We left the car in an empty supermarket car park shortly before 1 am and set out to walk to Millhouse School which we had estimated as being a little over a mile away. The rain had stopped. Patchy cloud heralding more showers was continually obscuring then revealing a partial moon, but there was sufficient light from occasional lampposts along the road paralleling the seashore for us not to need the torches.

On reaching the driveway to the schoolhouse, we took to the lawns to avoid our feet crunching the gravel. We stopped for a moment facing the front doors. The whole house was in total darkness.

'We never discussed how and where we are going to make our entrance,' whispered Poppy.

'The study is, I think, around the back and near to that big sunroom. It's all lawn there is no gravel to cross, let's try there first,' I replied in a similar whisper.

Our paces became slower and softer as we approached the rear of the building; again, no lights were to be seen. The moon came out briefly as we looked at the sunroom and we saw that it had a glazed door which was directly facing us. I went up to the door and very gently pressed down the polished metal handle. There was a gentle click and the door swung open smoothly towards me.

'Hooray,' Poppy expressed almost as a sigh.

We were both wearing rubber soled sports shoes which we wiped silently and very carefully on the cork matting lying just inside the doorway. The moon was hiding behind clouds once more. Poppy switched on her torch and led our way through the sunroom, into the reception hall and thence along the short corridor leading to Muhler's study. The study door was open, but the room was shrouded in blackness as we stepped inside. I turned on my torch; Poppy turned off hers and put it into one of the pockets of her anorak.

Using her hands, Poppy indicated to me to shine my torch onto the photographs standing on the bookshelves behind the desk. I illuminated each of the six photograph frames in turn while she studied them without touching. Satisfied with what she saw, she took two of them off their shelf and put them face up on the headmaster's desk. I bent over the desk and illuminated the photographs set into the frames. The first photograph showed a fit looking Muhler standing with four boys, the second showed just three standing boys. She took the envelope containing the photos of both the Simons, Krugman, Holtom and Maclean out of the inside pocket of her anorak and carefully compared each image with the two frames. I was looking at the photos from the upside-down perspective so was unable to help with the identification of the boys. She put her gloved index finger on each of the four faces shown with Muhler and mouthed 'Simon, Simon, Krugman, Maclean. She turned the frame over and pointed to the year *1929* written in black pencil by itself on the cardboard backing; she returned that frame to its correct position on the shelf.

She turned her gaze to the second frame, put her finger on one of the faces and mouthed 'Maclean again'. She scrutinised the other two faces, comparing them with the photos in her hand, turning them to various angles. 'Strangers,' she whispered to me. She turned the frame over, as she had done with the first photograph, again a handwritten date, *1930,* but nothing else.

She removed the cardboard backing, which was secured by four tiny rotatable catches, took my torch from me and shone it very close to the reverse side of the photograph. I could see some writing.

The light in the study came on. I whirled around and saw Kosler standing in the doorway behind me; one hand was on the light switch by the door jamb, the other held a small revolver pointing straight at Poppy.

Poppy barely raised her head; she was re-reading the back of the photograph and I could see her mouthing words in a desperate attempt to commit them to memory.

Kosler's voice sounded very angry and more guttural. 'That will do, Mrs Parsons. I am sure those names are now firmly in your memory, which is a real pity for you. Now, put that photo back into its frame, put the frame back on the shelf, then stand beside your husband.'

Poppy did as she has been instructed and took her designated place by me as Kosler moved towards the desk and behind us both.

'I told you to go away, I thought that you were two interfering journalists, but maybe you are something quite different. It doesn't matter because now we all have to go on a little journey. Yes, the gun is loaded so stay in front of me. We are going out the way you came in through the sunroom, then round to the other side of the house where my car is parked.'

The car looked similar to our Chevrolet, now parked in the middle of the local town. Kosler ordered Poppy to drive, with me to sit in the passenger seat by her side, and told us to keep our gloves on. This, I presumed, was to avoid our fingerprints appearing on the interior of the car and I suddenly realised that Poppy and I were on a one-way journey.

Kosler started the car and turned on its lights by leaning across Poppy, his gun pressed firmly into her stomach. He then climbed into the back of the car. I saw, through the rear-view mirror, that he had placed himself in the middle of the seat, so that he could both see through the windscreen and control both Poppy and me at the same time.

I started to protest. I felt the muzzle of his gun in the nape of my neck as he told me to shut up. 'No more noise from either of you; and if you try any tricks, Mrs Parsons, your husband will immediately pay the price.'

The only words were his as he barked out intermittent driving instructions to Poppy, 'Right out of the driveway.

'Follow the coast road through the town.

'Turn left at the signpost coming up this side of road bridge ahead.'

The signpost read *Little Qualicum River, Fish Hatchery*. Poppy turned the car onto a gravel road passing through flat fields. Moonlight appeared briefly and I could see a rushing river glinting on our right. After about five minutes the road started to climb and the fields gave way to tall trees that in the darkness appeared to be trying to smother us. The road twisted this way and that, seemingly following the convoluted path of the river which I could no longer see as it had dropped from my sight into its valley. At one point the sound of cascading water became so loud that it drowned out the sound of the car's engine and I guessed that we were passing a large waterfall. I glanced at Poppy's face, it was set in grim determination, a look I remembered from the episode with her Japanese father in Western Australia. I knew that her mind would be racing, striving desperately for a means, a plan at least, of escape.

We were driving into wilderness and I became certain that neither Poppy nor I were going to emerge alive from the *Fish Hatchery*, whatever that was. This man Kosler was not just a carer for Muhler, he was something much more. Perhaps placed by the Soviets to guard a person who had served that country well in the past and had secrets that were never to be revealed. In that context Poppy and I were likely expendable.

I began to voice my thoughts loudly, as much to act as a warning to Poppy as an outlet for my fearful frustrations. I was rewarded by a very hard blow on the side of my head by the gun and collapsed unconscious.

I don't know exactly how long I was out to the world, but somewhere between five and ten minutes I would think. The car was drawing to a halt as consciousness returned and with it an unexpected clarity in my mind. I could feel a trickle of blood making its way from a wound in my skull, down my sideways-bent neck and onto my collar. I made no attempt to touch the wound or to move from my seeming lifeless position. I reasoned that if I stayed limp and unresponsive, Kosler would have to get me out of the car before he visited any more violence on me or Poppy. And that might present a problem for him and an opportunity for us.

Through half opened eyes I could see that the car had stopped near to a single lamp post which was flood lighting a large concreted area. This flat area appeared to be punctuated with rectangular ponds or culverts and there were some single-storied huts on its far side. I could hear the very loud sound of cascading water coming from somewhere behind and this was intermingled with the sound of heavy rain on the roof of the car.

Kosler had got out of the car and now opened my door. I closed my eyes as he bent to examine me. 'Mrs Parsons,' he said. 'Get out of the car now and help me to get your man onto the ground. You take the shoulders and I will take his legs.'

I felt Poppy's hands touch my upper arms and opened my eyes to her.

'David, David,' she called softly. I gave a little groan as if I were just waking up and stared straight into her face. I knew that look on her face. It was the one she used to give me when she wanted me to extract her from some unwelcome company, usually an intoxicated *Hooray Henry* in the Zetland. It was her 'do something now' look.

'I'm OK,' I said. 'I can get out by myself.' I put my legs out of the car, made as if attempting to stand, and landed on my knees.

'Move towards the light, both of you,' ordered Kosler. I could see that he had his pistol pointed at Poppy. I used the bonnet of the car to lever myself up onto my feet and I shuffled slowly by Poppy's side. We moved towards the lamp post which I could now see was set on the edge of a deep concrete culvert; powerful, turbulent water was racing down this channel culvert through a spill way and into the main channel of the Little Qualicum River.

I deliberately fell to my knees coughing and retching. Poppy, disregarding Kosler's pistol, dropped down beside me. Kosler moved up beside her and bent over to look at me. His pistol was no longer pointing at Poppy and she took her chance. As I raised my head, she swivelled half around and delivered a kick directly to the rear of one of Kosler's knees. His gun went off as he fell backwards and into the culvert behind him; there was one cry of '*Hilfe*' and then nothing except the sound of the bucketing rain and the streaming river water.

Kosler's shot had not touched me. 'Are you alright?' I asked as I picked myself up and bent over Poppy.

'I'm fine,' she answered as she, too, got to her feet. We approached the edge of the culvert cautiously. The lamp post light fully illuminated the flowing water six feet below our feet, constrained by the narrow passage into a raging current. Kosler was face up in the direction of the flow, his head trapped between the edges of the sluice gate. He was completely under water. Trapped by the driving current, his arms and legs were flailing helplessly, his eyes were wide open staring up at us and his lips mouthed what I took to be '*Hilfe*' again, then the flailing stopped and his eyes stared lifelessly up through the raging water.

The gun was by my feet; I kicked it into the culvert. I embraced Poppy, kissing her hard on her lips, chastely but with love.

'What now?' she whispered to me as the rain eased off.

My words came tumbling out. 'He's dead, we have to get out of here, away from the school, back to Vancouver, talk to Paul.'

Poppy looked at her left hand which had been holding my head; she showed me the blood on it.

'It will stop bleeding soon,' I said. 'I'll cover my head with my anorak hood to give it a chance to dry. That was a very neat move you made on his leg.'

'Something Stephen taught me. But you got my message and created the necessary diversion to his attention. I guess we just leave him there … and don't tell anyone.'

'Except Paul. When Kosler's body is found which given the hatchery is shut at this time of the year could take several days, it will look like suicide or an unfortunate accident. We have to leave his car here to make it look like he drove himself to this place with the clear objective of killing himself. Our prints are nowhere inside this vehicle so we are clear, I think. Now all we have to do is walk all the way back to Paul's Chevrolet and get the hell away from Vancouver Island.'

'Just one more thing,' said Poppy, speaking very deliberately. 'Remember these names, I found them on that second photo, John Newby and Richard Hargreaves.'

'John Newby and Richard Hargreaves,' I repeated.

'Those are who we came looking for.'

---///---

It took us well over an hour to retrace our journey back to the supermarket carpark in Qualicum. We walked in single file, mainly in silence, taking it in turns to lead using just one of our precious torches at a time. Occasionally we were helped by moonlight filtering through the gaps in the cloud cover and penetrating the tree canopies; occasionally it rained on us. We were wet, very tired, but not at all miserable when we climbed into our car at 3:30 am. Poppy said that with my head injury I was in no shape to drive. She started the engine and waited for the heater to start blowing hot air onto our wet clothes, shivering bodies and squelching shoes.

'We could just go back to the school now and steal that photo,' I suggested.

'Bad idea,' rebuffed Poppy. 'At present that study is as we found it. We don't want to do anything that could even vaguely connect us to Kosler's disappearance which a missing photo might indeed do. Muhler and that woman, Patricia, knew that we were interested in schoolboys. She will turn up tomorrow morning to give him his breakfast or whatever. She will be the one that will raise the alarm over the missing Kosler, and that will bring the police to the school and probably to Muhler's study. A missing photo would point them straight at us.' She looked at her watch. 'I reckon we have about four hours before his absence from the school is noticed. We must get away now. Can you remember those two names?'

'John Newby and Richard Hargreaves,' I replied.

We headed off to Parksville where we very quickly changed out of our wet clothes, repacked our luggage and left the motel room behind us. As we drove and began to feel more physically comfortable, the reality of what we had just been through hit us. We swapped expressions of disbelief, then relief, and finally anger with how we had been set up by Noakes and Co in London.

'Do you think they knew? About Kosler I mean?' asked Poppy.

'That question is, perhaps, our natural reaction to what just happened. But no. I think we were used as innocent, untainted information gatherers and were not deliberately sent into harm's way. And having escaped with our lives, we now have proof that both Kosler and Muhler have murky pasts. We have fulfilled what was asked of us.' And I was certain of my answer because I knew my father, who surely had some knowledge of what I had been doing, would have liked me to be tested but never to be put in harm's way.

When we arrived at the ferry terminal at Nanaimo and paid cash for our ticket, we were told that we would be sailing on the 7 am boat. We had half an hour before boarding was due to start. The only phone we could find was in the rather dingy passenger waiting area which was already getting crowded with foot passengers. Speaking freely with Paul was going to be difficult, but I volunteered for the task with Poppy entwined around me and so, hopefully, muffling my voice from being overheard. She held the business card with Paul's number in front of me while I dialled, and then loaded the phone cradle with coins on my signal. Paul was clearly an early riser as he answered almost immediately.

'Paul,' I began. 'It's your *parson*, talking in the open. We are about to catch the 7 am ferry from Nanaimo. Major complication here causing a death, involvement by us but not easily connectable to us. We have two names of interest, John Newby and Richard Hargreaves, a third name will be given to you in person.'

The reply was terse. 'All noted, recorded but not understood. I will meet you in the Horseshoe Bay passenger terminal. Wait for me there if I'm late.' Then he rang off.

'I got what he said,' said Poppy. 'Let's get back to the car ready to drive it onto the ferry. There is something about that second photo that I haven't told you.'

There was a slight lightening in the sky to our west as we sat in the car, in the middle of a long line up of other cars and next to two lines of heavy trucks, all waiting for the ferry to start loading.

'The second photo showed three boys together,' Poppy reminded me.

'Maclean, Newby and Hargreaves,' I replied correctly. 'The names were written on the back with the date.'

'Yes, 1930. But unlike the first photo, Muhler was not present and the boys were not in school uniform. And they weren't boys anymore but young men. When I first looked at the photo, I thought they were wearing school blazers, but they weren't; they were wearing sports jackets and they looked like university students.'

'At Cambridge perhaps?'

'Maybe, but I don't remember their names coming up in all that stuff we read which described what happened at Cambridge in the 1930s.'

'Me neither,' I concurred. 'But Maclean was still at school in 1930, wasn't he?'

'Yes, I think so,' said Poppy.

'So, it was a get-together of some sort, somewhere else. Perhaps the 1930 date was not the year that the photo was taken but the year when all three were being tutored by Muhler at Gresham's. They sent it to him as a reminder and he put the date on.'

'Yes,' exclaimed Poppy. 'It was a meeting-up of Gresham's School Old Boys. It's a great pity that we didn't nick that photo.'

'Yes,' I agreed. 'But that might have led us into even more trouble than we are in now.'

---///---

Poppy and I had to wait in the Horseshoe Bay for nearly an hour before Paul turned up. 'I've been somewhat busy, as you might imagine, but let's get into that car you have been using so you can tell me what happened in privacy. That's my usual car you've got so I came here by taxi. Then I'll tell you what has to happen.'

Poppy and I took it in turns to relate the full story of everything that had happened to us during our two days on Vancouver Island. As well as emphasising the seeming importance, as we had seen it, of the photo of the three young men together, we also expounded our theory about Kosler perhaps being mixed up with the German émigré anti-fascist activists in the 1930s. Once or twice Paul pursed his lips, but he did not once interrupt us; this was a person, I determined, who knew how and when to listen.

Poppy ended the saga with 'And so here we are.'

Paul held his hands clasped together up to his mouth, his lips seemed to be kissing an index finger, perhaps nibbling a piece of stray flesh. After what seemed a very long silence, but was probably no more than two minutes, he spoke.

'I told London about your predicament as soon you phoned me from Nanaimo. Of course I only had the very bare bones of your story. About an hour later I got a call back containing instructions which I had immediately to act upon. Thankfully, now that I have the full story, I think the instructions and actions given me are still appropriate. Firstly, the names of Newby and Hargreaves have created a great deal of interest in London and wheels, of which I have absolutely no knowledge, are now in motion. So, congratulations to you both for that part of the Millhouse School story, although you have created quite a mess which now has to be cleaned up.

'Of course, at this time London knows nothing about the demise of the man called Kosler, I shall be telling them about him as soon as I get back to my office. However, and it can only be my opinion at this time, you seem to have disentangled yourselves from his supposed suicide. I think your ideas about his background or something similar may be right, in which case I accept that you were both about to be shot and acted as you had to. He would have fled, probably to Europe and to his masters, actual or historical. People in his line of business usual have an escape plan and another identity in their back pocket.'

Paul pulled out a notebook from the small leather bag he had been carrying when he arrived at the ferry terminal. 'And now we come to your escape plan, or rather, plans. You, Poppy, are going to Singapore to see your parents, it's about time! You fly out this afternoon from Vancouver. I will take you to the airport as soon as we leave here and you will have the use of the VIP and Diplomats lounge there to pass the time, get cleaned up and eat.'

'Singapore?' queried Poppy, clearly surprised and sounding a little annoyed.

'Yes, via Tokyo I believe. We will pick up your tickets at the airport. There can be no argument about this. We, that is principally me, have to erase your traces as much as I can and Task One is to get you away from Canada as quickly as possible. Now, David, you are going back to London. You are leaving at lunch time today on the earliest flight I could arrange, by a fairly tortuous route via Edmonton, Winnipeg, and Toronto. Saturday is a hard day to fix flights at short notice and no VIP lounge for you I'm afraid. Again, your tickets will be at Vancouver airport when I get you there with Poppy.'

Paul opened his bag again, extracted two passports and handed them to Poppy and me. 'And here are the passports you will be travelling under.'

I opened the passport up, it was the one that I had been given to travel with Poppy from Hong Kong and thus in my correct name.'

Poppy had looked at hers at the same time. 'Oh!' she exclaimed. 'I'm back to being Mrs Shawyer again. How did you get hold of these passports?'

'In the Diplomatic Bag,' answered Paul. 'They were, in fact, sent to me as soon as London knew that you had agreed to travel to Canada. I have had them since before you first arrived here. It was thought that these passports might be needed in case you had to be extracted in a hurry, which has proved to be the case. There is always a Plan B. Now, let's get going to the airport, I'll drive.'

Chapter 19

While traveling back to London I spent more time in Canadian airports waiting for my so-called connecting flights than I did in the air. My taxi from Heathrow airport deposited me outside of my Earls Court apartment in the early evening of Sunday the 26th of November. I was exhausted but knew that I had to stay up as my first stroke against incipient jetlag. I unpacked, took a shower, drank a couple of beers at the Earls Court Tavern, not nearly as noisy as on Friday and Saturday evenings, and ate in my favourite local Italian restaurant. Returning home, I was tempted to phone Susan but thought better of it when my addled brain realised than she may not have known anything of what had happened in Canada. This was a relationship, if that was what it to be, that I did not want to start out in an atmosphere of evasion or lies. I was fast asleep before 11 pm.

At eight the next morning I was awakened by the phone ringing in the lounge. Staggering up, literally, I managed to get to it before the caller gave up.

'Good Morning, David,' Jean Hathaway began. 'I won't ask you about your flight which I know would have been a trial, but at least you are safely back. We are still working on the names you uncovered so can't tell you how significant or otherwise they may turn out to be. But let me personally just say that you and Poppy did a good job in the circumstances, and we are all very relieved you are both safe.'

I bet you all are, I thought, *otherwise the shit would really have hit the fan if we had ended up as corpses. A hard thing to explain away to our Canadian friends.*

Jean continued. 'I know that you might be tempted to give Susan Anderson a call, in my world we are trained to pick up subtle signals, but I urge you not to just yet. She is very engaged in what our little team is doing with your information and in liaising with the relevant Canadian authorities, so it would embarrass her and could easily compromise her work. We will put you and Poppy back in the picture in a little while. In the meantime, I suggest you go back to your life in the world of insurance. You know what to tell your colleagues about your temporary secondment to the Government, don't you?'

I said that I did, and the call ended.

I mooched around the apartment, did my washing and slept for the remainder of that Monday, and on the following day I went back to my office for the first time in over two weeks. Using the excuse that the work I had been doing for the Government was Commercial in Confidence, I avoided having to invent any cock-and-bull tales for my colleagues.

What could I have told them in any case? That just four days previously I had been kneeling in the rain by a river in Canada with a loaded pistol held to my head convinced that I was about to die?

I sat at my desk and started to catch up on my real work, to go through mail and phone messages mostly concerned with my Singapore harbour portfolio. James Harrington came into the open-plan office where I worked and welcomed me back; he had a knowing look in his eye but did not ask me into his office for one of his cosy chats. He, like Henry Souch who I think had no more than a slight inkling of what I had been up to, also knew better than to ask questions that could have caused me embarrassment.

My life, both working and social, soon returned to its usual pattern and Christmas loomed ahead. My parents phoned to say that they were coming over to stay in the studio on the 22nd of December and would not return to Spain until well into the New Year; they were looking forward, they added, to having a family Christmas with me and my assorted uncles and aunts.

'I've already made most of the arrangements and I'm expecting you to join in fully,' my mother insisted.

There were no questions from them about what I had been doing since the time we had last spoken by phone more than a month previously. That there were none made me immediately suspect that my father knew at least something of what Poppy and I had been up to.

That phone call nearly prompted me to phone Poppy in Singapore. But not having heard from her caused me to think that she was tacitly warning me that it was too early to renew contact via her parents' home telephone, our only means of communication other than airmail. She would get in touch when she was ready, I convinced myself.

However, on the evening of Wednesday the 13th of December it was Susan Anderson who phoned. We exchanged brief pleasantries then came her question: 'Are we still on for a date.'

'Of course,' I replied. 'Whenever you want … this weekend?'

'Yes, Friday evening, 7 pm at that new Bistro, Chez Maurice, between Covent Garden and Leicester Square. Do you know it?'

I replied that I didn't, but the place couldn't be hard to find. 'But why there?' I added.

'Because Eugene Russel has reserved a room there for all of our little team. While having dinner, on him he says but more likely the secret office fund that everyone knows about, he is going to tell us what has been done with the names you and Poppy gave him.'

'So you know already?'

'No, not everything. It's all been a bit compartmentalised. Typical need to know. I don't think we should talk about it anymore. I've been assured that all will be clear on Friday evening. You will be there?'

'Of course, at seven.'

---///---

I took the tube train to Convent Garden station, which was a mistake. If I had got off at the preceding station, Leicester Square, I wouldn't have had such a long walk to the bistro, getting slightly lost on the way, and I wouldn't have been ten minutes late for the 7 pm date. I was shown into a private dining room of much the same size as the office Poppy and I had been holed up in at the Old Air Ministry Building. There was one empty chair at the oblong table filling the centre of the room, clearly mine as the other chairs were already occupied by Mr Noakes, Jean Hathaway, Susan Anderson and Poppy, with Eugene Russel seated at the head. The table was laid, it seemed, for a considerable feast. I greeted everyone in turn with a handshake, except for Poppy who accepted a brief kiss, and sat down next to Susan. Poppy was at the other end of the table next to Eugene, Noakes was facing him at my end. In reply to my question after the greeting kiss, Poppy said that she had arrived back in London only the previous day.

A waiter filled the flutes by each person's lace-edged white linen place mat with champagne, then retired from the room closing the sole door behind him. I supposed that Eugene had a hidden electric bell near him to recall the waiter whenever he decided.

Poppy looked splendid, dressed simply and expensively with just a touch of makeup garnishing the beautiful face that I had loved so much. Susan's looks were rather more restrained, but the glasses were gone and the contact lenses, I assumed, were in place. I smiled at both women. Poppy's return smile was one of sharing a secret with me, just one more of the many we had accumulated since childhood. Susan's was cool, sophisticated, and then she dropped her eyes.

Eugene's toast was simple. 'A toast to us all,' he proposed, 'and damnation to the villains.'

We all stood up, lifted our glasses, echoed the toast, drank some of the champagne, sat down expectantly and looked at Eugene.

'I propose,' said Eugene, looking at each of his audience in turn. 'that I now tell you what the information unearthed by Poppy and David has produced so far. Jean and Noaksy know what I know, Susan has some inkling, but our two detectives not at all. And after that we will eat and drink some more. The only door to this room is now closed I see, thus we should be disturbed no more until we are ready to eat. What I tell you and what we may subsequently discuss is absolutely Top Secret and I remind you Poppy and David that you are bound by the Official Secrets Act, as is everyone else in this room. But first of all, welcome back to London, Poppy, I hope that you survive this evening without becoming too tired.

Eugene finished off the champagne in his glass. 'Let's start off with the late Mr Karel Kosler. The British Columbia police are satisfied, they say, that his death was suicide. They think that he was going to shoot himself and let his body be washed away by the river. But the gun somehow went off prematurely and he shot himself in the foot causing him to fall into the river and drown. It's a good story and I think it will stick. In any case, the Mounties want the case closed off as they need to get on with investigating his past working in conjunction with our MI6. And from MI6, with which organisation Noaksy and I are once again on speaking terms, I'm glad to say, it seems that the theory that Kosler was some type of anti-fascist, communist activist holds water. It appears that he was active in the Balkans during the last war as, of course, was Klugman, so there is a very possible Gresham's link there. Which brings us now to John Newby, he of the photograph with Maclean and Hargreaves.

As we now know, Newby was at Gresham's with Klugman et al, and from the photograph appears to have had a post-school relationship with Maclean and Hargreaves, whom I will come to in a minute. Now remembering what I just said about Klugman and Kosler, it doesn't come as a huge surprise that Newby was also working in the Balkans with partisans during the war and there he died in action. In other words, there seems to have been a little nest of Gresham's associates fighting the Germans and aiding the putative Communist government in what is now known as Yugoslavia. So Kosler becomes even more a person of interest as they say. MI6 have taken on his case with relish.

And lastly Richard Hargreaves who, until very recently, was First Secretary in our embassy in Prague, right in the heartland of the Iron Curtain countries. Susan was the person that drew the connection within hours of us receiving his name from Paul in Canada. She realised at once the sensitivity and potential ramifications of that knowledge and immediately informed me. I then contacted both MI6 and the Foreign Office who, together with Noaksy, drew up a plan of action which I authorised. We all agreed that what had to be done would be done. I have just been briefed on what has occurred and Noaksy will now tell you the tale, after our glasses have been recharged.

Eugene bent down and I heard the clink of ice cubes as he pulled a champagne bottle from out of a bucket concealed beneath his chair. With a very deft and clearly well practised series of swift movements, he had the cork out with a satisfying pop and charged his empty glass. He signalled to Susan who took the bottle from his hand and topped up everyone else's glasses as Mr Noakes rose to his feet.

Tuesday 28th November (3 days after Kosler dies):

Charles, the man who was driving Noakes when he first made contact with David, is now taking him an hour and a half west of London to RAF Benson, an Air Force transport airfield in Oxfordshire. He stops the car at the horizontal pole barrier blocking the passage of vehicles into the base. A military policeman steps out of the guardroom into the wind and rain of a blustery afternoon. He exchanges some words with Charles and then moves to the car's rear door; Noakes winds down his window and shows the policeman a pass. 'Do you know where you are going to, Sir?' the policeman asks.

'Yes, thank you Corporal,' Noakes replies. The policeman moves slightly back, salutes, raises the barrier and waves the car through.

Charles takes the car through the administrative area of the airfield, past some looming hangars in front of which can be seen numerous large transport aircraft, and parks by the side of the Air Traffic Control building with its high tower constructed so as to overlook the whole of the operations area of RAF Benson. The two men, carrying small suitcases and raincoats folded over their arms, make their way into a room identified as Air Operations. They are the only occupants of this room which resembles in one part a small auditorium with a large screen and with the remainder set out with desks, chairs and blackboards.

Two men in flying suits enter through a door marked 'Flight Planning'. One is a Squadron Leader and bears a pilot's brevet on his left breast, the other a Flight Lieutenant with a Navigators brevet. Brief introductions are made, the pilot identifies himself as the captain of the imminent flight.

'So, Berlin tonight, to RAF Gatow direct,' begins the pilot. 'Take off is scheduled for 1600 hours, 30 minutes from now. Weather is reported as gusty and wet for the whole route, so we are in for a bumpy ride. And as you two will be sitting on para-seats attached to the inside walls and we have freight on board to block your views, your ride will be boring and uncomfortable I'm afraid. I'm told that we have to bring you back as well Mr Noakes, whenever that may be.'

'Hopefully, I won't be too long in Berlin, just a few hours if all goes well.'

'OK. The co-pilot and the flight engineer should have finished the pre-flights by now and the loadmaster the securing of freight. The crew bus is waiting outside, so let's head out to the aircraft.'

The bus draws up to one of six Argosy freighters parked in a line on a huge area of hardstanding which is illuminated by banks of floodlights mounted on tall pylons. Four ground crew stand around and under the four engine turboprop aircraft with its already closed rear freight doors. The twin-booms stretching out rearwards from the wings to the tail structure make the Argosy resemble an aerial wheelbarrow. One man is attending to a large mobile generator attached by a thick cable to the aircraft's fuselage, two others are by the main wheels holding ropes attached to chocks while the fourth is in front of the nose of the aircraft so as to be visible from its cockpit.

Noakes and Charles climb into the interior of the aircraft followed by the Captain and the Navigator. These two aircrew clamber up a ladder into the cockpit while the loadmaster, wearing the rank of Warrant Officer, shows Noakes and Charles to their metal framed, netting upholstered, sideways facing, para-seats; there is a tall pile of loaded freight pallets within touching distance in front of them. There are no other passengers.

The engines are started one after the other. The high pitch whine of the Rolls-Royce Dart engines increases progressively to a near unbearable level. The loadmaster offers padded ear defenders to his two passengers which are gratefully accepted; he checks their full-body seat harnesses.

The flight takes the best part of three hours; it is noisy, bumpy and generally uncomfortable for Noakes and Charles. The loadmaster offers them coffee from an urn which, as both are feeling queasy, they refuse; he points out a toilet they can use and puts sick bags by the side of their seats.

After clearing West Germany, the flight of the plane is via the narrow, central air corridor over East Germany into Berlin, one of the three entry routes permitted by post-war agreements with the Russians. Noakes is not comfortable with going into Berlin although he knows that he will not be leaving the Allied Zone of that divided city. He has too many unpleasant memories of the clean-up tasks he and his ilk performed there after the defeat of Germany in 1945.

In preparation for the task that now awaits him on landing at the British controlled airfield of RAF Gatow, he reviews in his mind what he knows about Richard Hargreaves, having known nothing about him at all before that phone call from Paul in Canada.

Richard Hargreaves, career diplomat, age 54, three tours as First Secretary in British embassies abroad, has held his current post in Prague for two years. While effective and generally well liked, he is unlikely to make Ambassador because of questions about his character which started to surface in the last eighteen months. These doubts arise from his homosexuality which, although recognised when he first joined Government service in 1935, but suppressed and hidden since then behind the façade of a very loyal wife and two adult children, has started to become more overt. Could have joined MI6 when he left London University as that organisation had no bar on homosexuals then (and now? Noakes wonders) but chose (or was instructed?) to join the Foreign Office instead.

Hargreaves appears to fit clearly into the mould of well connected, highly educated men that were sought out by Philby and associates for recruitment to his cause (which at this time is a purely speculative supposition, Noakes knows).

And the reason that Noakes is sitting uncomfortably in that noisy warehouse of an aircraft is because, over the previous three frenzied days, MI6 reassessed personal files and case notes. This work developed a clear picture of Hargreaves being in places where he had no business to be, dealing with people that he had no cause to contact and mixing, unobtrusively it seems, with those MI6 defectors who are even now living in Moscow. But this investigation, Noakes knows, would never had been initiated had not that young couple unearthed Hargreaves' connections with Gresham's School, Muhler and Maclean.

Hargreaves' habit of going to Berlin for what he has described as business liaison purposes and recreation every few weeks has now come under scrutiny, and he happens to be in Berlin for those very reasons right now. Now is it Noakes' job to retrieve the person of Hargreaves and commence a forensic investigation of the secrets held within his head and those that he may have spilled to the Soviets; preparations for this task which were well in hand before he left Benson. He draws a small photo of Hargreaves from inside his jacket and studies it for a couple of minutes.

The aircraft approaches Gatow airfield, bucking and twisting through wind, rain and turbulence. The final touchdown is smoother than Noakes had expected, however. The aircraft stops on a remote area of the hardstanding; the high pressure and low pressure fuel clocks are closed in turn by the Flight Engineer and the whining of the four engines ebbs to nothing over a period of several seconds. Noakes and Charles remove their ear defenders and clear their ears by blowing hard through pinched noses. They emerge into a pool of floodlight, their raincoats on and their suitcases in hand. There is a very light drizzle falling.

An RAF Flight Lieutenant dressed in a thick greatcoat with brass buttons is standing by a car, an aircrew bus is alongside the car. The officer introduces himself as Maurice Stannard from the station's military police; he tells Noakes and Charles that he is taking them to see the Commanding Officer, RAF Gatow. The aircrew from the Argosy pile into the aircrew bus.

The Group Captain Commanding Officer is waiting in his large and military badge garlanded office, his Woman's Royal Air Force Flight Officer Adjutant offers Noakes and Charles refreshments which they both accept; a female corporal brings in a tray of coffees and biscuits. The door closes leaving only the CO, the policeman, Noakes and Charles in the room. They sit down around a small conference table.

'It's been a busy time here, arranging for your visit,' begins the CO. 'Lots of signals traffic between London, HQ RAF Germany and us. And I trust we will not disappoint; we get quite a lot of, shall we say, unusual comings and goings. We have a building here that stills bears much evidence of what it was in the 1940s, a holding area for people of special interest. It's quite comfortable these days, in fact some visitors prefer it to the Officers Mess for short stays; we now call it our 'Guest Quarters'. Anyway, there are no visitors staying there at present, although Stannard has placed three men there to help you in any way you might need including getting food and drink from the NAAFI if required. When you are ready to return to Benson, your aircrew will need an hour or so notice to complete the flight planning and prepare the aircraft.'

Stannard drives Noakes and Charles to the Guest Quarters where they deposit their suitcases into a twin-bedded room with bathroom facilities. He then gives Noakes a small manila envelope saying, 'This was deposited for you at our guardroom at 15:00 hours this afternoon.' Noakes moves away from the others and opens the sealed envelope to check its contents; satisfied, he puts the envelope into his jacket pocket.

Stannard introduces Noakes to a man in civilian clothes. 'This is Corporal Haynes, he is to be your driver and general helper. He knows his way around Berlin, both East and West. When do you need to go out?'

Noakes looks at his watch. 'It's past seven my time, what do you have?'

'Twenty minutes past eight, we are an hour ahead of England.'

'Then we had better go right now if we are to make the reception. Let's leave our coats here so we don't stand out among the guests.'

---///---

The car pulls up outside the recently completed Hotel Europa, thirty minutes from Gatow and firmly in the American Zone of Berlin. It is a popular place to stay for visiting businessmen and is set up to handle conferences and the like. The driver, who prefers to be called just Haynes when out of uniform, is asked to park as near as possible to the front entrance to the hotel and keep an eye out for his two passengers returning out of the hotel.

'Well within an hour I would expect,' says Noakes.

Noakes and Charles enter the large and gaudy lobby of the hotel. A banner above the reception desk says 'Welcome to TRADEX 67 Delegates'. A similar notice on a floor stand bears an arrow pointing to 'TRADEX 67 Reception, Argos Room'

Noakes and Charles approach the Argos Room which is situated on the floor above the lobby. Multiple wide doors are fully open and past them the two men can easily see the delegates, all of which are standing in small groups spread throughout the chandelier garnished reception area. Noakes estimates that they number about one hundred. With very few exceptions, they are male and Caucasian. They hold glasses and talk easily with each other, occasionally nibbling canapes and other offerings taken from a posse of young male and female waiters. The talk is loud and the laughter louder, copious drinks are having their effect.

The two men stand in the entrance to the Argos Room and scan the faces of the delegates. They appear to be looking for a friend. No one challenges their presence. Almost imperceptibly, Noakes points a finger to a group of three men to the left of centre of the room. Charles picks up the signal and follows Noakes towards the three men. Noakes takes the envelope given to him by Stannard out of his jacket pocket. He taps the tallest of the three men on the shoulder from behind; the man turns to face Noakes with a smile.

'Richard Hargreaves?' Noakes asks.

'Yes,' replies the man still smiling. 'How can I help you?'

Noakes takes a photo out of the envelope and hands it to Hargreaves. The blood drains from Hargreaves' face; he clutches the photo to his chest, reverse side out, and looks around the room. Noakes follows the track of his eyes; they rest momentarily on the face of a young, blonde male waiter who breaks into a smile. Hargreaves looks hastily away. Noakes removes the photo from his grasp; the photo shows Hargreaves and the waiter, both nude, having sex on a hotel bed.

'Honey Trap,' says Noakes. 'To your room, right now. Follow us.'

The three men take the lift to the fourth floor of the hotel and walk a short distance along a wide corridor to Hargreaves' room which he opens with his key. Charles closes the door. Noakes opens the envelope again and spreads the contents on the bedspread. Six photographs of Hargreaves and the waiter engaging in sexual activity on that very bed. He grasps Hargreaves with one hand by the back of his neck and forces him to bend over the photographs for a moment, then releases him.

'Where did these come from? Who took them?' asks Hargreaves in voice breaking with tears.

Charles points to the fitting in the ceiling that supports the lamp immediately over the bed; it is askew, as if having been removed and then carelessly replaced. 'Little remote camera up there,' he says. 'Now long gone.'

Noakes speaks harshly. 'Who the hell do you think took them?'

'The Russians,' mumbles Hargreaves.

But that is not the truth that Noakes knows. Alex Hoffman fixed everything. A useful little man in Berlin who helped the British, with Noakes, clean up the dirtiest of Nazi scum after the war. Noakes doesn't know exactly what Alex did but he imagines it involved him, or a sidekick, acting as a waiter pushing a food trolley along the hotel corridor, entering the room with a stolen pass key when empty, fixing the semi-automatic Minox camera into the ceiling above the bed, returning the next day to retrieve it and then culling the metres of tiny rolled film for the images he needed. A simple manoeuvre performed the previous night.

'So we have to you get out of Berlin and back to Britain as soon as possible, before there is any attempt to blackmail you. There is a plane waiting at Gatow. You have five minutes to pack and get out of here with us.' Noakes gathers up the photos and returns them to his jacket pocket.

Charles carries Hargreaves' suitcase out of the hotel and signals for Haynes, parked across the road, to drive to the entrance. With no luggage, Noakes and Hargreaves walk past the reception desk looking as if they are TRADEX 67 delegates about to take a breath of fresh air outside the hotel.

By the time the car pulls up at the Guest Quarters at Gatow airfield, Hargreaves' mind has cleared. He accompanies Noakes and Charles into a room adjacent to the bedroom where their cases and coats are, and the questions come tumbling out. If it was the Russians, why have you got those photos? Can I contact my wife in Prague? Who else knows about the photo? … My Ambassador?

. Noakes ignores those and all the others. He tells Hargreaves to sit down and then asks Haynes to prepare for a take-off as soon as possible; the time in Britain is nearly nine o'clock, he notes. Haynes leaves to contact the aircrew.

Noakes sits down opposite Hargreaves, Charles stands behind him.

'Mr Hargreaves,' he begins. 'I personally don't care how many rent boys you cavort with although you know perfectly well that such behaviour, particularly when performed in the heart of East Germany, makes you vulnerable to a black mail attempt by the Russians. And such blackmail would include the threat, or the inducement, for you to provide them with sensitive information, turning you essentially into a spy.'

Hargreaves starts to protest that he would never fall for that, but Noakes cuts him off.

'Of course, that sort of honey trap would not be necessary if you had already acted in that capacity.'

Hargreaves begins to look panicky. Noakes continues.

'I, that is we, know about your friendship, started while at school, with the late John Newby and Donald Maclean, nurtured by your tutor Seb Miller. Your meetings with other people of dubious motives and actions over the years have also been examined ... and found wanting. Although I cannot formally arrest you, you are going to undergo a period of confinement during which time you will be given the opportunity to relate your life story. If you do this willingly, extensively and truthfully you will be allowed to retire gracefully and retain your full pension rights. But if do not cooperate fully –'

Noakes takes out the manila envelope from his pocket. 'Then these photos and your life story, as seen by us, will be leaked to the press. Which, apart from incurring the shame and embarrassment of your family, will likely lead to a substantial prison sentence. The choice will be yours to make, but if you now give me an indication of accepting that first option then I will not require you to be handcuffed to the uncomfortable aircraft seat that you are soon to occupy.'

---///---

Wednesday 29th

Hargreaves remains silent, with free hands, during the flight back to Benson. Once landed back in Britain, he and Noakes sit in the back of the car which had been left by the control tower just a few hours earlier while Charles drives them southwest through the early morning hours towards Guildford. The car enters the grounds of a large country house, the only light showing is that of a single lamp over the porticoed doorway. A man steps out into the light, opens the rear door of the car and leads Hargreaves away. Noakes and Charles head back to their homes in London.

---///---

'You mean he is being tortured?' asked Poppy.

'No,' replied Noakes. 'We gave up that sort of thing after the war and there wasn't much of that even then, on British soil at least. No, after his situation was fully explained to him once more, pros and cons, advantages and disadvantages, options and choices, he is singing freely. If he continues to cooperate and be useful, he will prematurely retire from the Foreign Office but receive his full pension, just as I had promised him in Berlin. But if he doesn't, then he will be dismissed as a security risk and lose everything, and if he protests too much, then perhaps what I threatened about the release of the photos may occur. But that sort of thing is very much above my pay grade. So, I echo Eugene, well done you two.'

'No more work questions permitted, let's eat,' said Eugene.

Towards the end of our lavish meal, as the port was being passed round, Jean spoke up, for almost the first time.

'I know that you have returned to your insurance career David, but what about you Poppy? What are you going to be doing from now on?'

'I'm going to continue in police work. I've been asked by both the Hong Kong and Singapore police if I would like to join their forces once I've finished about six months more training at Hendon, at Her Majesty's expense, I believe. But first I am going to get a divorce.'

'So you can marry Stephen?' I jested.

'It wouldn't be Stephen,' she replied. 'But it just might be Paul of Hong Kong and Canada. No, it's all for you David, so you don't have to commit adultery.'

And as she spoke from the opposite end of the table to me, I saw her left index finger trace letters on her side plate … L – U – C – Y; absent mindedly, I think, and not for me or anyone else to notice.

She was gazing straight at Susan, sitting by my side, as she spoke. I felt a stockinged toe lift my trouser turn-up and climb gently up my calf.

THE END

Authors Notes

George Blake

As the text of this book closed for print in April 2020, George Blake was still alive in Moscow, living on a KGB pension and 98 years of age.

The bare bones of his life and the events that led him to do what he did were extraordinary. He was born in Rotterdam the son of an Egyptian Jewish father of British citizenship who had served in the British Army during the First World War, and a Protestant Dutch mother. His family name was Behar and his later education took place in Cairo where he was influenced by a committed Communist cousin.

At 17 he was back in the Netherlands and working for the Dutch Resistance after the occupation of his country by the Germans. He then made his way to Britain by a devious route which included Gibraltar and re-joined his mother and sisters who had left Holland at the outbreak of WW2 and had changed the family name to 'Blake'. He joined the Royal Navy as an officer in 1944 and then was put to work for MI6.

When the war ended he was posted to Hamburg, then studied languages at Cambridge and in 1948 moved to the British Legation in Seoul, all under the guise of gathering intelligence information for MI6, where he was captured by the North Koreans at the outbreak of the Korean War.

He was incarcerated for three years in which time he became a communist (if he had not been one before), a devotee of Marx and volunteered to work covertly for the KGB. He returned to Britain in 1953 to a hero's welcome and to re-join MI6 where he married a secretary he worked with.

In 1955 he was posted to Berlin where he passed prodigious quantities of highly classified and sensitive material to his KGB contacts. He was arrested as a spy in 1961 and sentenced to three counts of spying each carrying sentences of 14 years of imprisonment to be served consecutively for a total term of 42 years. A draconian punishment which reflected the Establishment's embarrassment, rage and impotence of yet another MI6 mole being unmasked after Philby, Burgess and Maclean.

In some ways Blake was the 'perfect spy' in that his credentials would have been hard to believe if created within a novel. Born a foreigner, proven in resistance to a common foe (Germany), a linguist, a committed communist (probably covertly) and directly exposed to persuasion and pressure by an enemy (North Korea, China, and the Soviet Union) over a long period. Yet he, extraordinarily, was still regarded as a suitable person to be member of MI6. It is arguable that he damaged his country much more than his MI6 traitor predecessors in material and in loss of American trust (although that country had its own share of traitors then and other times). It is also almost certain that the information he passed to the KGB resulted in British field agents losing their lives, sometimes in horrible ways and, essentially the disintegration of MI6's covert organisation throughout Central Europe.

Footnote:

On Boxing Day (26th December) 2020, George Blake died in Moscow. The RIA Novosti news agency first reported Blake's death, citing Russia's SVR foreign intelligence agency. "We received some bitter news—the legendary George Blake passed away."

Russian President Vladimir Putin, himself an ex-KGB agent, expressed his, "deep condolences" to Blake's family and friends. In a message published on the Kremlin website, the Russian leader noted Blake's "invaluable contribution to ensuring strategic parity and maintaining peace on the planet." Putin went on to say, "Colonel Blake was a brilliant professional of special vitality and courage." The extraordinary debt Russia seemed to owe him was symbolised by him being buried with military honours at Moscow's Troyekurovskoye Cemetery.

No official statement was made by the British Government on the occasion of Blake's death.

Other Points and Disclaimers

Some of the people of mentioned in this book were (or are) real people. Apart from Philby, Maclean, Burgess and Blake, none of them deserve any adverse comment in this book, and certainly none was intended in its writing.

I was a pupil at Gresham's School for eight years and mostly very happy there. Gerald Holtom's son, Benjamin, was in my House although rather younger than I. Other people associated with the Gresham's part of the story, including Miller (Muhler), Kosler, Newby and Hargreaves, are products of my imagination as are all the other characters bar these two:

> Stuart (Beaver) Webster, who was my art master and a strong influence for my good.

> Mr (Scruffy) Burroughs, who was the handicraft master; he was highly influential in my choosing to be an Aerospace Engineering.

Both masters were much liked and respected by me.

The early relationship between David and Poppy is described in my book 'The Convent Girl.'

About the Author

Christopher Masterman was born in South London in 1942. His father was serving abroad with the British Royal Air Force; father and son did not meet until 1945. Christopher also joined the RAF where, with an MSc in aerospace technology, he served for 16 years as an Engineering Officer; at one time he was Prince Charles's personal aircraft engineer.

After leaving the RAF he worked for the European Space Agency in Austria before moving with his family to Canada where he joined a major aircraft manufacturing company where he rose to be an executive. In 1992 this company moved him back to the United Kingdom where he eventually retired. In 2006 he moved to Australia where he lives with his wife Elizabeth by the sea-side south of Perth.

Printed in Great Britain
by Amazon